CLOTHED, FEMALE FIGURE

CLOTHED, FEMALE FIGURE

stories

KIRSTIN ALLIO

DZANC
BOOKS

5220 Dexter Ann Arbor Rd.
Ann Arbor, MI 48103
www.dzancbooks.org

Designed by Steven Seighman

These stories first appeared, sometimes in slightly different versions, in the following publications: "The Other Woman" in *Alaska Quarterly Review*; "Millennium" in *Denver Quarterly*; "Ark" in *CURA*; "Clothed, Female Figure" in the *Iowa Review*; "Quetzal" in *The Literary Review*; "Announcements" in the *Louisville Review*; "Charm Circle" in *Mixer*; "Green" in *New England Review*; "Madrona" in *5Chapters*.

"Clothed, Female Figure" was reprinted in the *PEN/O. Henry Prize Stories 2010*.

Library of Congress Cataloging-in-Publication data available upon request.

ISBN: 978-1-941088-09-8

First U.S. Edition: August 2016

Printed in the United States of America

10   9   8   7   6   5   4   3   2   1

For my mother, Barbara
and my mother-in-law, Barbara

CONTENTS

Millennium   1

Clothed, Female Figure   13

The Other Woman   45

Announcements   73

Ark   87

Madrona   103

Charm Circle   127

Green   155

Still Life   171

Quetzal   201

CLOTHED, FEMALE FIGURE

MILLENNIUM

The summer before the millennium a coin turned through the air against the pewter lungs of a thunderhead. The grass where it would fall—tails up, in a moment—was cool before the torrent. By prior arrangement with myself, I set off for the city. My childhood was full of such solitary games and bargains.

People were talking about computer bugs, that summer. I pictured the seal-gray clumps of aphids in my mother's garden and the ants that marched down the brick to milk them.

I found employment in a Fifth Avenue apartment with a climate of dog's breath. From the fourteenth floor, the people on the street were as tiny as those aphids.

I worked under the hot wind of a little silver table fan, putting old auction house catalogs in new order. There was nothing but flat tonic in the refrigerator—it tasted like Freon. A corroded rubber band held the faucet together. The icemaker relinquished a plunk of cubes every quarter hour, and I melted them across my forehead.

The windows of the apartment were waxy, and had been painted shut in another era. If you pressed up against the glass you could see, as if at the bottom of a secret well, a murky courtyard where a few scorched houseplants had been left for the wife of the doorman. The same way, I thought, the people whose garden my mother had tended left us thin-ply garbage bags of clothing with an envelope that read: PLEASE SIGN ENCLOSED FOR OUR TAX DEDUCTION. I had seen the doorman's wife—the color of fried plantains, white creases in her bare armpits—pull the plants grimly away on the frame of a rolling suitcase.

The fleecy dust levitated like milkweed dander on the roadside. The apartment had once been grand, and I half expected to see a ghost gripping a lion's head cane with a concealed dagger, an antebellum maid with a slow step and a ruffled apron. Instead, slag heaps and cockeyed towers of catalogs, catalogs splayed and spiraled, pried apart with Post-it notes and old pencils.

Hillary Rice, my employer, worked at an auction house. She used the apartment for the spillover; she joined her husband at their country house in the Hudson Valley on weekends.

She made ceaseless, jagged forays in and out of the apartment in prim little suits with matching silk scarves in carrot, ginger, hibiscus. The Pernod she drank tinted her blond hair green. From my position on the floor I noticed that despite her blurred complexion and chronic bloating, she possessed perfect ankles. If I raised my eyes I could just make out the skiing scars underneath her sheer stockings.

She was pleased when I called her. She pegged me as the grateful orphan. "All the immigrants are nannies; the students will sue you for health insurance." She would hire me immediately to catalog the catalogs.

Her dog was an incontinent, rat-tailed wheezer the color of city snow (I would soon see) on an avenue. He scuttled behind me, toenails clicking and slipping, licking my sweaty imprints. The catalogs were full of furniture, but few actual pieces dared put their hooves down on the herringbone floors of the apartment. A chair shod in felt instead of iron, the husk of a horsehair sofa in the gallery entrance.

Once in a while, a bow-tied colleague entered the apartment with my employer. They didn't so much as nod to me, but I was impressed at first by their solemnity. They huddled worshipfully around a slide projector: a curly maple dressing table with Art Deco cutouts! I got tiny paper cuts on my fingers but the salt of my sweat cauterized them.

There was a wraparound balcony scrolled in wrought iron, but it was too hot to go out. Agile workmen from another continent flashed smiles and leers as they swung by on scaffolding. I imagined I could smell their thermosy lunches, hear their soda cans crack open. But I was neither friendly nor curious. A week of riding the subway uptown and back down at eight or nine (if she kept me past eight, my employer would begrudgingly offer me one row of her takeout sushi), and I understood, with relief, that in the city you don't have to make contact. The more people around you, the greater the buffer for your isolation.

I theorized that the millennium was like the Wizard of Oz— the moment before he reveals himself from behind the curtain.

I closed my eyes at night and my mind was a corridor—doors opened to room after room filled with antique furniture. An austere Shaker chair atop a lacquered, paneled wardrobe from a Chinese dynasty. A senseless jumble of ottomans and armoires, rockers and floor lamps. Toward morning my dreams quieted and there were intermittent oases around an Oriental rug, a spittoon, a bear skin with glass eyes and ivory molars.

I was a certified accountant, "between contracts." I was twenty, white-blond hair the texture of rose petals, still to my waist in the country style, a gardener's daughter. My mother had worked for the McNamaras, friends, for my purposes, of Hillary Rice. The McNamaras too had a Fifth Avenue apartment, although I had never seen it. My mother had been the resident gardener at their country estate, which was modeled after a chateau of the Loire River Valley. My mother had expended her last year sculpting a floating island in a pebble-bottomed pool dizzy with artificial ripples. Her cracked, square hands had woven the roots of dozens of hothouse belles into a ball of bobbing earth, like a surgeon re-braiding veins, compressing, coaxing them inside a body. The many-tiered bauble of flowers was given its own pair of hummingbirds at a debutante ball during which I passed appetizers.

The McNamaras let the gardens go for one full year in honor of my mother's passing. They excused themselves to Europe. When they returned they were eager to throw off the old earthy mantle. Some people in the town protested when I didn't inherit my mother's position—there was a spate of letters to the editor. The McNamaras, opined neighbors hotly, would use my mother's passing as an excuse to reroute the rosemary-edged paths I had grown up playing along; worse, bulldoze the whole thing for a personal golf course. The town felt it had protected my mother, like municipal property. Although, had I stayed, I would also have inherited the wide berth they gave her.

But the McNamaras had sponsored my course in accounting. I saw annuals—lumpen borders of marigold and impatiens—as non-deductible expenses; perennials were low-yield bonds. I took a few potted ancestors from the greenhouse behind the garage, humid with photosynthesis. My mother would have wanted me to have aloe vera for burns and rosemary—musky, stalwart, my namesake—for remembrance.

Having tossed my coin, I left the McNamaras with their year of weeds and leaves and undivided irises. I guess you'd say the garden's fully depreciated, I told Mr. McNamara. Our formal interview was over. "The accounting courses have taken root, then, Rosemary." He flared his nostrils at his pun but, just like my mother, I gave no sign of understanding.

I shared a studio apartment in the west Twenties with an anonymous roommate. She was a mutt: part waitress, part potteress, part student. She had the loft bed and I curled like a fern into the moldy pullout sofa. When fully extended the sofa blocked the kitchen sink, and so my roommate installed her coffee maker in the bathroom. I always plugged it back in when I finished blow-drying; this was the extent of the relationship. There was no shower, but the tub was gallantly rigged by the super with a chopped-off hose from a long-gone back garden. My roommate was industrious enough to locate a spray nozzle, and I donated the curtain. Indeed, our place was called the garden apartment, for it looked onto a postage stamp of a courtyard. We listed toward the one window with an accordion grate upon whose chipping sill my mother's houseplants teetered.

Old ladies let their cats out in the "garden" and a single slender tree dropped thorns on the concrete. If I couldn't sleep I went to the window and watched the neighbor with the chronically overstuffed mailbox smoking in an undershirt in the first gray light of morning.

I discovered a bar on a side street with a row of tired awnings. The drinks were three dollars, which fit my budget. I couldn't find a name anywhere, a dreamlike aspect that appealed to me. My calm increased until I could measure the exact tick, tock of my heartbeat.

Sometimes I watched the door for hours, until the dulled metal seemed to rub off like a silver lottery card you scratch with a penny. My mother drank California wine at noon and again in the evening. I squinted down the bar to count ice cubes in sweaty cocktails. I remembered how the floor of her little pickup truck rolled with empty bottles.

My mother was sunk in a clearing called Crepe Myrtle. The road became dirt, then two mud tracks, a path, a set of footprints, until it untwisted in the cemetery. My mother's ankles, in contrast to Hillary Rice's, had been starchy and tuberous as Jerusalem artichokes. The skin on her throat folded four ways like an envelope. The McNamaras wrote me a letter saying that for twenty years they had urged her to wear sunblock. And P.S., skin cancer has a heritability rate of X percent, Rosemary. I left my mother's widebrimmed straw hat with the blue jay feather in a carefully cultivated pink quince thicket.

The first time I addressed my employer by her name, she let out a strangled chirp and jumped back like a titmouse.

I was quiet for several weeks afterward.

But I began to notice that I wasn't getting anywhere. The sorting became resorting, reshuffling. It's called a circular reference, when the numbers get tangled and loop. A human error the formula can't account for. Numbers don't behave like that on their own. My mother had laughed when I told her the things I learned in accounting. The nurse, alarmed, retreated, and the doctor reading charts by the window began to fidget with his earlobe. My mother's laugh was too loud for someone who was dying.

"Sotheby's, '91," Hillary Rice pointed. "Over here. And here," she jabbed, "Christie's. Parlor furnishings." Sometimes a catalog demanded membership to two, or more, categories, and my employer flipped her stiff green hair between adjacent piles before she signaled. None were discarded.

"1999 will look so quaint in a few months," remarked my employer.

My mother was in charge of forty acres. No mule. I trailed behind her. When I was old enough to go to school the McNamaras arranged for the bus to come out to their property. I guess they were glad to get something for their taxes. When the emptied bus returned me to the dungeon-like entrance, I punched in the code on the alarm pad and watched the gate slowly stretch open. There was my mother surveying the pithy stalks of hydrangeas, pushing mulch over peonies.

Blooms browned and wilted and dropped to become compost for the very plant they came from. Winter turned mulch into a new layer of skin, a matted web through which the anemones poked up albino feelers. My mother raised her own vegetables, too, before she got sick, and sold them in town off her truck in the summer.

I thought of the nurse who had shown me how to rub my mother's purple feet for circulation.

"But you never get ahead in gardening," the nurse was saying.

We each held a foot so dense with blood it felt boneless. The nurse had demonstrated how to go around the ankle in a figure eight. My mother made an unfamiliar noise in her throat and I wondered if she could hear us. There were layers of voices in the hospital. My mother trying to clear her throat was the sound of a caveman. A static-filled page emanated from the ceiling and the nurse fled us. My mother looked a hundred. A dark, twisted-up root with the little root hairs still clinging.

Once, the McNamaras sent flowers. Not flowers from the garden, but chilled carnations the color of antacid tablets. I grabbed them out of the vitamin-enriched water and stuffed them in "biohazard." My mother made the noise again and her eyes tensed like she was passing a very bright sun in another solar system.

Hillary Rice began to talk in short yaps directed at some point on the blank wall behind me. "I'll be staying here this weekend." The dog had stopped going to her when she talked. He licked my calf contentedly. "You'll have to get the upholstered dining sets out of the bedroom." She did not mean real furniture. I suddenly realized I had never wondered where she slept during the week, and whether she took the dog with her.

When I came in on Monday the apartment smelled of cucumber bath wash and sweet, beige face powder. There were no food smells. I couldn't imagine Hillary cooking. Instead of chiseled pumps she wore tasseled slippers. I heard the icemaker in the kitchen bang out another glass worth.

Now I was fairly certain my work sorting catalogs had no cumulative intent, so I began to clock in at the bar on a daily basis. I sat on a stool, a neighborhood regular (the college kids sprawled in booths; I became old for my age at my mother's passing), and the bartender exchanged my melted drink for a new one without asking. I admired his mental calculations, the column of subtraction from a twenty slapped down on the bar by a peremptory patron. The couple next to me had come in with a bunch of Easter lilies from a bodega wrapped in white paper, and the bartender gave them a beer pitcher with water. The fragrance of the big, white flowers overpowered the bar smell of smoke and vinegar. I thought of telling my mother that every night they trucked flowers in through the tunnels.

Stepping into the dim of the bar was like entering winter. There was no work in winter. When my mother had carted away the Christmas wreaths and laurel roping we were free till March. My mother went to my teachers in her heavy boots, broad, chapped cheeks, and handed them the note that either I or Setta McNamara had written. Please give Rosemary the lessons she'll be missing.

There was something fierce and forceful in my mother's shyness—as I innocently named it—so that the schoolgirls with whom I missed forming friendships avoided me in the warm weather also.

I learned that regulars called the bar The Sign because there was none. But inside, the walls were plastered with bizarre and truncated language. I had to shut my eyes against the Lysol-slick graffiti in the bathroom. New York City slang was no different from the slang on the inside of the stalls at gas stations, rest stops anywhere across America. My mother used to come in with me and block the door with no lock, lopsided hinges. We never mentioned the women at the mirrors, patting on makeup, plumping a hairdo. She treated my long hair like a plant. Watering and dead-heading but never styling.

The bartender's name was Joe and he gave me a Greek coffee boiled in a copper pot. It was so thick and sweet it cut through the drinking. I noticed he bit his nails to the quick at the old-fashioned register. Once I tried to talk, offering up my employer, the over-warm, custardy smell of her dog. I offered up my mother, who had been fifty years old when she had me. She was raped in her own vegetable garden in the late fall, pulling out bean vines and the leftover tangles of tomatoes.

One hell-hot day toward September I felt Hillary Rice's gaze upon me. My movements down among the piles became haphazard, so that I had to stop and acknowledge her. She chinked her nails against the chlorine-colored Pernod and water.

Up to now she had voiced no complaints about my work. It crossed my mind she might have finally detected my heart wasn't in it.

"We can thank Setta McNamara," she said slyly.

Did she still think of me as grateful? To be safe, I kept my eyes trained on the catalogs.

"I'd like you to start answering the phone for me." My employer tapped her foot as if she were agitated by her own performance. "I'd like you to say, 'Hillary Rice's office.' You should drop whatever you're doing and answer."

"Sure," I said, on a level with her razor shin bones.

"Do you talk to Setta?"

Her shoes themselves were furniture. I tracked the white stitching in leather.

If the town had more or less "allowed" my mother to raise a child, and the McNamaras provided a stipend, then everyone had stayed silent on it—for my sake, it occurred to me—until my mother's passing. Suddenly it seemed like a great gift, even though I knew it had been granted more out of embarrassment than benevolence.

Several times I turned my duplicate key in the lock of the Fifth Avenue apartment and found Hillary Rice standing, stunned, in the foyer, wearing her gentlemanly plaid pajamas, at once gaunt and dissipated. "Pardon," I said. "I'll come back later." Her shoulders went up in a cringe at the sight of me.

One day she met me at the door dressed in a prune-colored pencil skirt and cropped black jacket. She flipped her bank of hair and blinked at me.

"You again." She had never before been loquacious. "It's too bad we're not best friends, isn't it." She blinked again, as if instead of laughing. "Do you think it's paying off?" She waved her hand and we surveyed the stacks of catalogs.

I didn't say anything. I was waiting, just as I had with my mother, whose speech was so rare that even Setta McNamara (my employer had a point: Setta was in everyone's business) had never heard it.

I thought of my mother sweeping her gnarled hand across the bedside table. The hospital phone that charged a fortune just to get a dial tone, the stiff-legged get-well cards, Dixie cup of water.

I couldn't tell if my mother was reaching for something or if she meant to clear the little table. That was the way she had worked, too: sweeping the path clear so I could walk there. Reaching for a yellow rose behind a spreading buddleia, tipping into the air a dozen blue-cut butterflies.

CLOTHED, FEMALE FIGURE

It wasn't my first family, and I don't have "favorites," but the apartment where they lived was closer to my old apartment than any other I'd worked in, and so I felt loosened, as if my whole body were the tongue of a sentimental drunk, susceptible to love and forgiveness. The mother, Ivy, was a civil rights lawyer, and the father, Wendell, was an artist. He was ten years younger than she—why should it matter? Because she wore the yolk of someone abused rather than amused by youth's indulgences. She had a boyish build in contrast to her heavy harness, and from my position (I admit there is some dignity in distance), here was a mismatch with which mischievous fairies entertained one another.

New Yorkers do not like to venture too far west or too far east, their compasses set to the moral equilibrium of Fifth Avenue. Ivy and Wendell's building, a narrow brownstone washed down like a bar of soap, was far to the west, between Tenth and Eleventh Avenues. Chelsea, Wendell insisted, which even I knew was an affect used to both mock and elevate his circumstances. From the roof, accessed by a hatch Pollocked in pigeon droppings, you could see the Hudson River. I had been able to see it from the roof of my own first apartment. A sense of hope never failed me, walking west, into the sunset...although when I arrived for work it was always ash-gray morning.

Ivy and Wendell slept on a Murphy bed in the living room. It hinged precariously off the wall, reminding me of Russia: cheap construction and close quarters. Leah, age six, occupied the bedroom, with a ceiling as yellowed and cracked as heirloom china. She wore frocks that twisted around her pencil body and her ears pushed through her hair like snouts.

She read to herself, poetry. By our Russian giantess, Anna Akhmatova, Leah had read "Evening"; she had also read Tsvetaeva and Emily Dickinson.

"She read at three," said Ivy, more dutifully than proudly, I noticed.

"Should I tell you the first words my parents discovered me reading?" Leah quizzed me. She had an un-modulated voice, as high as a sopranino recorder. In my previous life in the Soviet Union, I would have characterized such a voice as anti-social.

"Sorbitol," she enunciated. "Hydrated silica."

I suppose I raised my eyebrows.

"Toothpaste," declared Leah.

By that same first evening, I had read aloud half of the collected Grimm's Fairy Tales, cross-legged on the floor of the living room. When she was sure I'd finished Leah rolled over and her belly flashed: hard, green, like a slice of raw potato. "Natasha!" she cried. "I love to listen to your accent!"

Wendell did not like the modern children's books, the ones where you could buy the lunchboxes. Fine with Leah. Besides po-

etry and Grimm's, she loved lists of ingredients. She had something of a phobia—I use the term as a former professional—regarding compounds. She yearned for the simple.

"Bread and water sounds like a good diet," she said mournfully.
"But do you know how many things they put in *water*?"

There were no doors on the cabinets in the kitchen, due to
a campaign against the bourgeois in that house, and Wendell's
trumpeted belief in the art of the everyday object. Mismatched
student pottery was dustily webbed to dog-eared cereal boxes.

The window in Leah's room was on an airshaft with the di-
ameter of a corpse. I considered all of this close to depravity...
although in an unsettling way I wondered if I had brought it with
me, imposed a film of sorrow and poverty with my very gaze upon
Leah's circumstances.

It was true, she was my first only child. My research, in the Soviet Union, had for a time argued in favor of single-child families. In
terms of allocation of resources, at our stage of civilization, a single
focused beam of light, of calories, rather than the messy breadth of
competition, followed by dissipation among siblings and favorites.
Well, according to the posters that slickered my home city, there
were no Soviet shortages—of heart or of health—whatsoever.

Leah and I had walked down into the West Village, where she
was to meet a friend in a slice of park between two angled, inter-
secting avenues. We both drew to a stop in front of the window
of a florist. My English was excellent, but a bald spot in my vocabulary was botany. That spring Leah had found me out: I hadn't
known that ivy, her mother's namesake, was that dark diamond
creeper with tough stitches into cement and mortar.

"Natasha!" cried Leah happily. "I'll tell you everything!"

"Leah Halloran," I said. "Private tutor."

I saw her smiling down into her sweater, which was a habit she had, and sometimes she'd come back up sucking the collar.

I stood at attention. We let a couple of young women bob past us.

"Lilac," Leah pointed. "And hyacinth." Smugly, "I call them poodle flowers, Natasha."

Oh no, Leah Halloran was not a giggler. Her laugh was a serious matter, and as she pushed it out, now, I knew to remain silent.

The window glass through which we looked was as shiny and cold as chrome. Or, of course, a mirror. There we were. A small woman with short dyed hair beneath a boxy white hat, a triangle of wool coat, and a string of girl coming just to the breast of the woman.

Once Ivy said, testing the waters, "Did your mother work, Natasha?"

I didn't immediately answer, and so she added, needlessly, "Growing up in Russia?"

No, Ivy was not curious about my personal childhood. I understood immediately that she was taking the measure of my judgment of her as a working mother.

And, I suspected, she wanted to know what I knew about her daughter that she didn't.

But I simply winked. "Do I have any choice but to be a feminist in this apartment?"

"Feminist!" She laughed. "It sounds so—the way you say it— May Day! Sputnik!" She hit the air with her fists for our relics.

To wink, in those days, was my constant habit, if not directly, then atmospherically, or at an imaginary bystander, my alter ego, off in a corner.

I winked again. Ivy looked around to see if Leah was in the doorway. No, Leah was fast asleep, the tape recorder resting on her pillow, tape like flypaper catching flecks of sound-dust, so that if she talked in her sleep she could listen to it in the morning.

Before my employment, Wendell had stayed home with Leah, sacrificing his art, but leaving plenty of time to meet the drop-off mothers at Leah's school in the West Village who had just rolled out of bed and into those American blue jeans, pulpy and white at the knees and buttocks.

It was five flights up to Leah's apartment at the top of the brownstone, and the stairs were made of solid black rubber. The walls were tiled, with a black border, and the lights were so dim I supposed they cost the landlord a negative number. Leah never touched the railing, descending or ascending, but pedaled in the air, or rather like a drum majorette marching to her own, hectic heartbeat. I had no difficulty imagining what she had been like as a baby: a root face, an early, succinct talker, a body like a tail, too thin, too expressive.

Just as I don't have "favorites," I would say that I never become "close" to a child or a family. I have always suspected it's a work ethic left over from my previous profession; also, I prefer families who refrain from using intimacy as a means to wheedle extra hours. I prefer families who wish—and are cognizant of this wish themselves—to remain a rather closed unit, penetrated only by the specific terms of my contract.

And yet I would not characterize my particular style as "distant." In fact I have been accused, in one mother's fumbling manner, of "apocalyptic thinking," and by another, giggly with reprobation, "your weather eye, Natasha." Clearly, I've been, at times, overly concerned for the safety and well-being of my charges.

I stayed three years, until Leah's parents separated. I had begun to notice that Ivy seemed not so sad as tired, and I admired that, I thought to myself, a mother refusing sadness. I knew that money was tight, in fact Leah had told me, with a child's candor, and I suggested they didn't need me. Ivy said I was very intuitive and gracious. With Ivy's excellent letter of reference, I was able to find employment almost immediately with a family in Nyack.

It is true that over the years I thought of Leah. At first, it was practical: How would Ivy manage to take her to the museum class she loved so much on Wednesday evenings? Those lovely little leather sneakers—would they last through the season? Would she succeed in making friends with that laughing black girl at school she so admired? And once I even heard her voice, a rather comic announcement, "Whoever's in charge of me pours my soy milk." But then, of course, I had new sets of children to think about... and in my imagination the apartment between Tenth and Eleventh Avenues and my old, first apartment began to swirl together so that I had to think of both, or neither.

I certainly never keep records; in some cases I can't even remember all of the names of the family members. If there were previous marriages, children in college who visited their little half-siblings over long autumnal weekends... In one case, well, I can picture his two-seater sports car and the wrinkles on the seat of his suit jacket, but I simply cannot remember the name of the father. Why spend so much time on him? Why not his children? The boy, Harrison, wore a fireman's hat for a year, even—and I suppose especially—in the bathtub; the girl, Kimball, collected pandas.

In any case I don't take solace looking back. I don't take solace at all, and I take my coffee black, which is unusual for a nanny. Nannies are notorious for their sweet tooth, and while every Russian dreams of drinking coffee when he gets to America, he's without fail stricken homesick and tea-addled upon arrival. I am the exception, in both groups I claim membership, to such material and sentimental happiness.

It was last Saturday when I heard my employer's appraising step along the attic hallway that leads to the little room that comes with my paycheck. I have calculated how much is subtracted in "rent," but in this suburban neighborhood it is difficult to compete with the stream of au pairs from Thailand who accept a salary that assumes caring for children is as breezy as summer camp. They are accustomed to summer camp—back home, twelve little siblings are waiting.

I rose to greet her. My defense, as always, is formality. My current employer is a female doctor. She is tall and forced to bow her neck beneath the attic roof, the suggestion being that her own house oppresses her. As a hobby, she figure skates, and I believe figure skating is her true nature. That it fails to bring her recognition...

"Oh, Natasha!" Her surprise at finding me in my own private corner was unconvincing. "Here's this—" and she held out a rather bulky letter, laden with small stamps, as if someone had a tedious math assignment. I had the impulse to snatch it up, but it seemed essential that I measure my response: that it be equal, exactly, to my employer's.

"Thank you, Virginia." There was a pool of quiet around us.

"It's so quiet up here," said Virginia, taking a breath of air distilled by the attic. I remained expressionless. The envelope passed between us.

"Is Colin napping?" I inquired.

"A miracle," said Virginia. I nodded as if to excuse her.

"Oh!" She paused to signal that what was coming was such an incidental request it had only just now occurred to her. "Would dinner at six be possible?"

My day off was always cut short. If I pressed, I could get an evening to make up for it during the week, but I rarely bothered.

"Or shortly before..." she added. She looked at me curiously. I was aware that it would have seemed more—normal—if I told her from whom I had received a letter. It was true: at this address, I had never before had mail.

Very calmly I walked over to my desk with the letter. Of course I had scanned the return address. A woman in my position can't afford not to. I placed it on my desk and turned back to my employer.

She said, "Five forty-five-ish?" I nodded once, curtly.

Dear Natasha,

I'm writing you from college. Taking it for granted that you remember me, Leah Halloran? I would have written before but did you know that you are the invisible woman? I actually had to get a boy here to help me find you. He is the original computer geek, very sweet, will do anything because he is from Ohio.

My college is one of those Vermont enclaves that used to be all women, with a name that sounds like high tea in Britain, so that now it's not so much co-ed as college for the *sensitive*. I've given myself away—sensitive. An artist like my dad. My mom is still the only one who makes an honest buck in the family. I rent a room off campus, in the town, perched over a manmade waterfall. I look across the dam at the abandoned mill buildings from the 1800s. Sometimes I take pictures of townies from my windows. You know, girls with laundromat hair who walk like fat babies? Kind of voyeuristic, but what am I supposed to do, snap shots of trees and historic cottages? I impressed my photography professor, anyway, who is British. Gavin. He gets a lot of washings out of that accent.

You can see my photos for yourself, anyway. I'm sticking a few in the envelope.

I can only describe the sensation of reading Leah's letter as a welling up—was it self-satisfaction? I had done nothing to deserve it, and it certainly wasn't a feeling of completion. No. If anything, such a welling up (never would I have been so sloppy in my descriptions as a psychologist!) was a sensation of business *un*finished.

I do like my work, although I have been harsh, perhaps, in my description of Virginia. But I find it so demanding in its requirement of vigilance, that it would be unusual for me to allow a moment to feel "self-satisfaction."

What I felt was more like hope—already—that Leah would keep writing.

I finished the letter, and read it all over. I've received Christmas cards from a few of my families, Happy Holidays, the Xs, no more, and I've never expected it. But now I was absurdly, uncontainably excited. How could I rush through time and space to reach Leah?

All capital letters, slanting strongly toward the right-hand margin. Now I was almost sure I'd had a dream—Monday?—about Leah. Could I have predicted, or even willed the letter? How many dreams, I wondered, go unremembered if they are not *fulfilled*, somehow? How reliant are we on the world—I wondered, wildly, euphorically—to supply a coincidence to trigger our memory?

I searched my dream and it seemed, perhaps obviously, that the dream Leah was not the child I remembered (whose dreams are photographic?), nor was she a sort of projection, one of those artist's renderings of a kidnapped six-year-old, now grown up, and likely still tied up in a psychopath's basement, of what I would, in a lucid state, think an eighteen-year-old Leah would look like...

Perhaps I'm expressing myself clumsily.

It's one of the Russian poets who said this: Dreams ensoul lost love, for the fleeting lifespan of a flower.

You know, Natasha. I was just thinking—this may sound strange—but you were my mother's conscience. I don't mean my mother felt guilty about you—that you were an immigrant, or underpaid (right?), or the whole women-riding-on-other-women's-backs theory. I mean that she couldn't do two things at once, so she split the one thing off for you, (me), and along with it, her conscience.

Well no, she didn't turn evil or something when you left us. She was bereaved. I guess you should know that.

She's more or less famous now, as in people recognize her in restaurants. Certain restaurants. She still won't take my old bedroom.

Apropos of nothing, I'm going to Italy with one of my professors and her family for the summer. My mother is really upset about it. She wanted us to hang out on the scenic Hudson for August. I almost couldn't decide between Tuscany and Eleventh Avenue. My professor—sculpture—has two little boys, Roman and Felix. So I'm their nanny. Any advice for me, Natasha?

How I wished she'd sent a picture. Although her black-and-white photographs of local Vermonters seemed to me perfectly proficient, I wanted to see Leah. Regardless of my dream, at eighteen she must be tall and skinny like her mother, veering around somewhat absentmindedly, peaked skull, an adolescent crone with arms all wrist, legs all ankle. I admit, I can't imagine her beautiful. I always thought she was rather too shy to be a body. She used to have to hike up her saggy underpants. It galled me, the way it was constant, and that Ivy wouldn't go out and buy her fresh white ones with new elastic. Is that what Leah means by her mother's conscience?

All afternoon I anticipated writing, and my little boys, Jack and Colin, were revivified by my anticipation. They sat at their little red table clubbing their pale chunks of dinner and I was overcome with tenderness. Colin, the baby, called me Nata. His father joked, *Nada?* I even laughed along with them.

And suddenly it seemed to me that all my past successes as a nanny were thrown into relief, even exaggerated in the light of my new status. Leah had found me, and my good fortune seemed to radiate out so that any number of other human beings in the world were now also assured their reunions.

I was so eager to write that I skipped drying the pans after dinner (wondering how I ever have the patience to do it) and went straight to the attic.

It so happens that I am also taking care of two boys, I started. What are the ages of Roman and Felix? Mine are one and three, too young to travel to Italy!

I stopped. I looked around my attic room as if I hoped to describe it. For Leah's sake, was it a Grimm's fairytale garret?

The view over the street trees…I suddenly remembered the ring of lamplight on Leah's squirrel-gray pate, the crown of a gentle princess.

The single bed was too soft, a Goldilocks hammock. The walls were steep and ran right into the ceiling.

The little boys here are very good, I began again, although now it was some time later.

In the Soviet Union I might have become a prominent psychologist.

I wrote, My present family is very demanding.

Then I stopped for such a long time that I lost my train of thought, my intent, entirely.

Several days passed, although I was composing all the while. I almost felt like my own biographer. I wasn't so foolish as to flatter myself it was for my sake Leah found me, but even more, then, I felt a considerable pressure.

Once, I started: The little boys here have plenty of spirit! In fact, these are my first children who receive medication.

Or better this way? The little boys I take care of now can be very difficult.

No. She'll think I have allegiances, favorites, and she'll wonder how she stacks up against them.

Are you planning to major in sculpture?

All the children I've ever cared for are good children, Leah.

I laughed at myself harshly. Sometimes I dream they've been snatched—from the park, from the market, it's like a parallel life, really, the fear of it—and then I realize, in the dream, that it is I myself who have vanished.

Dear Natasha,

If you sent me a letter at school, I missed it, so now you'll have to spring for the stamps to Italy. My mother gave me a pack of condoms as a farewell present. Watch out for those Italians. Disturbing? Uh-huh. You know my mother. She's all about fairness to the point of being blind to human nature!

Emmie, my professor, says time zones are cathartic. We hope for rebirth when we travel. My God, we run ourselves straight into the knives of jet lag, whispers Emmie at takeoff.

It's probably obvious I have a crush on her. Ah! Not just her art but her whole life is talented. Her husband. And her children. Roman is three and Felix is one. Any tricks of the trade for me?

I have never allowed the maudlin aspect, but suddenly I remembered Leah's little sack of bones on my lap, her cinder hair beneath my nose, the Murphy bed latched high up on the wall above us.

Emmie hasn't bought a seat for Felix, so he's tethered to me by an orange seatbelt looped to my seatbelt. Roman effortlessly unclicks his life or death and stands up to regard the folks in the row in back of us. I peek through the seat crack to see if the trio of passengers is receptive. A nine-year-old boy (I'm guessing) encased in electronics is flashing and flinching on some other planet. His mother has newly plucked eyebrows. She might have done it with unsterilized tweezers. She clings to her paperback like it's one of the seat cushions that doubles as a life raft. She does a tiny wave at Roman and then closes her eyes against a death's head. The third passenger is a business droid with a newspaper complexion and goggly eyes like a housefly under a microscope. He says, Do you like flying? Roman falls

down as if he's been shot. Are these flying types really ubiqui-
tous or is it my own perception that lacks variety? Sometimes
I really just hate growing up. Not just, oh, things used to be
so simple, but things used to be so original. Now everything,
absolutely everything, is a repeat.

Which is why I find myself in Italy and not on the banks of
the Hudson River.

Rolls of gold straw, stubbly fields, combed and tufted pine
trees line dirt roads off the highway. I look over and Emmie is
closing her eyes at the wheel of the car we rented. The boys are
bobbleheads in their car seats. For a long moment I think we
will just lift off into the shiny sky which I've already decided is
the essence of Italy. Then I realize that we are slowing down
rather quickly and veering off the road rather dangerously.

I am too shy to wake up my professor! I put my hands on
the wheel where they won't touch her hands. I don't even know
how to drive in America, let alone *Italy*. I let the car swerve
off the highway and roll into a ditch gently. Then I don't know
what to do so I turn the keys out of the ignition. I tell myself
the car can't spring forward with the keys severed.

How's that for my first adventure?

Oh, that's very fine for an adventure, Leah. I don't know how to
drive, either. Perhaps you remember the way I scuttled you across the
streets in a state of clinical panic. I don't trust drivers. I close my eyes
against them, my breathing choked, irregular, not trusting death, either.

When we get to the compound (Emmie wakes up in the
ditch and looks at me strangely; my mouth corkscrews instead of
smiles), we are delirious. Felix begins vomiting. I stand back—
surely this is Emmie's department. Indeed, Emmie grabs my

arm and says, Oh my God, I throw up when I see throw-up. She turns away and hurls.

Did I mention that we're joining Emmie's two best friends from college? They've each brought their nanny. There's one nanny, hanging out a fan of laundry. The other is a button-nosed eunuch (I decide, cruelly) from Thailand (Emmie's friend Hedwig tells me). She turns the hose on the vomit in the courtyard before she's even said hello to us.

Hedwig, later: You're Emmie's student?

I wilt like a zucchini flower on the end of its phallus.

Certainly I was glad Virginia didn't choose this moment to quake up the attic stairs with some scheduling conflict. I've always thought laughing was worse than crying because laughing, you have to pretend to be happy.

I made my decision it was not appropriate to write back to Leah. There were a multitude of reasons. I owed it to myself to remain utterly free of children in my unpaid hours. There was never any *joy* for me, with children. Indeed, sleepless nights worrying over Leah left me distracted, even depressed with Jack and Colin.

And yet when I received another letter...

You should see the clear-skinned, glinty-eyed women, Natasha. And the dark gangly men with lovers' names. I get why my mother provided me with condoms.

We are invited to a dinner at midnight (I exaggerate the time but not the magic) and climb steep stairs, me carrying Felix, Emmie tugging Roman, to a sprawling red-tiled terrace furnished with monumental potted olives. Two cooks, three courses, faucets of wine in square juice glasses. All candlelight.

Then Francesca, the hostess, a tycoon's daughter, spies our children.

The little ones aren't tired?

Emmie swoons into the lovely commotion even as her children are dismissed from the party. Crestfallen, I pull them inside the "apartment."

But the sun is healthy, the Italian language is organic, the cheese tastes like meat, and the milk tastes like flowers! Smooth brown haunches in tiny swimsuits. I look down at my tissue-paper skin, grayish white, tattooed with the soot of NY City. Perhaps having inferior skin consistency makes me try harder at conversation.

Those other trees on the terrace are hazelnuts!

I told myself that Leah's letters were poetic, but not personal. I told myself that I was never more than a stand-in, a warm body, for any of my children, and so was not, categorically, entitled to any sense of guilt I might feel at not writing Leah.

Emmie spends the mornings in a studio she rented. She comes back to the compound for lunch, upsets Roman and Felix with her managing of their diets, and then calculates—as if, every time, it's a special exception—if I could put the boys down while she takes a breather, a.k.a. four hours. After siesta, she runs three miles with Hedwig to a polo field where they nuzzle the horses like infatuated schoolgirls. Then they walk back, all art and relationships.

Here's how it started. Last semester I had an idea for a life-sized sculpture of a woman. The whole point was she would be clothed, suggesting the *opposite* of clothing. Like naked bodies are less sexy, actually, than bodies in bathing suits. Uh-huh, that's my college for you. A clothed sculpture about nakedness, basically. Emmie was the one who drew me out, encouraged me. I told her about you, I admit, and I probably made you out to be some hammer-fisted, kerchiefed Stakhanovite. Emmie said my idea was very precocious. Then I had an idea that the body had to be yours, actually—I mean I became obsessed with likeness and proportion and even your particular wardrobe. I remembered, and it startled me, that you always looked as if you'd just stepped out of the collective closet of the Soviet Union. You looked as if you immigrated every day, to Chelsea.

(Not that my mother's wardrobe was ever up-to-date, but did she ever even offer to walk you down Hudson to the church thrift shop?)

Emmie argued that the power of the work was that it was universal, you know. Woman's lot and all that. I disagreed but didn't know how to express myself. I just felt like it was *mine*. Even though it was yours, in a way, Natasha. Emmie said I didn't understand art and I broke down in tears, knowing girlish capitulation was the only thing that would save the relationship. And here's where the relationship has gotten me.

I was holding Felix on my hip yesterday—he's the quiet one, with an amazingly gourd-like forehead. Roman hurled himself at me, across the lawn—his love is so boisterous. All of a sudden I remembered how I could disarm you by running into your arms, because you were so shy, for a grownup, and going for a hug was so unlike me.

I found myself wishing she'd return to the nanny on the lam, me, Natasha. I longed to laugh again imagining myself ducking some black market thugs, gumshoes wearing masks of Beria and Stalin. Admittedly, there was a hole in the logic of such letters—

why did Leah write me? But I couldn't pretend I wasn't exalted.
Emotions that would be embarrassingly simple in my psychology
days, but now...well, I told myself, there was the possibility that I
was a lonely old woman.

I came to New York at twenty-six and married the first man I
met, literally and proverbially. He stuck his head around the fire
escape. "Hey," he said. "Neighbor."

He had a loopy, charming grin and hard eyes the color of lapis.
I had just brought home a pot of daisies (margaritka, in Russian),
and I was setting them out on the little balcony. I wouldn't have
called it a fire escape. My English was good but not specific. He
climbed over, still grinning, as if he were shy of my beauty but
like a dog couldn't help himself. He had long legs in tight jeans and
white socks with holes in them. So already we were intimate. We
had one son, Arturo, named after my husband's father, the patri-
arch. The family business was Italian tiles. We were a mismatch
from the beginning, although there were never any lighthearted
fairies making fun of us.

It didn't take more than ten minutes for me to look through my
papers for a picture of Leah. With the way I move around so much I
don't have much of anything. No. In those days it seemed more exaggerated, deliberate to take a picture, and I wouldn't have wanted
Ivy to get the wrong idea. As I said before, there was already some
sense, among my previous families, that I could be too vigilant.

I have not thought of the Hanauers, for example, in many
years, but how clearly I recall Becky Hanauer, a quavery-faced
woman who had a great deal subtracted from natural beauty,
casting me from the servants' quarters. "I just feel that you're—
overbearing in the household, Natasha." I pointed out to her (I

had nowhere else to live, but she didn't know that) that most accidents happen in the presence of many adults because each individual adult assumes another is watching the children. Of course, a child can wander to the brink of an unattended swimming pool, I said, mistake the deep for the shallow, but more likely, it is when many mothers in oversized fashionable sunglasses like wasps at the nectar of gossip are present that a drowning actually happens.

Becky had fallen completely silent.

"Oh my, Natasha," she said, several long seconds after I had finished. All of her lipstick had come off on her coffee cup and she looked both pale and lurid.

It occurred to me she thought I was accusing her of the—well, the pre-death—of one of her children.

"I am sorry, Becky," I said somewhat woodenly.

"It's stressful being with children, Natasha," she managed.

My opinion was that, for her, it was, indeed, terribly "stressful."

"I think you should come in the mornings, you know, in the breakfast rush hour... " Half smiling, she indicated the warzone of toast and yogurt and mashed banana for the baby. "And then," she continued, "well, *go on home* after the baby's dinner."

I bowed my head until she said, "Natasha?"

"Becky, it's as you wish," I said. "Now please allow me..." and I moved in on the crumbly carnage, and the baby, who had been watching alarmedly, began banging with her bottle.

I came commuting in to Manhattan every morning by seven o'clock to get Leah to school by nine. Sometimes I volunteered in Leah's classroom, divvying paint or helping at the scissors station. I used to stay there, in "Chelsea," with Leah, until ten or eleven in the evening. A few times Ivy gave me cab fare but—I'm astonished at myself!—I categorically refused it.

Once, only a little bit less than a year after I'd left Leah, I had an opportunity to walk slowly past the front of her school at the dismissal hour. Many of the children who indiscriminately bumped and jostled one another were as tall as I was. I couldn't believe that had been the case when I used to pick up Leah. I felt a terrible clutching and sourness in my stomach: in anticipation of this very moment, I realized, I hadn't eaten anything since I'd left Nyack at six o'clock that morning. Suddenly I knew I was not in the right frame of mind to greet Leah. In any case I had no right to see her, none at all, it would be a compromise of context; like time travel, it was simply not possible.

I almost threw the next letter away as soon as I received it. I had intercepted it in the entrance hallway—Virginia need not creep up to the attic again, justified on her errand—and I stood beneath the chandelier that Jack had many times tried to leap for, holding the letter away from my body. I could see myself from above, too: I was very stilted and ridiculous in this action.

Such a correspondence need not continue, I heard myself whisper, as if I were, indeed, acting. I had a moment to myself—the boys were napping.

But what if I, Natasha, *weren't* just an adolescent idea for a clothed, female figure? What if such a statue…took on a life of its own, like a guardian angel? I wouldn't write back, that remained clear to me, but I must remain, somehow, *open*.

Dear Natasha,

Emmie's other college roommate, Lorene, hired a real Italian grandmother to cook ragu that smells like it has a hundred ingredients. The sauce simmers, thickens, reduces, and the grandmother-cook sweeps the patio with one hand and picks herbs in terracotta with the other. Emmie's all about: Don't come near me, I am a ladysculptor. Molly and Eveline have urged me to let the boys watch TV with their boys. Do you know what? All the children are boys, future kings and princes, and all the grownups are women. I'm the only woman with any future to speak of.

Lorene, actually, has just returned from a week of Ashtanga in the center of Italy. Emmie keeps teasing her about being strong and centered—obviously, Emmie wishes she were a svelte yogini. Lorene and Hedwig think it's very cute that I'm the nanny. They tease Emmie that she must really trust Mark, Emmie's husband. They tease Emmie that their nannies have to pick up the slack, like making the kids the lunchtime chopped ham and ketchuppy hotdogs.

A rash and fever called sestina afflicts our Felix. The poetry of it! cries Emmie. Only in Italy!

I guess that's where we are: the space between the verses.

Now it all makes sense. How he threw up upon our arrival, how he's been so clingy, not his usual self, Emmie assures me. Hedwig is a biologist. She calls sestina one of the last remaining childhood illnesses. As if the illness itself were an endangered species! Free to burn, perhaps to purify, intones Hedwig. It occurs to me to ask Hedwig how she feels about death.

Lorene is a fashion designer in Paris. She says, So did we approve of the spaghetti sauce? We did, didn't we. She has a way of pulling her ribs up off her stomach, as if to make more room for spaghetti. Hedwig comes in from wherever she has been with her laptop, wearing a bikini and the gauzy Indian tunic that all the ladies are wearing—really, another kind of housedress. Emmie hands me the sestina.

Mark's arrival. The big personality. Everyone feels loved and it's all worthwhile to be stranded in Italy. Yes, they're already starting to complain about their vacation. Maybe we shouldn't have listened to Francesca, maybe this isn't the best spot. Maybe this is second-tier, maybe we're missing the part where it's going to show up in a glossy mag stateside. Mark heads down to the beach hours after everyone else has already departed. I know because I must stay in the tiled quarters with maladious Felix.

I'm not really sure if I should talk to him. Only it makes me think of so many things to say when I *don't* talk to him. Last night I was so bottled up that I ended up telling Hedwig about you, Natasha, how you flashed in my mind every day after school, after you left us, and how I'd have to catch myself before running out to meet you.

All right, I'm beginning to recognize something of myself in Leah. I see how she's making friends with those women, her professor and her professor's girlfriends, by confession. She's baring her wounds as a way to be accepted. Sure, she tells them about her daddy, how he left them for another woman; she tells them about her Russian nanny, who left them for a family in Nyack.

Yes, there was a time when my "opening line," as they say, had something to do with losing Arturo. I didn't think I could get a job without it. A mother would show me around her big sunny apartment, and I'd kneel down and greet her children, and then the mother would have to throw in some extra, like a dog who had allergies and had to be fed cooked turkey. Well then I would make my confession.

I go around all day worrying about Leah. The other husbands have arrived too, and Leah calls them bigshots, and now she calls the women longlegs. She writes,

> They've all gone down to the salty still water. They're all parading along the eucalyptus avenue toward the umbrella colony. If I close my eyes I can hear the sound of scuttling maids coming out from the corners, taking back the house, the loud brusque whisper that can only be the sound of sweeping. Your maid is like your garlic breath. Molly, the Thai nanny, and Eveline share a closet with bunk beds. Molly puts rice in the mouths of seven siblings in Thailand. I don't know this for a fact but I sure can hear my mother say it. All Eveline will tell me about herself is that she hates the food in Italy.
>
> Have you ever been to Italy? I can't believe I forgot to ask you.
>
> One of Francesca's friends (Francesca, sorry: one of Mark's old girlfriends, how we heard about these apartments) arrives from Rome to stay in the apartment upstairs from us. Her name is Giulietta, which is a whole different kettle of fish from Julie, isn't it. Despite her name, she's all bourgeoisie and gristle. She wears a big floppy sun hat and movie-star glasses. She brings her terrible son Brando and an American au pair from Vassar College. Why does the au pair seem more like a houseguest? Because she has some Feminist Theory 101 in her back pocket?
>
> Last night we were hanging out on our dark lawn—Roman was waiting to catch a bat or at least hit one with the sand shovel he was waving—when a chair came hurtling through the air from the terrace above us. Brando was having a tantrum.
>
> Mark came out of the tiled quarters. Everyone looked to him to see what was called for.

Vassar slunk down, whining, But why don't they have shower curtains in Italy?

You lost a chair, said Mark, deadpan.

There's a little cutout in the pine trees through which I could see the twinkling lights from boats on the water.

Al-lie? called Giulietta from the terrace above us.

Vassar shivered.

Mark laughed at her and she flickered up for attention. He said, You must be Allie. He reached out his hand for an introduction.

He said, Baths in the sea, Allie.

I happen to know he's forty. He swings his hips when he walks, which might be embarrassing in a younger man but it makes him seem youthful.

My employer, Virginia, asks me, "Who are all the letters from, Natasha?"

She cocks her head, fleetingly curious, "I've never even asked you. Do you still have family in Russia?"

I look down at the letter in my hand, with its *Italian* stamp and *Italian* postmark. But my employer is not really a classy person. She works hard, she's a doctor, but she started medical school when she was about fifteen (this is her joke, actually), and hasn't seen the real world since then.

I am no longer in the habit of confessing anything. Oh, I'm friendly, and at once gentle and vigilant with the children. I'm always getting told by the mothers that I'm not like the stereotypical Russian nannies with spare-the-rod-spoil-the-child ideas about discipline. It's funny because that phrase of course comes from the Bible, and wouldn't be known to most Soviet Russians of my generation. Also, Russian mamas notoriously spoil their children. As if they had multiples, which they don't, categorically.

I just stand in the hallway not knowing what to say to her. Which is the lesser of two evils? That I'm corresponding with one of my old children (like an affair, almost!), or that I do have family in Russia, with whom I have never, since I emigrated, exchanged so much as a sentence?

Of course, I am not, technically, corresponding.

Luckily Virginia doesn't have the time to pursue it. She is already explaining to me some glitch in her schedule, some scheduling conflict, that is a favorite term with her, that overlaps with my afternoon off... All I can think as she's talking is something from her boys' swim lessons, to which I accompany them, which strikes me as very funny indeed, "bubble bubble breath," which is Virginia talking.

It's all about the women, here, Natasha. The men are spoiled and paunchy, spreading out in the vacated cities, sleeping late, earning money to pay the nannies. There was one flashbulb of awareness when they were teenagers, and the rest of their lives they try to get back to it. Their bodies were strong, a sheer drop. Their hair was black, they drank black coffee and liquor indiscriminately. The only consolation now is to make mad money. Yes, Mark has gone back to New York for a week in the middle of his vacation to make money.

And no, Mark isn't paunchy. He's spoiled; but he's the only one who really pays me any notice. He watches me with Roman and Felix. I figure he'd say something if he didn't like the way I was treating his heirs. They really look like him rather than Emmie. Mark says that one way to travel is to love everything, revere it. I tell him I think the sunbathers on the rocks look like browning dumplings. I tell him I love to watch the family picnics beneath the pine trees. He smiles as if I've just said something very esoteric and he alone understands it.

I don't think she can see it coming. I don't think she's old enough, or pretty enough, to see it coming.

And if I wrote her?

I laugh at myself harshly. I'd disappoint her with my old woman's voice, I'd hurt her with my lack of belief in her beauty.

This Mark, her professor's husband, will come back from his business having justified it to himself—every man can justify it—and Leah will be a bird in the hand before she's even sited properly in the binoculars.

I take my afternoon off in Central Park. The commuter rail is empty at one o'clock on a Wednesday, and so I have the sense of swooping silently upon the city. I take a little picnic, and Leah's most recent letter. After I finish eating, I wander around for a bit until I find a nice shady rock to sit on—private but not too private—and listen to the xylophone of bird voices. When I close my eyes for a moment, they seem to be elongated, like raindrops, and when a gust of wind comes up, there is a sudden discordance as if the notes are all struck together.

Dear Natasha,

I'm on the lawn again, looking through the keyhole of hedges to the marine blue (today) Mediterranean. Felix is sleeping. Roman is watching the idiot box with Lorene's kids; Hedwig's husband has actually taken his boys out fishing, so that he won't have to do another thing with them all of August. Everyone else (if I say "the others" it will really sound like a novel, won't it) is out on the count's sailboat. Breezing along the Mediterranean in their sexy skins beneath their sexy sail. Molly and Eveline went into the town—I offered to watch Eveline's charges. I could have taken Felix in his carriage. To town. But I thought I might get points from Emmie for reaching out to Eveline. Ah! I feel like the Christian fundamentalist in an apron and a bonnet making quilts past the year 2000. Life is a sacrifice of the soul; children are the refining fire. Mark said that, with a half smile.

I really can't say you *shouldn't* have left, Natasha, because that's worse than underpaying, or paying for a single doctor's visit instead of health insurance —you can be sure my mother's all over labor violations. I can't say you shouldn't have left, because it sounds controlling. But when is love not controlling?

Here comes Mark. Ah! It seems like he's smiling in spite of himself, you know? Like he genuinely likes me.

Yes, I've been to Italy. My husband took me, and Arturo, when Arturo was a ten-month-old baby. There was a great hassle about my passport. I had been planning never, ever to leave America. That was my thinking. But with the problems at the consulate, my husband began to suspect me of a covert Russianness.

"One thing," he said. "If you're my wife, you don't draw this kind of attention."

We fought all the way to John F. Kennedy Airport. Arturo wailed in the backseat and I twisted around to look in his wobbly eyes. I reached my hand back to his soft knee and he hiccupped. I looked in his wet light eyes and thought to myself that there was no reason under the sun, as they say, why he should stop crying. I knew that things were never going to be good between me and his father. Indeed, Arturo began to wail with renewed passion.

"Oh you're a good a mother!" my husband shouted.

I was always the crazy one, as if it had to be one of us. My husband said he should have seen it. He claimed that I mumbled certain things in my sleep.

Indeed, whenever we fought, my English failed me, as did the entire body of my psychologist's training. This fight was something to do with the way I'd left the apartment. I hadn't tidied up sufficiently. I hadn't put away the clean dishes from the previous night's dinner, for example. My husband was suspicious of everyone and everything, and he somehow thought the likelihood of our apartment being broken into—by the police, that is—was greater because I'd left it in shambles. I knew a little bit about the drugs, but I never said anything.

Arturo was just beginning to walk at the time of the trip to Italy. My husband was very proud of him. My husband wanted to take him out and show him on the streets, in the bars and restaurants, as a son of Italy. We visited various cousins of my husband, and my husband always pulled Arturo away from me and presented him as if he belonged solely to my husband.

The last three days of our vacation we spent on the Mediterranean. It reminded me of the Black Sea, where I'd been as a child: so calm, like a bathtub, families like porpoises picnicking on the rocks, riding bicycles down piney paths, eating late and lavishly. We went to the shale beach in the afternoons and my husband would swim out to the boats while Arturo clapped and paddled in the shallow water.

Our last afternoon there was a terrific thunderstorm. As I remember, there was an ominous warning rustle through the pines and in a matter of seconds the sky was cracking like ice on a river in springtime and the air was throwing off shards of electricity. I could see my husband's slick black head dipping way out in the water and I began waving frantically. Then the sky dumped out its buckets.

What should I do? I tried to shield Arturo, but I had nothing on but a bathing suit. I'd left our clothes and towels at the hotel, in the midst of another fight with my husband. The rain was surprisingly cold and hard, like one of those "massaging" showerheads. Arturo began to whimper.

Just then, a teenage boy appeared at my elbow. How can I describe it? He was like a courtier in a castle, he had that air of grave attendance. His hair was jet and he had a low forehead and fluted nostrils. His gaze was intent, as if *I* were the sole reason for this moment. His tanned body in a swimsuit was strangely flat, almost one-dimensional. He held out his big towel. I nodded gratefully and wrapped up Arturo. My baby's slightly droopy eyes, one was what they call "lazy," his copper hair like mine in a delicate ridge over the crest of his head (now darkened with water), his soft bare body…

"I am Seryozha," the teenage boy bowed to Arturo. Arturo smiled from beneath the towel.

"Come on!" He gestured for us to follow. He pointed to a big pine on the beach of which one half was charcoaled, branded by lightning. "That was last summer," said Seryozha, by way of a warning.

He herded us along the path. Lucky it was wide, because you could hardly see past the curtain of rain in front of you, and I was sure I would have stumbled with Arturo. When we got to the little hotel where we were staying, I held Arturo away from me to unwrap the towel and return it. Seryozha shook his head vigorously. "Tomorrow."

This seemed at the time the kindest thing that anyone had ever offered. He bowed again, and disappeared into the rainstorm.

I'm sorry, Natasha. This has nothing to do with you, really, I mean you shouldn't be concerned for me like my mother.

Maybe you're *my* conscience, actually. Did you get the letter where I said you were my mother's? I admit I was kind of proud of myself for figuring out that little piece of psychology.

I admit it's kind of funny to keep writing to someone who doesn't write back to you, but in a way it reminds me of some art project sanctioned at my college. Anyway, feel free to destroy these letters. I certainly never want to see them.

Last night we went to a Medieval town about an hour's drive away for a late dinner. Francesca had recommended the restaurant, with outdoor, torch-lit tables in a cobblestone chasm walled by stone churches. Emmie and Mark had a bad "row," as Hedwig calls it, beforehand, so Emmie stayed behind with Felix. Mark wanted to take Roman. Hedwig and Lorene urged me to come along in order to help Mark with Roman. I would have stayed home out of loyalty to Emmie, I know I would have. Ah! Could you see this coming? Please tell me you couldn't. Have you ever felt like all that was surreal in the night is a curse in the morning?

It was in the car on the way home. We took a different car from Lorene and Hedwig & Co. because of Roman's car seat. It was with our clothes on. I kept thinking of that diamond-shaped view of the ocean through the hedges, and our keyhole of nakedness. I said, Please don't tell Emmie. And Mark laughed, Emmie and I tell each other everything! The kind of slippery teasing that writes a reprieve for everything. That covers all its bases. Do you know what I mean? I know my mother would say that's not teasing, Leah, that's an abuse of power. Can you just hear her?

My husband roared at me, "You left me in a thunderstorm!" Oh, I needed to laugh. What a baby my husband sounded like. What a stupid baby. It came to me that I would not tell him about Seryozha—whose name couldn't, I realized, possibly have been Russian.

I suppose it was in that moment that I knew I was leaving.

Here is the truth, Leah. I would be the crazy one if crazy was what it took to get free.

I told myself that I did not want to "go down" with my husband, certainly that was his slang, and again I needed to laugh at the evocation. For example I had not the least intention of being at home when the police arrived heaving with petty resentment at having to climb four stories. Ours was a walk-up, just like yours, Leah. I would not pretend I wasn't terrified of those black-nosed German Shepherds, police dogs with thick muscular tails used, like kangaroos, for superior balance.

"Where was I supposed to have thought you'd gone, Natalie, Moscow?" my husband shouted.

Yes, I called myself Natalie then. Assimilation. I thought it sounded odd, harsh, nonsense, but that's what I thought a professional immigrant would do. Not a housecleaner or a nanny.

When I take too many painkillers now there's a side effect of my uterus contracting, and I think, mincing down the stairs to Virginia's children from my attic, that children are truly our penance for being, once, ourselves, children. But then I think, why should you, Leah, have to pay for being Leah?

The storm cleared and my husband said he would take Arturo to the town center where there was an arcade with many small shops, cafés, and a fruit market. They would spend the afternoon making friends with the shopkeepers. Fine, I said. Goodbye, Arturo. I had to kiss him in my husband's arms although I did not want to go near my husband.

I allowed one moment of silence in our little hotel room.

When I think about my son now, it's not the way I knew him, held him, and held onto him when he was a baby. I try to imagine him as a grown man, that he's tall and kind and handsome, that he's been a good son to his father and his stepmother, that he's gone into the tile business or gone to college, that he says with curious pride he's half Russian. Even if he doesn't, that maybe he thinks it's his secret.

I must add that as far as I know he has never tried to find me.

No, I never allow myself to think of him like that—in my arms, on the beach of the Mediterranean, in a wild thunderstorm. Because in that moment, I was sure Seryozha (and I know I didn't hear Sergio) was our guardian angel. I was sure he was a sign. That this was the beginning. The cleansing rain, the hotel room with its welcome, stuffy warmth, Arturo's eyes gleaming with excitement at our rescue.

THE OTHER WOMAN

My mother played piano, oldies and Chopin. Twice a year she played Happy Birthday, once for me, once for my brother. She woke up early for it—the one day she could wake us up early without risking her life, she said. Hah. You weren't allowed to kill your mother on your birthday.

Did we happen to know that Happy Birthday was the first song ever transmitted back from a spacecraft? This was exactly the kind of stray-dog fact her boss brought home, and my mother couldn't get over how every ugly mutt of information looked purebred in the light of the university. She laughed, wheezed, pretended she wheezed on purpose. My brother wanted to know what model spaceship, trying to impress her, and my mother said, "That would not be the question, genius."

Affecting the fatigue if not the vocabulary of the educated classes, my mother elaborated, "You get a blob of information, Zack, and the question you don't ask is, What's this fucking blob of information?"

I gave him a glare; naturally I agreed with our mother.

Drama. My mother stepped back to make room for her declaration: "The question you ask, Zack, is the *why* question."

Professor Shemaria, aforementioned "boss," saw the world through why-colored glasses. Professor Shemaria connected everything, in her classroom and her research, through why questions.

"What do you think I do all day," said my mother, "empty wastebaskets?"

My mother was on the custodial services payroll. My brother stroked his chin. "Is that a why question?"

"Smartass-holery," said my mother. "Why do I work? So Zack can eat donuts."

I hooked my toes on the back of his sneaker so that when he lunged he lost it. Flat tire. We were out to get each other, the three of us.

Nan Shemaria was a professor of sociology. Everything she told my mother about the human race ended up being something bad, something snide, something derisive.

Or something doomsday. Professor Shemaria was politically childless, my mother informed us. You could defeat anything, said my mother—biological imperative, winsome little babies—with the right term for it.

If why questions weren't already anti-faith, Professor Shemaria's defeat of religious holidays was the institution of wine-and-cheese Fridays. On the department's nickel, reported my mother, a spread of Swiss, Brie, butterfly crackers, chunks of unripe cantaloupe like something from a dermatology experiment. Adjunct faculty debated Head Start vs. stipends for home tests administered by stay-home mothers, grad students dangled their theses like undergarments, a pair of humid undergrads stuck their heads in, only to recoil when they gauged the naked distance across the room to the wine and cheese table.

Fridays my mother got home after midnight.

Our house was a one-story box, like the little green ones in Monopoly, but with a sun porch. My mother rented half the driveway to a neighbor for the neighbor's son's Yamaha. My brother played on the bike incessantly, and my mother yelled through the louvered slats of the sun porch. We were right across the street from Our Lady F, Efraimia, where we did not go to church, because of questions handed down from Professor Shemaria.

Happy Mor-tal-ity to you, Happy Mor-tal-ity to you, you act like a monkey, 'cause you came from one, too! That was my mother's version.

Truthfully, was it Happy Birthday or death itself that was transmitted from outer space? Death, for sure, when it was beamed down through the middle school PA system, as if the space shuttle *Challenger* had exploded in real time, in Social Studies. It was the same January week of my mother's first diagnosis. "Not too shabby compared to Christa McAuliffe," said my mother. I thought of the air-beyond-the-air that hosted Russian spy pods. The stars like streetlights on foggy winter evenings.

Anyway, my mother played it loud and raucous. She played with exaggerated fermatas, *derisively*, from the sun porch, not an ideal place for an instrument, and she winced and cursed when another key mutinied, the pedals swollen at the root so they were nothing more than footrests. Or she sang in Spanish. We were basically Italian. Singing in Spanish mocked Spanish, for no good reason, mocked birthdays, made birthdays part of the running joke on the banality of love in families.

My mother was tall and spidery, all transparent joints, pipe-cleaner legs in off-brand blue jeans. Her cigarette leaned out of her mouth dangerously—she liked to scare us. She kept a big glass jar of pennies on the kitchen counter, as big as those jars of jelly beans you're supposed to count to win prizes: a gift certificate to Newport Creamery, a shampoo-color-cut by Trudy.

Trying to guess the pennies made your head spin, like an optical illusion.

For a couple of reasons the pennies were more or less impossible to steal. This was one thing my brother and I agreed on. First of all, you didn't have time to count to a hundred. Second, you didn't steal a dollar, you faced a hundred counts of stealing. That was a lot of wrongdoing for a stinking dollar. That was the point. That was the hard lesson. Another hard lesson was our father leaving, but to our mother it only proved there was no love in families. The Alimony Asshole, our father.

Truthfully, he didn't just vanish. My mother said he was a long slow death like cancer. She was the expert.

He worked at T.F. Green Airport. My brother used to think he *built* T.F. Green Airport. The Unions squeezed him, and same as our mother, he wasn't a joiner. He was snuck on a construction site in Dorchester. Then there was a gig in Lowell. Each job a little farther from Providence. When he stopped by, unannounced, he always brought a box of donut holes. "Hah!" our mother would cry scornfully, and tip them straight into the garbage. "Did they sweep them off the floor for you, champ?" she'd say then, getting in his face, softer.

We got a long-suffering, bearish stepfather after a while; our mother teased him without mercy.

Whenever we found a penny, exempting in a public fountain (because Professor Shemaria had catalogued the "wishing well phenomenon"), we were supposed to pick it up and save it for our mother. Pennies were different from donut holes. All the lost pennies on all the gummy floors and cracked sidewalks in Providence belonged to our mother. Her eyes were copper. Green spots appeared with her illness.

My high school yearbook voted me most likely to keep my figure. It wasn't necessarily a compliment. It seemed to me you wanted, at that age, to *spend* your figure.

My mother was balancing on the kitchen counter—lemon yellow with sparkles, a 1950s dessert, what was floating island?—on one elbow. My mother said the sparkles were mica. Another thing that cracked her up was how kitchens had evolved from the fucking fire of Prometheus. "The Early Peoples actually used three hundred and sixty degrees of their cooking fires." My brother and I rolled our eyes behind her.

The pattern in the tan carpet was like worm tunnels in tree bark.

My mother was idly paging through my yearbook. I remember thinking, What if you were thirty-seven, instead of seventeen, when you graduated? What if you could calmly flip through your yearbook, pointing out, "Hah. That's Diane Orabona's daughter. I remember when Diane Orabona peed her pants in gym class." Or, stabbing at a bleached blonde in a homemade anarchy T-shirt, "Look at the birth-control boobs on that one!"

My mother talked fast, and she only ever smoked half her cigarette.

She said, "Didn't they lower the hormone dosage? Didn't I read that?"

I laughed nervously. Those girls towered above me in popularity.

"In my day birth control was a fucking horse pill."

What if you were a certified know-it-all and you had something to say about everyone? My brother and I called each other doho, for the failure of the donut holes, for the failure of anything that was, in and of itself, a hole, a negative greaseball.

What if, at thirty-seven, you had already had two scares, including chemo, surgery, and remission, and you could still say *boobs*? As if you still possessed them?

And how could I laugh with you when you said it?

"They couldn't say anything about your grades?" my mother persisted, thumping the yearbook. "Nothing cute about straight A's is there. Nothing hot about a four-point-oh, four years running."

Why did I choose this moment to notice that my mother had, since yesterday, become flat-chested? But I could easily see her chucking the post-mastectomy bras the insurance company paid for on a one-time-only basis. Her vanity was never sartorial.

One Saturday morning I found her on the sun porch engrossed in papers, fanned, stacked, and scattered around her. The sunlight through the slats blinked maniacally. She was kneeling, using the piano bench as a table, furiously marking across the pages of what could only be, I realized with horror, Professor Shemaria's students' papers. Her left hand was pulling out hairs, strand by strand, a habit of which she was so deeply ashamed that my brother and I had never even mentioned it to each other.

"What are you doing?" I surprised her. She snapped back like a measuring tape into its metal locket.

"Maybe you'd care to help me here, genius." She recovered quickly.

"Okay." I didn't move. I tried to look without looking, as if the pages were love letters or a diary.

"Intro to Sociology." My mother's voice went up—she couldn't conceal her excitement. "Her TA had to go home to Argentina."

My mother smacked the page in front of her. "Are you kidding? Anybody could do this."

I reached for a single sheet of paper and I saw that my mother's impulse was to stop me. She caught herself. I looked at it without reading. A college paper. "What?" said my mother.

"You were supposed to rest—more—I thought."

"Do you see me on my feet?" she said. "I'm poolside, genius." She let her big eyes droop for a moment. She grabbed a handful of papers and made for the sofa. It was mildewed, it was on Zack's list every weekend to get rid of it, but she rolled herself out luxuriantly.

"I could do this in my sleep," she said, closing her eyes again, for my benefit.

"Or I could farm some out to you," she called after me. I couldn't recall ever having heard her so hopeful.

I could live at home and put myself through college. I could choose—two years, secretary, four years, teaching certificate. Never a nurse. I had done my fair share of nursing. Besides, those were girls who smoked since seventh grade, starred in slumber parties, and were now forced to cup their cigarettes in the wind tunnel against the north side of the hospital annex.

I met Phil because we attended the same teachers' conference in my home city, and he mistook my parked car for his Rent-a-Wreck.

He'd lost the keys and was jimmying ineffectually with a coat hanger. "You're lucky you're not trying that outside Planned Parenthood," I said, sounding for all the world like my mother. He jumped. He made an embarrassing little sound and I blushed for him.

His quavering defense: "Who actually owns a— a well, a Taurus?"

"Girls from Rhode Island," I countered, guessing correctly that he wasn't a native.

He happened to be standing in a significant array of pennies. I pointed. "A hole in your pocket?" Just like my mother, I said stupid things when I was nervous.

He ducked; he shook the pockets of his sport jacket; he came up underneath the pockets to gauge the sewing project (not that I knew then he did his own sewing); he stepped out of the loose circle of change around him.

He surveyed the sidewalk and smiled helplessly.

I had to smile back at him. But still, my innate tactlessness. "Are you trying to poison the pigeons?"

He laughed, but I could see he was baffled.

"You can't feed the ducks anymore because of complex carbohydrates," I babbled. "You can't throw an apple core on the highway because a skunk will risk his life for it." He was staring at me, but not unkindly.

"Phil Lebed," he said, holding his hand out. What a round face—and was he crossed-eyed behind his glasses?

His hand was soft like a Kaiser roll from the supermarket. What was so odd about him? He talked like a white man, and he was shy like a white man, but his skin was the muted black of an old backyard tire swing.

"What's your name?" he said finally, when I didn't offer it, and—I knew intuitively—at great cost to his temperament.

Before I could stop myself, out came my standard, "Hey, that's what people always ask me." He only looked baffled again. "Swan," I said. "I'm Swan." I was not accustomed to speaking gently.

Between Phil's thick eyebrows and mat of dark hair was a sweatband of tight forehead. His eyebrows kept edging the sweatband upward. "Swan!" he said, clearly delighted.

"You got it," I said, covering my bases.

He put up his arm as if to shield himself. I would have to be even gentler!

A cunningly visored meter maid came sneaking along the sidewalk. I glanced down—yes, she had chalked my tires. I began to fumble instinctively in my pockets even as she stepped back and made to write out a ticket. The nerve. I put myself between her and the meter. Without looking up she said, "Better hurry." I opened my mouth—I was going to lay into her—but out of the blue—

"It's our car," said Phil Lebed, outrageously.

To make a love story short? As of that very moment, I was no longer alone against all the meter maids of this world.

From Rhode Island to the island of Manhattan—Phil was a New Yorker—was like jumping octaves. There were actual geological gorges—Phil was a geology teacher. Truthfully. Glacial ravines, used like garbage dumps. The train from Providence bore right through them. Once it stalled (the lights went out, and there was a long sighing sensation) and I saw a man sleeping under the pitted girder of the highway above us. The slope and the tracks made a perfect vortex for eternally blowing garbage. It was hard to shake that off, gliding into Penn Station half an hour later.

But there was Phil, so glad to see me. His glasses were yellowed like calluses, his dark hair shiny with lanolin, packed on his round head like a yarmulke. His eyes were not crossed, it turned out, but magnified.

For Phil, I described the view of water from the train: slate and onyx, white birds like paper boats, tawny sea marshes. I told him about the real boats that looked like they'd been shrink-wrapped for the winter, and the beautiful old houses on the water—*waterfront*, the obsession of all Rhode Islanders.

I told my mother, over the telephone, which she was sharing with a dying woman pastor from Olneyville, that Phil did the dishes.

"Do you cook suddenly?" bit my mother.

I hated cooking, just like my mother. Hah. The banality of genes.

Phil cooked, Phil did the dishes. It's not tit for tat, I wanted to inform her. But I was immediately ashamed of myself. I knew she didn't think that. I knew it wasn't an even exchange, her giving me life and me using it.

She was ignoring me, talking to her roommate. Stupidly, I'd betrayed a trace of self-importance in my marriage, and I was paying for it.

"Hello?" said my mother.

I said, "How's Jeannie?" The pastor.

"Here's a coincidence," said my mother. A sudden shift—her voice was rich with feeling. "Jeannie majored in geology!"

She didn't say, of course, "Like your husband," but I was fairly certain she was speaking of him—richly. And it occurred to me suddenly that my mother never said anything bad about my husband. My mother! Who cut into everyone, who butchered everyone into simple terms and stereotypes.

I had to try her. "He overcompensates for his masculinity," I heard myself saying.

But had my mother heard me? She crackled, and I could hear Jeannie laughing in the background.

I told myself I didn't see how Room 743 could be all that funny.

I was leaning on the counter in Phil's and my new co-op apartment. The countertops were a lifeless white and showed every single ring of coffee. Phil had promised to take me to Bear Mountain on the weekend. There was a soil test kit in his backpack. I told my mother I wouldn't be coming to Providence till the following Monday.

I hung up, pretending to be businesslike when a nurse stole her attention with tubes and cuffs, a bowl of ice cubes. I could hear the rustle and slump of a great pile of newspaper the nurse had pushed off my mother's lap unceremoniously. My stepfather always left her the newspaper, which, as she said, deprived her of her only reason for a field trip to the hospital gift shop. At home, my step-father used to read on his back, feet up, pages splayed across his privates. Sections would slide out for my mother to retrieve, the dog to skid on.

Phil read his newspaper at his desk, back rounded like a drum-lin. In a halo of Pleistocene light he was a protective examiner.

Sumi was handed down to us, I imagined telling my mother coolly.

"This girl is A++," read the note, with her name and tele-phone number scribbled on the back of a register receipt from Love Drugstore. The previous owner of our co-op had purchased Dramamine, Gatorade, and shoe polish.

I found Phil in the would-be bedroom, looking happily and blurrily about him. "Look at this, Phil," I waved the receipt in front of him. His good glasses had been misplaced in the move and these backups were from a high school prescription—thick, milky safety-goggle plastic. They say when one of your senses is compro-mised, your other senses kick in to compensate. Not in the case of my husband. He was packed in cotton. He couldn't see, hear, taste (all we'd had for three days preceding the move was Chinese takeout), or smell. (Our pores were Chinese. Our clothes and the two towels we'd kept out till the last minute.)

I spent part of every week in Providence. I kept the house up for my brother and stepfather, meaning I made one stop for milk, dog food, toilet paper. Then back on the train, most often with an empty seat beside me on the aisle, as weekday midmornings were not a popular time to travel. Trackside backyards bearing a family's series of big purchases—aboveground pool, trampoline, boat on blocks, pre-fab tool shed with a single, barren window box. A series of disappointments. My fleeting association with sandy scrub, folded paper birds on the low water was part of the all-around sadness.

One morning while I was on the phone with my mother (and the woman pastor, I complained to Phil later), there was a loud knock on the door. I hung up apologetically (although my mother hung up before I could apologize, quick as ever to slip out beneath the weight of emotion), and rushed headlong to answer it.

I peeked through the spy hole to see a woman's face, distorted by the miniature lens, nose first, huge, dilated. I retracted. Could she tell I was looking? Had she heard my eager footsteps, and then the appraising silence as I pressed my face to the door?

Somebody must have recognized her and let her into the building. I couldn't tell her from a psycho killer, but I opened the door anyway. I, who could barely cross the street in New York City without blushing, sensed immediately that I must act casual and—somehow—generous with my apartment.

"Sumi Creech?" she said, as if I were to approve a password.

She was white as Elmer's glue, with tomato-colored blemishes along her cheekbones. She smiled—a space between her small front teeth—but she wouldn't be the type for a conventional handshake. She wore a jersey skirt and an oily-soft, drapey T-shirt beneath which her abdomen showed like a week-old balloon, or the lax pouch of an out-of-work belly dancer.

"To clean?"

"Oh!" I cried, ratcheting up my sisterly smile. "Come in. I was just—"

She moved in on my little apartment.

I shrank back toward the white counters. There must have been a hundred henna rings, quite beautiful if you didn't think "coffee."

"Did they not tell you I was coming?" She lugged a duffel bag the size of a two-week vacation.

"Who's in there?" I said, before I could stop myself.

"All homemade solvents." She ticked them off on her fingers. "Vinegar for the glass, grapefruit seed extract for the bathroom, hemp, aloe vera. I bring my own rags unless you want me to use yours. I don't use paper towel." She squatted down and began to unzip the body bag.

"Wait," I said, and my voice curdled in my ears. Surely she hated me. For resisting? For everything.

That was it. I did not want her to hate me.

"The thing is," said Sumi matter-of-factly, "I know this apartment. I can do it in under two hours. On this floor I do Harriet's, the Kims'..." She trailed off. "If you want to ask anybody."

I studied the view from the kitchen window: all angles and blocks, hues of brick slashed with shadow, baked in sunlight. Sky, brick, street. It was so easy not to see the people.

I tried not to watch her. I tried not to listen to the roar of the vacuum—Phil and I didn't have one, but Sumi had let herself nonchalantly into "Harriet's" (I didn't know any of my neighbors) and borrowed "el Hoov."

When she got around to the kitchen, I retreated to the bedroom. She had picked up all the clothes and folded them neutrally, neatly. She had opened the blinds. How had light found its way down a brick chasm and then L-shaped like a periscope into this window? I stood at the bared glass and looked slantwise toward another brickscape. My apartment was beginning to smell like a dewy garden. Was there anything to say to her, if I made it out to the kitchen? Was there anything *not* to say to her?

Now I know you can divide womankind by those who clean feverishly the night before and those who leave oatmeal parchment curling up the sides of a pot, not unlike dried semen.

Before Sumi's arrival, I arranged flowers in casual mugs "here and there," as if I had an easy, spontaneous relationship with my apartment. I brushed crumbs from countertops, stopping shy only of sweeping the kitchen. I lined up my expired acne creams even though I no longer needed them, being a Mrs.

She cycled around to me on Wednesdays, some time before eleven. I made our bed, even placed a thrift-store ashtray on the white coverlet. I hadn't smoked since I was fourteen—behind the roller rink, just the once, with the girls who became nurses.

I always had the water boiling. While Sumi sipped her tea— cranberry, she had advised me, for urinary tract infections—I discreetly placed the two twenties half in, half out of her patchwork coat pocket.

We talked about Sumi's childhood. Her parents had dropped out in the seventies. They were back-to-the-landers, a revised farm in the Northeast Kingdom. Vermont, I learned, which was a place I'd never considered. What was it like to pad across the cold crooked floorboards of a vintage farmhouse in the middle of the night to the unlocked door of the outhouse? To meet boyfriends by the pond for skinny-dipping? I imagined them all, the boyfriends, as carpenters, or traders from the nineteenth century.

Sumi's wardrobe—I'd never seen anything like it. She wore anti-clothes, I decided, things that were ugly on purpose. But truthfully, was there anything more to style than purpose? Garishly crocheted shawls on top of leotards, peasant blouses stained from breastfeeding, a pair of drafty, unlaced high-tops. Her hair was thin and scabby from veganism, a practice in alignment with her political brand of poverty. She dyed it with a natural plant, and it was a righteous, premature gray at the roots. Sometimes she brought her baby, a little twist in tie-dye she called a sling, who swung like a third udder as she cleaned my apartment. "He was a persistent soul," she said admiringly. "He's been trying to get in on this world since I was fifteen."

"What's his name?" I asked gingerly.

"Goose," said Sumi. I noticed the baby had red-rimmed eyes like she did. Was she making it up on the spot? Did she remember my name was Swan?

Of course there was something crackpot about Sumi, but she was so easy to talk to, and her gappy smile.

She took canned goods, loose change, toilet paper, a load or two of laundry detergent in a Ziploc bag like a tiny blue waterbed.

Phil's mother, Alex, was the famous feminist. I had seen Phil scuttle for cover when our neighbor, Harriet, a lawyer who wore a margarine cardigan over her tennis dress, struck out down the hall ahead of us: Alex had put into Phil a fear of women. She didn't believe in marriage: it had the "unmistakable contour of oppression." But what mother believes in the marriage of her only son to the wrong woman? Alex had sculpted, hooded eyes that she blinked slowly (her eyelids had a color all their own— bloodless, lilac), and her burnt-looking hair fizzled at the ends like tassels of an ancient prayer rug. I couldn't decide whether she was ugly or beautiful. I couldn't decide whether I *wanted* her to be ugly or beautiful.

But I thought I knew what *she* wanted —if only I were a bona fide hayseed, pure and oxidized. No. I came from a dissipated line of White Zinfandel drinkers, bulk soda in the garage, tracksuits out of T. F. Green to no place farther or more tasteful than Disney.

I was traditional without being original, poor without being salt-of-the-earth or spendthrift. I was guilty of putting a post-wedding stretch limousine on plastic. I had whined until my stepfather caved on a real live pianist.

I didn't correct Alex. Truthfully, I hoarded it—the fact that my mother had moonlighted for Professor Nan Shemaria. Had capably—brilliantly?—graded Professor Shemaria's papers. From Professor Shemaria's office windows you could look down over the whole settlement that was Providence. My mother had described the barnacled tenements on treeless streets, the state buildings set in over-large parking lots, honeycombed on the inside with countless bureaus of busywork, with sleazeballs and pension-plodders staring out of nicotine-stained single windows.

Professor Shemaria studied Azorean immigrants. She staked my mother out at City Hall, where my mother was a regular Studs Terkel. She had no problem killing time with peroxided Marie Antoinette hairdos on coffee runs and the like while she waited for her subjects. Azoreans were forced to surface at City Hall eventually, in defense of a plat and lot number, a lush vineyard, perhaps, that thrived inside a city square of chain link, painstakingly trained and clipped up over a carport.

Professor Shemaria gave my mother a reporter's notebook. It wasn't necessary to be scribble-scrabbling as they spoke, she said, but it was also easy enough to stick the thing in a coat pocket. My mother might feel more natural herself if she engaged first and took notes later, Professor Shemaria suggested.

I used to imagine my mother was recording words of wisdom, social prophecy in broken English. Once I found the notebook set carefully on top of the piano. My mother was taking a shower, and

I swiped it almost without thinking. My thumb rifled the pages and a receipt fluttered out. I bent to retrieve it and saw it was for $2.83, from Dunkin Donuts. Suddenly I could hear the wall of street noise, loud static of car engines, horns, jackhammering in the background. I imagined air brakes, a city bus, a near accident. I felt my mother's gaze on me. There she was in the doorway.

"Gendered attitudes toward indigenous agriculture," said my mother dryly. Her long wet hair had soaked her shirtfront. I tried to shoot the notebook toward her. She took it almost graciously. A half smile: "It's not what they say but why they say it."

Alex was right about the hired pianist: poor taste.

My mother had always wanted to play at a wedding.

Oldies? Chopin?

She used to joke that she would wear black so you could tell her from the bride. At Phil's and my wedding she was in a supposed period of remission. But she came in late and sat at the back of the church, a promiscuous ghost among the distant cousins and old neighbors.

At the reception she sweated through her mascara like a maudlin prostitute. I made sure she and Alex did nothing more than shake hands with each other.

Alex never wore makeup. She smelled like her own sweat. A patchy, backyard smell—raking leaves, flaccid November grass coming off on your sneakers. I thought about mother animals rejecting their young after the cubs or the kits had been handled by humans.

I couldn't seem to tell my mother about Sumi. I told myself I was thrown by my mother's take on Phil, her uncharacteristic lack of judgment. But I decided to come clean—about Sumi—to

Alex. She was grading papers at her kitchen table as Phil prepared a dinner of stir-fried vegetables.

"Safe, Swan?" she said. "Vegetables?"

There'd been a little hullaballoo the week before. The noodles were made of the same thing as brown paper bags, I'd claimed. And I'd gone on, ridiculously, at my mother-in-law's table, that such noodles were "an insult to spaghetti."

To my surprise Alex said lightly, now, and without looking up from her papers, "That's too bad. I wanted to give you Ana Maria."

Twice a week, I learned, Ana Maria let herself into Alex's apartment in the West Village. Her shadow was a wafting blue mist of Windex, her tracks were white as soap flakes. As if by magic, bagels and milk were replenished, the thick dandruff of cat hair dealt to the throaty vacuum, toilets transfigured. "She was here today, I think," said Alex.

I excused myself. Indeed, the bathroom shone, all traces of Alex vanquished. I couldn't resist touching up my hair in the mirror polish of the toilet handle.

I had to admit I was morally stymied. I had seen the cash Alex left for Ana Maria on the kitchen table, blunt and rumpled.

Maybe, I thought, trying to excuse Alex, being a feminist just meant being busy. But there were contradictions. Alex considered her single motherhood a religion, but called herself an atheist. Phil's dad was "a friend of a friend's friend" who agreed on a whim. And yet hetero sex was never whimsical! It was grave, said Alex. Even violent.

Phil had the same hooded eyes as his mother, vein-colored eyelids. But his skin was dusky instead of halvah. He had the sweetest way of pressing his grapey lips together to suppress his giggle.

He smelled like pie. He was heavy-boned and barrel-chested. He closed his eyes when he took off his glasses. I rubbed gently around the bone; impossible, in love, to call it an eye socket.

So maybe feminism was just another word for contradiction. I sounded like Alex. Alex would say women were shape-shifters, fluid. If you wore high-heeled shoes, you were hobbled by the male race, but there was no race *happening* but the male race. I cringed when she tried to sound black. High heels or fleet sneakers? Alex would say that question was the kernel of feminism.

You passed off your broom, your rags, only to enslave another woman. Or were you saving her? From rice and beans in Tijuana? Phil copied his mother, careful to use the name of the city. You never said *Mexico*.

Once I heard Ana Maria retching. Alex stood in the doorframe of the bathroom in enormous slappy sheepskin moccasins and a man's dress shirt that came to her kneecaps. Her bare knees were dark and oily-looking with arthritis. Ana Maria's broad back pitched forward so that Alex had to brace herself to hold her. *Now my husband he say no more times. Always you losing the baby.* They lurched as a single form, a weird rocking horse.

Later Alex told me, "She sat down on the toilet and the baby came out like a pomegranate."

I guess I imagined we were in cahoots, Sumi and I, sharing the load of womanhood. I made the tea while she took a toothbrush to the shower grout. She did my laundry while I made confessions.

For instance, I'd gone off birth control. That was a confession. So many milestones of womanhood have had the taint of shame, secret, I said to Sumi. God, I couldn't bear to remember first menstruating, couldn't even use that word without feeling squeamish. "Sat on a berry?" my mother had said, offhandedly, without looking, or looking elsewhere, so I had followed her gaze across the room instead of around to the seat of my own nightgown.

Sometimes I lay upon the marriage bed and listened to the sounds of sweeping and spraying and vacuuming like they were the ocean. By the way, I said once to Sumi, there was no surf in Rhode Island. It's all bay where I'm from, fish heads and tampon applicators washed up on gravel beaches.

Sometimes I helped her with the other apartments on our floor. I believed my service was inconspicuous. We might have been a coffee klatch or a book club. I pretended I had to keep my hands busy polishing the silver picture frames on Harriet's display shelf. Waterskiing with a blond sister (or mother?), a boyfriend with a dinosaur jaw, Washington Square Park—law school graduation. Sumi called her the lawyerette and I laughed conspiratorially, stopping short of telling her how Harriet still terrified Mr. Lebed.

Of course I had cleaned the house for my mother, I told Sumi. My mother's weakness came in waves. My mother said, with wry distaste, that the nausea was like morning sickness in pregnancy. She said she never wanted to be found dead with her head in the toilet.

When I thought of my mother now, my every motion became obvious, garish. Like finding yourself on very thin ice, in the middle of a lake, in the middle of a nightmare. Even the decibels of your voice crying for help can break it.

My mother's illness? I said to Sumi, my tune suddenly cool and catchy, trying out the verdict. A long siphoning of housework, love, money for college.

I had an ancient snapshot that a maternity ward nurse had taken after my birth. "No breastfeeding in Rhode Island!" I declared, as I handed it over to Sumi. Did I want her to feel sorry for me?

I looked at it again, over Sumi's shoulder. There was a crease, white and soft, the stuffing of the photograph, right across my mother's abdomen.

My mother was propped up on the cot, self-possessed enough to have composed a scowl for the camera. The streaked johnny was more or less pasted to the front of her. My father was peeking out from behind her, clutching the paper bag she breathed in to stop hyperventilating. She puked in it later, she once told me.

To Sumi's credit, she studied the picture longer than was required of a housecleaner.

"No one's holding you, Swan," she said finally. I grabbed the picture. I suddenly didn't want her to say anything woo-woo about hospitals. Anything midwifey. Sure, I wished my mother could have died in my lap in a creaky farmhouse in the Northeast Kingdom.

But it was true. In the picture, I'm apart—above my mother, as if I haven't even been called down yet. From the heavens—is that how it works, really? Was I a "persistent soul," like Sumi's baby? Was I to take that to mean many abortions? I'm stranded on my back, on what looks like a metal steam table from a basement cafeteria. I'm a miniature monster. My red mouth is stretched at the corners, my bluish face contorted.

I imagine my mother rising from the cot coolly. Affixing a pad right to her jeans, no panties, like she always used to. Twisting her black hair off her neck first, then smoothing it from her forehead.

Okay, she says to the nurse who snapped the picture. I'll be back later.

My mother's funeral was the October after my marriage. My brother, living at home, watching football with our stepfather, eating our stepfather's red sauce, which he called gravy, came through, meaning he arranged it.

Alex offered to go up with us. She said, "Breast cancer is politics."

"Is she going to make a speech? Is she going to run for president of breast cancer?" I asked Phil later.

Phil told Alex we'd go by ourselves. She gave him two pink ribbons to pin on our funeral attire. I stuck mine onto my stepfather's dog's collar. I couldn't help it.

As if he hoped I would remember our meeting, Phil rented a Ford Taurus.

Alex lounged on Phil's side of the table, books on theory between them. Sometimes she asked me questions thinly disguised as conversation—I knew better than to answer by now if I didn't want to be a case study. I got up and cleared the Saturday lunch away.

In the kitchen I opened my refrigerator in a grand sweep. "Professor Lebed," I called. "Can I get you something?"

"Jam, Swan," came her tuneless voice. She always put it in her tea, like her Russian parentage, slyly asserting herself in my dominion.

But she was striding into the kitchen. I could hear her breasts lapping from side to side, her hair crackling with static. She kept a bowl of homemade jam in my refrigerator. Now she pulled it out and sniffed the uncovered surface.

"You don't know what to call me, do you," she stated.

"Well, Mother's a little awkward."

"The Other Woman," she said. She moved to toss the spoiled preserves in the garbage. I lunged.

"I was saving it." Of course, I wasn't.

Her eyebrows went up.

"I told Sumi to cover it," I said peevishly, before I could stop myself. Alex gave a short, harsh laugh. I stared hard at the flap of a mole on her chin. Once a month the single hair would have curled out long and wiry enough to hopelessly distract me.

I took a long time doing the dishes. "Swan!" called Alex. I came to the doorway. "What was the name of the professor your mother worked for?" I looked at Phil, whose forehead was working. I couldn't be angry with him for explaining me, or defending me, to his mother. But somehow, I'd wanted her to go on thinking I was tracksuits and spaghetti.

"Oh, shoot," I lied calmly.

"Not by any chance Nan Shemaria," said Alex.

I had to cough to unchoke myself. "Truthfully, I never paid much attention."

The moment I said it I knew I was damned if I was lying and damned if I wasn't.

I was certainly reeling, though. I'd gone from orphan of a janitress to devious daughter-in-law in an instant. I'd lost my cover, my mother uncovered...to get all academic about it.

Alex was looking up at me very carefully. "It was a frustrated life, your mother's."

Suddenly I wanted to beat my mother's life into Alex. I made a desperate grab for my wits. "My mother was always more interested in my life." It was meant as a rebuke, but it came out pathetic.

"That should tell you something." I heard condescension in her voice.

"Excuse me?"

"That should tell you something," said Alex.

"That should tell me I should have been there!" I was choking again. Stiff with rage—I was never agile as a fighter.

Alex said evenly, "You were the dream daughter. Let go of it."

I turned out of the doorway, disgusted with myself, with Alex. Death was sickening.

But then, all of a sudden, I got it. My mother's strange silence on the topic of Phil and Alex, her suspension of derision. She had hoped these were the people who would take care of me.

In the early evening I was to meet Phil at his mother's department, at a dean's tea where she was to receive an honor.

This is years later.

Alex was at the center of the coil, her olive-green eyes lit by the little amber-shaded university lamps on polished surfaces.

I heard her bray above the usual modulations and I thought, Alex has spent her career practicing laughing louder than any man in academia.

I watched her make her way to the cherry podium dollied in for the occasion. She seemed to sense me watching, and she found me in the crowd and nodded curtly. She had been hoping, I suppose, that Phil and I had come together. What were the famous feminist's true feelings about the ramifications, in real time, of fifty-fifty parenting? When it meant that there was equal likelihood of Phil or I being held up at home, even absent, on a night like tonight?

An X of a woman—cinched waist, flared, Victorian collar—was heading toward me. I hadn't counted on talking to anyone. The woman's features were deep notches, and as she came closer I decided she looked like Abigail Adams, first lady, with a beak chin and a sly, fetal old Englishness.

"You must be the Double Swan," she declared, holding her hand out.

She was presumptuous, and I wanted to recoil. Phil's private name for me, as Lebed, of course, is swan in Russian. So the woman must have had some intimate access to Alex.

She had an overly firm grip. She shook my hand as if women had been doing it for ages.

"Nan Shemaria."

It's not too nineteenth-century to say I nearly fainted.

Nan didn't wait for me to recover. She waved and gesticulated to Alex, pointing to the crown of my head when she caught Alex's attention. Alex lost no time zooming in on us.

"So?" said Alex, taking both my hands in hers.

"She looks exactly like her mother," Nan said.

Alex stepped back and squinted.

I found myself standing very still for their inspection.

"Shall we sit?" Alex directed us. I followed almost meekly. A grad student of Alex's, effete and fawning, passed with a tray of wineglasses filled one-third with red-brown liquid. I traded in my teacup.

We settled on a sofa. "Well first, here's to you, Alex." Nan raised her glass in the same way she had shaken my hand, as if toasting had always been women's provenance.

People were watching. My skin prickled. There was the dean, blundering toward us expectantly, burnished with alcohol. Alex rose to greet him. I cast my eyes around for Phil. What was keeping him?

Nan exhaled loudly when Alex set the dean on his course. "Such an intimate setting." The faux living room. "Alex, really. Congratulations. You do so deserve it."

Alex performed a sort of extroverted shudder.

It had not quite dawned on me that such stagecraft was for my benefit. Pointing to my wineglass, Nan said, "You might want another one before you hear this."

God, I thought, gradually recovering, and anticipating how I'd tell Phil that the two of them had the bedside manner of 1950s male gynecologists.

Nan said, "Alex and I have known each other for years and years."

Here came a grad student behind a platter of cheese, and suddenly I thought of departmental Gouda. My mother had brought home Friday leftovers under the thin shroud of a paper napkin. The cubes of cheese hardened back up in the refrigerator, or Zack would microwave a sandwich. The crackers were useless but I always buried them near the bottom of the trash. Even before my mother got sick I wanted her to think we were grateful.

"Casablanca," said Alex.

Truthfully, she uttered it. And I wanted to laugh, perversely. What a ridiculous name, as if I'd almost forgotten it.

"La Double Vie de Casablanca," said Nan. "Drink," she instructed. She was convincing. I thought I knew what was coming but nevertheless I brought the glass to my lips.

"A single mom with no education, recurring breast cancer," she faded off, shaking her head. "We women." I could see that she meant to cry but she had to reckon with her immense self-satisfaction. "I had no idea," she said, "that Casablanca was a cleaning person."

"It took us a while to piece it together!" said Alex. "That she passed herself off to Nan as some kind of—"

"Post-doc!" cried Nan. Again, wondering, "Post-doc. It never occurred to me to check out what—transcripts? W-2s?" She looked at Alex. "Our bubble, right?"

Alex nodded.

"It involved an extraordinary number of hours," said Nan, "my work. Casablanca's work."

Professor Shemaria really was shocked. I had to give her that. And Alex—it was unlike her to be overwrought. Was she? Was this the first time I had noticed her translucent skin, dark-edged features?

"Nan calls her Lucy," said Alex, then. "I just call her the Ur-feminist."

I waited. How they longed for my shock in return. For my approval of them in their discovery.

Truthfully, I hadn't known the extent of my mother's deception. I washed and ironed those smocks, and the navy-blue uniform slacks, several times a week. Her nametag said C.B. I imagined her swiftly, surreptitiously, stuffing the uniform in her locker, changing into jeans and a cheap blouse.

I heard Alex swallow. I had to swallow too, my laughter.

I had to swallow my mother's laughter.

"Either of you geniuses been digging around in my pennies?"

My mother is cawing. She's holding the big glass jar up like she's about to smash the clay tablet. Not just her voice, her whole face is hoarse.

I'm stricken for a long, awful moment. Did I do it or did I only dream I did it?

"This other woman at work?" says my mother. The jar is too heavy to hold up over her head much longer. Like an old freight elevator it jerks and drops down to the counter. "Fresh from the fucking Azores. Skinnier than I am." She pinches her waist, which is like a windpipe. "She doesn't have papers—she's covering for her aunt. That's the word. They all cover for each other. We're in the big closet in Tabor Hall together. I have to show her how to change the mop head. Tina, I say. We call them all Tina. She's dragging the Medusa out of the gray water. Her people are fishermen.

It's like she's hauling a whale. She says to me, 'Back in the Azores have I small sons and daughters.' How old is she—thirty? 'I'm savin to bring em hea-ah. I'm workin and savin.'"

My mother pats the counter till she bumps into her cigarettes. "I can't do that weird accent."

"But you know, geniuses?" Her voice rises. "Wait till she gets a load of this piggy bank."

ANNOUNCEMENTS

The idea for a baby is an inner light. Never before has Elena sensed her spirit. As if the white mist/fire of it were cloned? Divided?

She gets a little queasy when she thinks about that speckled ovum, like a red-checked tablecloth waiting to be laid with a picnic.

Tim says, Whoa. Elena.

The conversation drops off a cliff and they can hear its tiny ring-ping-ping when it hits the metal bottom. What kind of cliff is like a sink, stainless steel?

But she can't help herself. Since when has life offered such perfect resourcefulness? Since when has life collected all its lost buttons and suggested: two eyes, a nose, a mouth...

They've joked before about women friends who quit their jobs. When the babies come, their faces look like pansies and their fists like fleshy clubs. Both the babies and the mothers.

It's not that, says Tim, determined.

I'll stay home and pair socks! Make authentic pita between feedings!

She hears herself say "feedings," and it gives her courage and a kind of musical machismo, like she used to get from dancing drunk.

Or I'll go back to work and drop—him? her?—off at a daycare that keeps the babies in pens till they soak through their pants like a Romanian orphanage.

Rumanian, Tim corrects her.

At work she tells Sheri and Anita. They take her out to lunch and insist she order a virgin margarita. Sheri insists; it's what she wishes someone had done for her, she says, dangerously plaintive.

Anita says: In *other* countries, where they don't have, for instance, a certain family-values recovering-alcoholic president, tequila does not impact the future neuro-psych test scores of your baby, Elena.

Anita, of the amazingly slender flanks, like a greyhound, has three children. Elena realizes with some shock that she has never thought of Anita as a mother until this moment. In fact, she's never thought of women in general as mothers, and she takes a quick glance around the restaurant. It makes her woozy to imagine all of these dowdy office types in poly shells and rusky skirts—well—having the same inner light as she does.

The margarita is a slushy bowl of fruit punch. The corn chips in the basket are greasy, unsalted, and Elena already feels like a cow craving a salt lick.

Anita: So, are you going to find out?

Elena says she doesn't think there's anything surprising about being surprised by the gender.

I used to think it took nine months for the baby to decide for itself, says Sheri.

Do you have names yet? Sheri is like an eager little calico, ready to knead your leg if you let her jump in your lap. But it's not kneading—of course!—it's nursing, thinks Elena.

We're scaring her, chides Anita. Elena pushes the salad in a deep-fried shell toward the center of the table.

Then Sheri says: I had to give up my first.

All three women are silent. Needlessly, and helplessly, Sheri says: Baby.

Is this some kind of initiation? For ten years now, Sheri and Anita have been her best friends at work. Elena is suddenly furious. Why has Sheri kept her dirty secret?

Then Sheri says, genuinely embarrassed, I don't know why I just told you.

Elena doesn't think the ball should be in her court. After all, it wasn't her idea to have lunch at a Mexican restaurant.

But Anita is fluent: Was it your parents?

Sheri sort of breathes, Yes, and adds, Another lifetime. There's a flare of recognition between the two coworkers. Elena is left out of it.

Most days she takes the MBTA home, to its last stop: Providence. A couple of times a month, when her timing is off, she takes Amtrak. It's twice as quiet and five times as expensive.

There's the canyon of colonial houses, the tall white point of the oldest Baptist church in America, the golden dome of the Old Stone Bank. The train station is right against the statehouse, which she used to call the Taj Mahal when she first moved here, for grad school. It strikes her that every day she makes these same tired observations.

She says: I broke the news at work. Anita and Sheri.

And? Tim says guardedly.

They approve, I guess, says Elena.

Tim's already told a few people. He hasn't told anyone that Elena had been insistent in sex, not exactly aggressive, but as if she were at some sport. Perhaps rowing. But he has said that they were sure about the due date. And he's told his brother how Elena had wanted the lights out, a first, as if she were going to be able to actually see a conceptual spark in the darkness. And then he'd been embarrassed, sensing his brother's embarrassment.

When Elena is six months pregnant she hangs a rainbow-shedding prism in the clerestory window above the bassinet of the future infant. Little pixels of color will twinkle over her baby's skin like non-denominational haloes.

It's a Saturday in September and she calls her mother. Whimsically she says, What's it going to be like?

Her mother replies, Joy is an acquired taste, Elena.

What? cries Elena, laughing incredulously. It's not the first time her mother has issued warning. Elena understands it's mitigating, almost superstitious. Since when has Elena become ridiculously, heartbreakingly optimistic?

The baby's room is on the fourth floor of a typical triple-decker on the East Side of Providence. Quadra-decker, Tim calls it, the attic converted to make a duplex apartment, a small study under the eaves for Tim, and an alcove for the baby. Elena and Tim have lived here for eight years. Unmarried, except for the last three months. Tim's colleague married them, and the oriental rug in his living room shows up in all the "wedding" pictures. Tim and Elena trading rings, raising modest glasses of apple cider. They had walked home along the brick sidewalks, up and down over tree roots, holding hands, wondering separately at love's sudden practicality.

In the ninth month, December, Elena gives her notice. Not three weeks of paid maternity leave, but goodbye forever to the deliberate clatter of her high heels bisecting the commuter rail platform. She doesn't tell Tim for a full week afterward. Not because she's being devious, nor does she dread it, although he will be shocked and he will have to hurry up and finish his eighth-year dissertation so he can earn their keep.

Elena has to admit she doesn't tell him because she's superstitious. Just like her mother.

When the day comes, Anita and Sheri watch her pack up her desk from a respectful distance. They make a show of being strictly professional about it. Sheri has since apologized for her outburst over lunch: For stealing your thunder, Elena. She was sixteen and she was sent to a home for wayward adolescents. Sheri lets her starched blond hair sheath her face as she—bravely? pitifully?—finishes. Elena thinks maybe Sheri hasn't told enough people this secret. It seems as if there's a threshold for secrets.

Then Sheri says: I live for that day I hear a knock, though.

And the light inside Elena gyrates like the beacon of a lighthouse.

Anita says, Is it all the propaganda about breast milk?

Elena shakes her head, mute, as she passes under the office mistletoe. It's plastic, and the berries look like tiny egg sacs.

Because you can pump, one; and two, some babies just don't take to it.

The day she comes home with her briefcase and a tote bag stuffed with personal effects, she says to Tim: I broke the news at work.

And? Tim says, to cover for himself—he's not sure what news she's talking about, but he sees the bursting tote bag.

She waits for him to make sense of it.

He bends down and cradles her belly that is not a belly anymore it's so freakishly distended. When he stands up his face is
glowing from the contact. You're not a Mayzie, Elena, he says in
all seriousness.

She laughs uncertainly to hold the place where laughter could
be inserted.

No nanny/elephant sitting on your nest. Producing a kid who's
half kid and half nanny, Tim pronounces.

They've always had a sense of being together because they're
different from other people. But maybe it's no more than a biological trick to get them to couple, thinks Elena.

Tim is tall and fair, verging on redheaded. He bicycles to his
university office. He will always harbor a little disappointment
he can't wear black turtlenecks—he looks like a corpse—but he
consoles himself with a real tweed jacket he bought in Scotland.
People like to think he's Scottish.

Elena has been described as gorgeous, because she's dark and
dramatic, with first-class, movie star eyebrows, and as Tim said
once, eyes that talk. Her mother says: Isn't it wonderful. People
are comfortable these days with ethnic.

Elena's mother would never dare call a daughter of hers gorgeous.

The linden tree in front of their triple-decker is skuzzy with
pollen and the metal stair rail is sticky with sap. There are young
flies all over it. Even the sky seems yellow-green.

The baby is three months old, and the baby is three hundred
years old, and the baby could care less about arithmetic. There
is only—as in, in this world only—the bassinet in the converted
attic. Because now that Elena knows the searing hypnosis of pain,
the slick catapult of a full-sized dolphin shooting through her en-

trails (stomach is the least of it), the kinetic energy of the bare wet worm on her blood-spattered chest, she would never leave this baby alone for an instant. Not to mention the panic she felt when they brought the baby home and the entire triple-decker—not just their apartment, but the apartment of the urology resident, and the apartment of the downsized retirees from Maine with their vanity plates (NVR2LT)—was cast in utter darkness. So she sleeps in the gliding rocker by the bassinet, watches the linden tree outside the three-quarter-sized attic windows, reads through his naps in the same rocker with her varicose lower half propped up on the changing table.

The baby is three months old and Elena has the sense that Time itself has a three-month-old's consciousness. Time cannot, for example, roll over, and Time's blue eyes are still bleary, even flat, marked by a previous universe. She supposes Time can hear—her baby passed the hearing tests—but can't or won't pick out the words of her specific pleas, spells, sentences. It seems irrelevant to say Time is going slow, or Time is going fast. Time, like her baby, moves spastically, with a startle reflex.

Anita visits. She takes one look around the overheated apartment: Elena. As if staying home were a still life, and going back to work? Some kind of action-adventure movie?

Just ask people to touch his feet, says Anita. Anita herself squeezes the baby's tiny white tube sock.

It takes Elena an hour to get ready to leave the apartment. Anita pretends to be very patient. Elena tries to do everything with the baby strapped to her chest. Finally Anita says, Here. Let me hold him while you brush your teeth.

Reluctantly, Elena unstraps. Anita says, We'll just walk up to the park.

Anita says, You can't let this take over your life. He's his own guy. Really. Anita snorts. Elena has never heard Anita snort. The bright yellow forsythia is overflowing the wrought-iron fence, and the ground looks tender, like a new scar. The park is a box of sunlight. The baby tries to blink and squinches his eyes shut.

You're lucky you dropped the weight so quickly, says Anita.

Anita leaves from the park. She admits she has to do something with her own kids—sports event? birthday party?—and Elena slowly gathers herself and makes her way back to her apartment.

Later, she feels prurient gazing at the pinched bud of his face, picking the yellow beeswax scabs called, as in a fairy story, cradle cap. Even saying his name out loud seems intrusive.

Around five months, newfound energy. She can hear her mother call her spunky. She compares her baby's life to the life of a Third World orphan. Not that she has firsthand experience, but there's a general consciousness, dispatches from courtrooms and orphanages in China, Ethiopia, in the women's magazines at the OB where she'd been stationed weekly by the end to hear the prenatal heartbeat. Or, she wonders, how many babies out of a nursery crop (she thinks of the twenty or thirty infants swaddled in their shiny little basins, along with her baby, all of them lighter, wetter versions of their parents) would be abandoned to daycare from the get-go? Or witness the beating, maiming of an animal?

Her baby bunches himself around his crib like an inchworm. Now he can push up on his little arms to take a look. His eyes are clear and kind. His hair is coming in, fine and dark and surprisingly stiff, so that it looks like he has a buzz cut.

Oddly, it seems there is no time to follow the instructions to knit a "bonnet with chin strap." It's as if just to be a mother takes up all the time in the world.

She looks out of the fourth-floor window past the State House, toward parts of the city she has never visited. Beyond the city are the purplish hills of——Massachusetts? That she doesn't know what goes on in the square office buildings decorated each by a necklace of cars glinting and signaling in the sun seems to be an indulgence. It's not because she worked in Boston. Where are the big gassy city buses going? Dirty seagulls fly over a yellowing park that was supposed to provide low-income kids with——an alternative.

She thinks she'll take her son there, to that defunct park, when he is one or two and toddling beside her. An ice cream cone will once again mean what it meant when she was a kid. At the pop-down window, hopping impatiently on one foot, she will buy ice creams from the singing truck for all the low-income children.

When Alexis is six months, they go to an island for a long weekend.

Look at that, says Tim, the bed and breakfast has port-a-cribs.

It does seem amazing. That anyone would know what they needed.

It's difficult to pack. Tim hangs in the doorway watching.

Diapers, diapers, and tiny undershirts.

They park near the ferry dock in one of the dirt lots where a chowderhead kid in an oversized T-shirt and flip-flops waves them in as if he's been waving cars in for eternity. Tim carries everything on board while Elena bears Alexis. Her heart is in her throat. He's not going to drop, she tells herself.

She watches Tim leaning over the railing out on the deck. What does he see? The diving gulls, three brothers with identical hollow eyes throwing potato chips, the deep fur of white water the ferry churns behind it.

Or, with eyes on the back of his head, his wife and baby?

It seems miraculous that Alexis goes down in the port-a-crib. Elena sits on the edge of the four-poster watching him. She is almost stunned, actually, that all this—the baby—still exists when they transplant it. She wears her damp nursing bra to bed, goodbye sexual dignity, her eyes are too dry since pregnancy to wear her contacts.

When she closes her eyes she feels the subtle rollick of the ferry.

She is a ferryboat leaving a white trail, flat as a cake, holding steady.

In the morning she watches the sea from the porch of the bed and breakfast. The pitch of the ferry (another one making the crossing) is almost imperceptible from this distance. But the knowledge of capsize is in the body of the boat, thinks Elena.

She has hardly allowed anyone to visit. Tim's mother has been held off, Tell her I have postpartum.

Her own parents have made the drive from Queens only once, when Alexis was two weeks. She hasn't encouraged them, and they've sort of settled back into the fact that they already have ten local grandkids. Her offering seems minute. Her mother cleaned and cooked for forty-eight hours and her father folded newspapers that Tim left butterflied on the kitchen table.

Tim suggested having one of his grad students and the grad student's lonely British wife over—just drinks, he promised. Elena scanned her kitchen through the eyes of a female stranger and saw ridges of black dust on her high cabinets, a tacky film on the range hood.

Listen, Elena said. I am not a yogurt-eating housewife who whisks away dust instead of reading contemporary fiction or the—the op-ed pages. And I am not a career-chasing feminist who hires a Guatemalan housecleaner and then doesn't even notice her own spanking clean range hood.

Tim looks utterly defeated by the logic.

She knows she's privileged to be a housewife looking down (from above) on a housewife.

When Alexis is nine months, Elena decides to send out announcements. Friends from college with whom she's fallen out of touch, Tim's department, a high school boyfriend she hasn't seen since she was twenty-one but suddenly, inexplicably, misses.

Well, yes; now that she thinks about it, that's who she wants to tell: Ryan. She is a gummy-faced adolescent, her dark mane of hair unstyled like a peasant's, her slender, grooved neck, and she and Ryan are eating her mother's spinach pie and having a staring contest.

She doesn't think they had a lot to talk about, but there was unmistakable kinship.

She chooses a snapshot in which Alexis bears a striking resemblance to her, to his Greek side, as Tim says: Telemachus.

But Alexis is not exactly Homeric, or bronzy. If his skin has a color, it is chalk. Elena thinks of science class: is white a color? The color wheel, the periodic table, the Bunsen burner, the rainbow. Ryan sitting directly behind her so she felt she had extrasensory nodes budding out of her shoulder blades.

In the picture Alexis has morello cherry lips, dark lashes. His eyes are big and tragic. What would Ryan think?

Of course Elena Theodoro had a boy who looks like a girl. That's what Ryan would make of it.

And why of course? And why can she read Ryan's mind, in memory?

Actually, Tim thinks Alexis looks more Indian. A maharaja (she cringes, Tim with his complexion like strawberry shortcake), a princeling from *Arabian Nights*. Other babies are stuffed animals compared to elegant Alexis.

She has intended to put a crayon in his right hand, from the start. She admits her bias: the lefties in grade school were bad spellers and when they wielded scissors it looked as though they were cutting backward, into themselves. She puts her dry, chalk-purple hand over Alexis's underwater grip.

He already knows the scope of the apartment. The table legs and chair legs and clatter of his own fork when he lets it go on purpose. He stops to watch Elena at work on his birth announcements.

She has never done anything like this in front of Alexis. Never shaved her legs either, or mixed a drink: how can a set amount of alcohol make two people drunk? And yet she has not dared to drink a drop for fear it will spike her breast milk. She feels this project as a risk. She must be able to clean up fast, hide the evidence. If she is needed by Alexis.

The Crayola colors are paler with paraffin than she remembers from her childhood. She had imagined a more primary rainbow. She's going to glue the snapshot on card stock and draw a crayon frame around it. Now that she's started she feels a tremendous rush. Not to finish, she wonders, but never to stop.

In warning, Alexis starts to huff and puff on the floor below her. Why have I been deprived—for ten whole minutes—of body contact?

Oh, says Elena. She feels her color rising. Her double life, these birth announcements. He keeps huffing. His mouth begins to collapse but he remains bravely upright.

She never feels really free. In fact, not even as free as she used to feel on her lunch break. She has made an analysis of the verb phrase, "to put a child to bed," and decided it is not an action, or a series of actions. It's a presence. As in, the presence of the mother. Tonight, however, after Alexis is down for his first shift of sleep, she anticipates getting back to her little art project. She edges away from Tim, who is slightly flushed from wine and standing across the sink from her.

She says, I'm making announcements. Tim clears his throat. She says, You know, Alexis John Gamble. Seven pounds five ounces.

Alexis is twenty-eight months. This is absurd, says Tim. Do we count in months until he moves out of the house for college?

The birth announcements have just come back from the printer. There were several false starts, so that in the end, Elena had them printed.

Should she include a more recent picture of Alexis? He has long dark curls. She can tell that Tim feels conflicted about a haircut: the problem of baby and man in the same little body. The problem of mortality, already. She finishes up the dinner dishes. She takes the printer's box—several hundred announcements— and places it carefully at the back of her closet.

ARK

Caryn and five children are snowed in. The kitchen windows are iglooed with translucent bricks of opal, aquamarine, and rose quartz. The house feels different. Bigger—because it is all there is—and smaller for the same reason.

It's Friday, the kids' third day home from school, and Tori, the oldest, has strep throat. Caryn suspects it's from kissing another seventeen-year-old, a boy with a silver stud in his chin like a hard, shiny blemish. The oldest's story always gets told first, as if it were universal. Tori's friend is named Leo and Caryn suspects it may be his name her daughter likes, more than his kisses.

The kitchen is at the back of the house, with an abrupt face-off onto an imposing escarpment built recently, stone by stone, at great cost, by shy and seemingly peaceful crews of Azoreans. Caryn's husband, Dom, pointed out that they don't tell her their real names, and as if it were related, Caryn regularly complains that she can't see anything out the kitchen windows.

But now she can see snow, like light's body. Striated, blue-bright, a cross-section of a cliff. Light's body? The way all of her children have been entranced, at some point, with stamping on each other's shadows. "You're dead!" she can hear them yell, as they leap away from each other on the sidewalk.

Dom is away on business. If they were a Venn diagram, the two circles representing her and the children would be almost perfectly stacked, while Dom's would appear adjacent.

"Snowed in?" Dom caroled when he checked in last night. Caryn pictured him pinching his square buttocks together, a tic of merriment, standing at the plate-glass window of a hotel room on a high floor, looking out over twinkling lights. The particulars first. The shovel lost in a drift: couldn't she borrow from a neighbor? His ardent practicality came barrel-rolling through the darkness and he'd laughed, "Like *Little House on the Prairie?*"

When he's home he reads out loud (inviting himself inside their Venn circle), his trim gray head propped on his furry arm on a child's pillow. Caryn can tell that he likes the sound of his own voice. Once, after wine, she'd said she found vanity in men endearing. He'd claimed to be baffled and wouldn't let her apologize. He doesn't necessarily get sucked into the story like she does, but he loves it that she cries at the prairie deaths, the disasters in the Big Woods, and he is, in his approval of her, relentless.

Her younger children, Louisa, Anne, and Thomas, are occupied for the moment, quiet. There were births for each of them, thinks Caryn, but the individual strands of memory have been worried and felted. Like a blanket put through the wash cycle. Like the snow, its little lint hairs and fibers getting denser by the minute.

The boy at the kitchen table clears his throat: Paul, her sister's child. His hair is skull gray, and at five, he already has an Adam's apple. A year ago Ellen called in tears with the news of a scoliosis, and before Caryn could say anything, Ellen accused her of having four—*four*—as if it were an inoculation against the spinal curve of the only child. As if Paul, thought Caryn, a specimen, had to be a Frankenstein's monster of many disparate perfections.

Caryn's kids treat him with preternatural coolness, like an invalid. When Ellen drops him off, once a week, for an overnight, he perches on his hardbacked suitcase until Caryn escorts him up to Thomas's room, where she pulls a cot out. Why does she persist in putting him in with Thomas? Her son is eight, with rain-colored eyes and straight blond hair in a bowl cut. She knows his teachers think he is a devil; he's always being typecast by grownups who've loved or hated some other little hellion. He shines a flashlight in Paul's eyes whenever Paul betrays sleepiness, he has been known to guide Paul's sleeping hand into a bowl of warm water. In the mornings Paul waits for Caryn at the top of the staircase, his scoliotic, geriatric little form wrapped in a plaid bathrobe and corduroy slippers from Paris.

Caryn and Ellen are petite and blond, prettily of Irish descent. Ellen has a delicate, even precarious neck that will always present as girlish: as if she's at once carefree and in need of protection. They have analyzed their differences with no small amount of wonder. Growing up, they believe, they were meant to feel like the same person.

Caryn's hips are slightly flared, but they could still trade slacks, if Caryn wore anything but jeans and Dom's running sweatshirts. Motherhood is economical, the way it forces out all adult drama— for instance, a serious conversation with her sister. And it prevents her, when Ellen drops Paul off, from picking the fight she knows Ellen is waiting for.

She holds up an accidentally purchased box of lemon cookies. Maybe Louisa is right, and the fussy *biscuits* and the fussy cousin go together. Louisa's deft logic: "French people like lemon stuff."

It's Paul's dad who's French. Da-*veed*, croons Louisa. Once, last summer, Caryn took Paul into the yard to inspect an ant colony: the kind of patient, hands-on parenting she wishes she'd done more of with her own children. The kind of thing, Dom says, that would ensure their children ran for office on a save-the-insects platform. She peeled away the lawn, a lacy, desiccated layer of turf, to expose the precise sand kingdom. Paul said in his trill voice, "If I had one for a pet, it would die of grief, Aunt Caryn."

She'd tried to tell Ellen, but Ellen wasn't captivated. Maybe Ellen was simply distracted, rushing to work, but Caryn had been hurt, and sorry for herself, also, for the effort and tedium of confronting the mystery of the ants' existence compared to her own and her children's. She's gone to great psychic lengths to cultivate a token memory of each of her children. Token diminishes it; it's more like a cue. An unerring prompt from the unconscious, so that if her house burned and she lost every archived finger painting, hooked-rug potholder, autumn leaf like an unreadable old map between sheets of waxed paper...

There was a single mother with a boy in Tori's class in kindergarten who lived in an incongruous California-style apartment complex near the old Sunbeam Bread in East Providence. It was rumored that the boy took Ritalin and dressed up after school like a princess. So that the image of a plastic rhinestone tiara is luridly linked in Caryn's mind with a sort of pre-criminal, Child Services hyperactivity. The single mother—Caryn remembers her as too tall, full of shoulders—lost every single princess photo in the apartment building fire.

Caryn thinks she heard the boy made varsity as a freshman.

She can leave Paul for a moment. The front of the house faces north and the north wind doesn't allow drifts to accumulate. It looks like neighbors have decided shoveling is useless. Early this morning Mr. D'Amata got out in his pickup; now it's three o'clock. His parking spot is a shallow white basin.

The plow hasn't even made one pass on their street. Caryn catches herself listening for its rumble, the clank of its metal udders as little jet sprays of salt and gravel hit the messy roadbed. There is no wind now, and the quiet snow tumbles straight down to earth. Time accumulates with no pretense. Each hour feels like an hour, each minute feels like a minute. The snow is the sand in an hourglass.

There's a cascading crash from Thomas's room upstairs and suddenly she sees Thomas at fifteen months, his Dumbo ears, hot, red cheeks, quick fists, bullfighter's tight little rump. "I'm paying my dues with this one," Caryn used to repeat, not exactly plangent, but needing an incantation, on the playground, in the checkout line at the supermarket.

Caryn and Dom joke that their family keeps the pediatrician in business. The practice takes over a rambling, Victorian house in the cramped and shaggy university neighborhood. Caryn found herself there weekly in those early years—Louisa, Anne, and Thomas are all less than two years apart—and she used to chat up the bank of receptionists, women of a certain age, tugboat-bottomed, presiding over Brach's butterscotch candies, for whom, despite her conspiratorial chitchat, Caryn reserves a subversive, daughterly hostility. The Arletta pack, she bantered, should endow an extra couch in the waiting room.

She remembers breezing in for Thomas's fifteen-month immunizations, calling out to the receptionist panel, ever ready with trench humor, and being ushered into the empty office of a doctor new to the practice. She set Thomas, in a diaper, up on the white-papered table, and Thomas immediately—obviously—slid off it. He was so much like Curious George Caryn wondered if she could have been inseminated by a children's book. Dom used to roar at that. Even the short legs and long torso. Thomas made a beeline for the trash bin bristling with live germs and ta-da, thought Caryn, we'll get a month of green snot, disease of hoof and mouth, the tongue infested with yogurty white blotches.

Just as she started after Thomas, the doctor appeared in the doorway. Thomas's cheeks—it was eczema, actually, and not spirit—went instantly tomato.

"Not so fast, my man," said the doctor, scooping up the toddler.

Thomas stood straight up on the doctor's lap, his bowlegs locked, alarmed, but possibly interested.

Caryn produced an exaggerated sigh for the doctor. She rose and held out her arms to receive her baby. She shook her head as if to say resignedly, fourth child. It occurred to her that there was a lot of bluffing that went into a relationship with a doctor. Come on, she said silently. Hand him over.

But the new pediatrician seemed to have his own agenda. "Please sit down, Thomas's-Mom," he said gravely.

Caryn cringed. The doctor looked at her over the top of his glasses. "The terrible twos at fifteen months."

Taking her seat, Caryn told herself it was standard issue, the way he crunchled his short beard with one hand and appeared to hold the child effortlessly with the other. But still, she sensed the floor of her stomach.

And then the doctor made his now-famous comment. "The ears don't have to be a badge of courage."

At first she had no idea what he was talking about. She was already on shaky ground: a new pediatrician, and Thomas performing agitated knee-bends on the fellow's quadriceps. For a second she wondered if she had misunderstood words of wisdom; then she saw the pediatrician's long fingers pulling Thomas's ears out.

It's true that she has replayed the scene so many times it's become rote. Stilted. The way the light through Thomas's distended ears shown crimson, like his cheeks, the way the doctor's white coat was almost blinding, a well-planted movie shot, really, and she had momentarily thought that maybe it wouldn't be fire or flood, after all, that destroyed her family, but something she learned from a doctor. And she knew, at least for an instant, that fear of death generated all other fear in the world.

The pediatrician—she'd said to Dom: *the fucking doc*—had wanted to pin Thomas's ears back. Stitch them, albeit temporarily, to the sides of her son's head, so that he would look like *Go, Dog, Go!,* a Dr. Seuss hound in the perpetual headwind of a drag race.

"Like a Doberman Pinscher?" she'd demanded.

"Train them," the doctor had sort of correctively mumbled.

But even as she was stabbing her things back in the big boxy diaper bag, Caryn was considering. What would it be like if her children—not just Thomas, but in the abstract, *children*—were perfect? Would it make for a storybook that was somehow easier to remember?

Of course, her brain ticked, it would be a simple outpatient procedure. Maybe it could be done right here in this office. Would insurance cover it even though it was cosmetic? Would Thomas claw at the stitches in his sleep or when he was bored in his stroller or his car seat?

Then Caryn caught the doctor keeping keen watch on her. And she had harnessed her fear of death, a moment before so lucid, and as if to mock it, she'd choked out: "You should have been a veterinarian."

At four o'clock the snow stops and Caryn finds herself strangely unsettled. She can almost hear the low roar of the highway, a science-fiction river in a one-dimensional, fictive distance.

Louisa and Anne are playing cards in embarrassing British accents and Thomas has exiled himself to the basement in order to yell, because yelling is particularly not allowed when you're snowed in, says Caryn. She catches herself getting chippy. The house is a hive, self-contained. She has cans and cans of tuna. She has raisins and M&Ms, apple-cranberry juice. She leaves Paul in the kitchen and mounts the stairs to check on Tori.

Her oldest child is two weeping, watermelon eyes at the top of a snow-colored comforter. "How did you collect five water glasses?" says Caryn before she can stop herself. She goes to the window. The sky has thickened once more and snowflakes like the soft undercoat of a shedding mammal begin to spin and arc around the big linden. "Believe it or not," she says, "a couple of ice skaters are coming up the hill at this very moment." Tori's comforter rustles.

The snow against the glass is like a wave breaking. The cars are prehistoric mounds, the wind is now a giant. Caryn opens the window a crack and then pinches the storm window to slide it open. The woman ice skater is carrying brown leather skates in her gloved hand. The man must have his skates over his shoulder, under his coat. They would've needed a bulldozer to get to the ice, thinks Caryn.

"You can't go skating in this." Tori's voice comes out creaky. Even when she's sick she doesn't trust her mother.

Caryn sticks her nose out, miming deep breaths. The sound of a snow shovel—no longer a scrape, the snow is too deep to get down to the sidewalk—comes from inside the earth. Finally, right behind it, is the deep rumble of the snowplow. "I'm sick," her big daughter says, drawing her head off the moist pillow, long-suffering, indignant.

The snowplow is a woolly mammoth. Caryn closes the window. She puts her hand briefly on Tori's forehead and Tori accepts it faithlessly. Caryn takes all five water glasses between her fingers.

In the kitchen, Paul is steadily pouring his milk onto his placemat.

It's not like him, usually she wants to shake him for being overly polite, and Caryn is more concerned than irritated. She puts a dishtowel on the white lake but doesn't say anything.

"That airplane sounds like blades in the sky," remarks her nephew. His calm is false. Caryn knows he's been using all the powers of his imagination to make it stop snowing. The snow is coming down in chunks and curtains.

She knows it's the wrong thing to say but she says it anyway: "There's no way a plane would fly in this."

Paul speaks French with his dad like an angel. Too sweet, almost. Louisa, who mines her jealousy with lewd pleasure, sings from the radio, "*Voulez-vous coucher avec moi, ce soir,*" and Paul blushes. Caryn guesses Louisa feels encompassed by her sisters, even suffocated. She has no cold edge against the world like Tori, the oldest, and Anne, next to a brother. She never gets new clothes (she complains bitterly, predictably), and she doesn't even get to keep the hand-me-downs. Louisa could be the unhappiest of her children, just because of birth order. Caryn chides herself. She's not a fortune teller. She's a parent.

Anne is the most like Caryn. Fair-skinned, open-minded, usually quiet. Always dependable, the one who puts the new toilet paper on the roll, reminds them to stop humming Christmas songs in February. Caryn suspects Anne is Dom's favorite. A father can have a favorite.

For a moment she wonders what it would be like if Dom were here in the snowstorm with them. The point is they're *out* of the storm, she corrects herself. But it feels like they're within it.

She used to call Dom Big Man on Campus. It amazes her suddenly, seems passive-aggressive, almost, in today's careful rhetoric. Also because he's short, although back then she didn't think so. Dom the sprinter, fireball, speed demon: top-rated college athlete.

A gentleman jock. If someone twisted his ankle in a meet, Dominic would give up his time, his rank, his flow, and stop midrace to help the injured runner. When Dominic slowed, his body gave the impression of unwinding. Caryn loved to watch the high light blur of his run break apart, become mechanics. The decelerating, effortless jog, the torso slanting back against the very wind he'd just created.

He watched over his moods as carefully as his muscles. He said it depressed him not to help his fellow human. He was also prelaw; Caryn was lost somewhere in the Art Department. In fact, you could fall in love and call it art. She would have liked to major in watching Dominic Arletta's races.

One blowy winter day in her senior year Caryn entered the art studio and beheld the track star, stripped down to shorts, emerging from the janitor's closet. He appeared neither proud nor flustered. He ran his hand through his hair, which was warm brown, wavy, and long for a jock, and took his place on the pedestal.

"We have a new model," the professor remarked, and then off-handedly gave the assignment.

"What about the shorts?" said a big, coarse, boarding-school girl next to Caryn.

Caryn found herself infuriated. She glared at the girl and the girl snickered. Of course he wasn't naked. That was for middle-aged women, who, for the very reason they were ashamed of their stippled stretch marks and hormonal flushes, displayed themselves in front of college students. Perverted. Not Dominic. And she didn't need to see any more to know she loved him.

He said he was five ten so more likely he was five eight. He was slight but strong, skin a luminous olive. There was nothing extra about him, as if his heart, too, were pure in its race. His light eyes were full of amusement at his predicament.

He wasn't hard to approach. He was used to sporty female friends, they all massaged each other's charley horses. He was a boy, funny and careless, and a man, careful and serious. Caryn learned that he was modeling for credit: a semester in her drawing class so that he could get away with more track meets, fewer liberal arts courses. Caryn learned that he had a girlfriend—a runner, they did ten easy loping miles together on Saturdays—who was beautiful, black, and taller than Dominic by practically four inches.

In the spring Caryn showed her senior project. It only took her one night to assemble a clutch of driftwood like furniture. It was totally unusable. Her advisor said she should try to follow through on a concept. Was she trying to posit, her advisor queried, that conversation was a conceit? Ironic? So Caryn called it Conversational Grouping. Art was all in the title.

Ellen was coming up right behind her, in textiles. She gave Caryn an old-time train conductor's cap she prescribed as Caryn's handle. She would fix some couture-ish concoction on Caryn and then have to scissor Caryn out of it. She'd wail, "Why am I designing fabric for airplane seats?" Ellen wore her own clothes like she thought she was starting a movement.

During graduation week, between magnolia and lilac, the university was all send-off receptions. The Greek Revival and

Georgian brick university houses, with their high-walled gardens and miniature avenues of boxwood, were opened to students. Caryn and Ellen bought a structurally sound if prom-queen-like wedding dress at a secondhand shop. Together they sewed on seven layers of skirts in varying shapes and textures. The bodice was tight, opaline, and the petticoats were shell, snow, yellow, bone, smoke, dust, parchment.

The evening of the art department party was balmy and bowered with ornamental cherries in huge pale tufts and grass freshly clipped and fragrant. Caryn, in a rainbow of whites, went barefoot. The white wine seemed to be just another petticoat, and she got very drunk with very little effort. An hour into the party she was more or less incapacitated. Ellen had vanished, and who should appear but Dominic Arletta.

She has to ask herself now, in light of Tori in high school, was this an era before date rape? Was there really any chance goodness preceded badness in history? But the truth is, Caryn had been rescued. Dominic took her to his room, which smelled of clean laundry and plain seltzer, and, while she lay where she had fallen diagonally across his bed, he talked about running professionally versus law school, and how he did remember her from what he called his "ersatz modeling." He turned out to be as kind—straightforward, unassuming, he wouldn't have read anything into her ridiculous costume—as she'd suspected.

It occurs to Caryn now that she'd like to say it with grace. With gratitude, even. Not to invoke the near scandal, the heartbreak she caused her parents. Because that first night with Dom—that was Tori. Ellen Victoria. How ornate, amateurish, the name seems now.

She and Dom were married in August. She didn't wear the dress of many whites; her mother chose a disgraced-fat-lady tunic.

Raising her eyes again to the blanked-out kitchen window, think-ing about her parents, Caryn realizes she'd choose to be snowed in without them. She doesn't want them on her ark, her houseboat. Why isn't it enough to do what you think is right, Mother? How does imposing your right on me make you all the righter? Her mother, as if apologizing for her: "That's just college gibberish, Caryn."

Ellen had shown her support by shielding her eyes from the tunic of shame, and their love—Caryn and Dominic's—was trans-formed into an ongoing state of relief, thinks Caryn.

The phone rings. "It's six o'clock," snaps Caryn, catching her-self when she sees Paul's forlorn aspect. "He's sitting right here at the kitchen table."

Ellen drives a tiny, lime-green Beetle that would be better suit-ed to France, or a golf course. There is no way she is driving in this. It's not an apology, notes Caryn.

The only reason Ellen does not live in France is to be close to Caryn. Otherwise she hates this mini Mafiosi municipality, as she calls it, and Da-*veed* hates it, and they are always cracking on the mayor, who looks like Mr. Toad from *The Wind in the Willows* and possibly inflicted cigarette burns on his wife's lover. Secretly Caryn takes offense when any Italian name is parodied.

Ellen says defensively, "I'm not going to *walk* over."

No. From one side of the city to the other. But here is Paul, grieving at the kitchen table.

They're snowed in. The universe is snowed out. If there is no more universe, it doesn't matter that they are the five children and she is the mother. They are all on equal footing. It's a regular commune. A utopia, as the founding fathers would have had it. As she strides from the kitchen into the body of the house, she cries, "Anyone for minestrone?"

"What is a state of emergency?" Paul bleats from behind her. He won't eat canned soup. Da-*veed* makes his own stock with bones and parings. She should set Paul up with paints or Play-Doh. Thomas has refused all contact. She pulls a book of busywork mazes from under a pile of library books.

"Here, Paul," she says, handing him a pencil.

"Thomas!" she calls down into the basement. "I'll take you outside, Thomas!" She places her palm against the wall to descend the narrow staircase. There are the snow shovels against the stone wall, looking sheepish.

The basement is one big room with wobbly homemade shelves in deep corners. At first she doesn't see Thomas in the gloaming. He can't reach the chain on the bare bulb, and she suspects part of the allure of the basement is the semi-darkness. There are the hammers and nails, the cordless drill, the sodden bags of MiracleGro like blue salt, the pickax and handsaw have a life of their own. There's an instinctual fear, a surprise element about childhood.

He tackles her from behind. She screams before she can help it. His monkey limbs around her middle. "Thomas!" She pries him off roughly but he's incited, ready to go body to body. She can hear her daughters' running steps through the house. They heard her scream. She hopes she hasn't scared Paul. She doesn't think he'd budge from the kitchen table without her.

"Hello-oh," says Louisa in a deadpan down the stairs.

"Mom?" Anne, younger by twenty months, calls pragmatically.

Caryn calls up, "Sorry!" She shakes Thomas off.

Halfway up the stairs she smells fire.

The soup? She wastes time trying to relive the moment she turned the gas off. But it's not a food smell. There's Louisa guarding the doorway. "Hurry?"

It takes Caryn a moment to understand it's not her they're worried about. Paul seems to have ignited several pages of the maze book. He's solving mazes with trails of fire.

Thomas is on her heels, pushing around her, beneath her, panting with excitement. "Where did you get matches?" There is real awe in his voice. Caryn doesn't allow matches. Not in any drawer or cabinet. Not locked away, call her paranoid—they don't have candles. They have a single, disabled hearth known as the Santa Claus fireplace. She knows Dom thinks it's neurotic, but he's good at picking his battles.

Louisa and Anne are gathered close. All of a sudden, the whole tabletop is alight. There must have been grease, a feast fire. Paul stumbles out of his chair, backward, giving over his rights as a guest, his spectacle. For a critical moment, Caryn is motionless. What would it look like if the fire wound down the legs of the table? What would her floor look like? Would it be tempting, somehow, to walk across it?

Caryn's mind goes blank. This is fear, manifest.

Or relief. Thomas in a fireman's hat. He's wielding a dusty red canister with a mallard beak. In countless dreams Thomas has practiced.

When the fire is out, Caryn has a tremendous need to escape. She's been inside for three days now. She finds Thomas's coat and snow pants and her own long wool coat that she never wears because it's supposed to be a dress coat. She bunches an orange scarf around her neck that Anne knit for a favorite teacher. Caryn and Thomas push the front door together. It seems to push back against them. They're stymied for a moment. Anne says, "The window—" and Thomas, newly capable, authorized, set in motion, is already hoisting it, jumping out over the sill as if over the rails.

Caryn follows.

Jumping into the storm is like jumping into water. She goes deep—deeper than she's ever swam in any lake or ocean. She hears the distant thrum of the highway and her own pulse in her ears like water pressure. The snow is coming down sideways, a scrim, and she almost can't tell the shore, the sidewalk. She looks up at the house and finds her bearings.

MADRONA

The air was watery, snow by afternoon. Taylor clubbed her hands inside her coat pockets. Her building, with a gray awning that seemed to corral the cold, marked the spot where the tree-lined street lost its trees and sidewalk and became a route-numbered highway that coursed through acres of big-box stores and family restaurants. Taylor set off on foot: the little townish town was in the opposite direction.

She'd had no idea she had poor circulation until she watched her freshman-year roommate running around all winter in dishabille, in camisoles. Emily Linder looked like she was peddling bra straps.

People thought distant places were colder. "Seattle!" As if it were remote and frigid as a star. She never tried to correct them, regarding the climate or the fact that she was from Lynnwood, in mall-ridden Snohomish County. She was twenty-three now, she'd stayed out east after college.

She passed the gabardine public library, payphone under the exaggerated, modern eaves, cat door of a bookdrop for those, like cats, who avoided civic confrontation. Even the evergreen landscaping bushes, here, lost their pigment in the winter. There were law offices in a row of historic white houses. Taylor's sopho-more-year roommate had gone on to law school.

She felt as if she were holding cold rocks in her pockets. In western Washington Lenten Rose bloomed celery, eggplant, eggshell at Christmas; camellias budded by New Year's. But she wasn't nostalgic. An astrology column had once informed her that resignation was her coping mechanism. She pictured neat little gears inside her. Resignation was a form of low self-esteem—it didn't take a rocket scientist. She thought of Emily Linder throw-ing herself across the bed freely, a smooth roll of back fat exposed between her jeans and tiny tank top. Emily had given up on Taylor in the first twenty-four hours.

She could circumnavigate the municipal park and be back home by nine thirty. Ten seemed the earliest he might call her. She wished she didn't have to take her hand out of her pocket to check her watch. She was freezing but she couldn't bring herself to wear one of the pompom hats East Coast people pulled on nonchalantly. She was shy, vain, bored, boring. She didn't fight it. What she did fight, now, was the monkish depression. On a Saturday morning. Getting out of her monk's cell, walking to the village.

The park was designed in rays that went out from a bandstand. Taylor had watched children tumble across the concrete dais in the summer as if it were a giant bed, slightly forbidden. Now there were frost crystals in the pores of the sidewalk. She drummed over a petite footbridge and she could smell moldering blackberry in the streambed. A plaque described the provenance of the rose bushes, the brave and childish way the first settlers came from Holland, via New York, and the fact that a few of their diminutive farm buildings were still looked after by the Preservation Society.

She curved around the decorative pond where a heron like a close-up of a mosquito had spooked the fish all summer. There were ducks in pairs in the wicker bushes. They would have walked arm in arm if they had them, thought Taylor.

Her sophomore-year roommate, Adina, was an Ambassador of the College. She had insisted Taylor join her for the Orientation Week cookout, and they swung by other dorms on the way and collected a group of girls like a wedding party. It had taken Adina a full week to give up on Taylor. Taylor knew she could have saved her the trouble.

She checked her watch again. There was a chance she'd mis-calculated—her walk or his timing. She couldn't help falling into an awkward trot. Her left leg was noticeably longer than her right, she was terrible at sports, her senior year of high school she'd been forced to take the remedial PE class for girls who always had their periods. The teacher had added a comment to the passing grade: "She should try to make stronger movements."

She reached her building and sunk her key to the hilt. She felt as if he were watching her. Up the stairs, she used her arms for lever-age on the railing. She pictured him reading her number off a scrap of paper that would be regurgitated in the wash if he accidentally left it in his pocket. The library, its inner lights slightly orange, the payphone with its sleek dark neck and gleaming umbilicus.

The first time he called she'd been dozing in a chair in her living room, bare sun across the floorboards. She'd been kept up all night by the young professional couple directly above her: how many times could two people cross their apartment? Living alone, it seemed like the phone could ring out of nowhere. No storm warning, clouds bunching together, wind smelling different.

"Is that Taylor?"

She was cold despite the sun on the floor, and disoriented.

"Is this your street?" he'd marveled, laughing.

He'd invited himself up to her apartment. What was the first thing she did when she came home from work? he'd asked her.

She'd protested.

"No, really."

She imagined a stock version of herself moving down the thin hall to the kitchen. Her unsteady walk (X-rays and MRIs, it turned out leg length discrepancy wasn't a sign of anything) had always irritated her mother. Her billowy socks and fallen ankles. Water for tea. Secretly she found coffee disgusting.

"Well, what kind of tea?" he'd teased her, and she knew he was more entertaining to himself than she was. She'd tried to block his view of the chair where she habitually hung the sweatpants and T-shirt she slept in.

The kitchen had an electric stove, a mismatched fridge and warped cabinets, as if the plywood were fifty percent polyester. She ate discreetly, plain and dry, she was a budget vegetarian.

He said, "My wife's a vegetarian."

She felt like she was walking into a trap as she took down a Goodwill teacup. He pointed at it. "You're not having any?" She took down another.

"You've got terrific southern exposure up here," he continued. She looked around, bewildered. "I love apartments. I don't know why we give them up when we turn into so-called grownups."

She had never imagined living in a house. It seemed as foreign as living in China. He seemed to be serious about evaluating her whole setup. Silence.

"Your turn." Was he mocking her? "*So tell me about you, Andy.*"

He was a playwright with a playwright's ritualized way of looking at the world. "Do you see what I'm saying?" The teakettle

MADRONA   107

started hissing. Taylor surprised herself by knowing he wouldn't care what kind of tea she poured him.

He had short gray hair and eyes like wood grain. He wanted to write plays, but he collaborated on TV series. He was never the "based on the book by" or "based on the idea." He wasn't in LA, there was that little problem. He unsheathed a dark silver cigarette lighter. He weighed it. "Come here," he said, and she brought the tea over. He put the lighter in her palm and it was heavy, like water.

He waited until the tea was almost cold and then he took a single swallow.

"Do you know your neighbors?" he asked her.

The couple who kept her up all night—"Maybe they're sleepwalkers," he suggested. But most of the occupants of her building she had never seen at all and she imagined ticking them off a master list of human beings.

"That's actually quite creepy," he said with admiration.

Now she cleaned her apartment constantly, she felt like she was in a movie, even when she slept she felt like she was "sleeping."

She worked part time in the office of the private school where his daughter was a fourth-grader. Weekend afternoons she filled in at a boutique decorated with hand-painted scarves and quilted dopp-kits on the cakey little main street; both jobs came through the older lady she'd done errands and bills for through college. In any case, he had walked into the school office looking for his daughter's teacher.

She wasn't supposed to leave the front desk unattended. Confidentiality, litigation, and the children of centamillionaires and semi-celebrities. But he just stood there after she explained that she could help him set up an appointment, and to escape his stare she'd excused herself to go looking for the teacher in question.

The windowless teachers' lounge was crowded with dented cupcakes and super-saturated pineapple left over from class parties. For a moment she was caught up in the desertion of broken oatmeal raisin, carrot sticks gone to sawdust. Her parents had been teachers but they'd shielded her. When she returned to the front office he was grinning over the biblical ledger.

"Did you just start here?" He didn't wait for her answer. "Where have I been?" he said, still grinning.

She shook her head, she had no idea.

He laughed. "I don't know either." He studied her. "Inside information here." He lowered his voice. "Everybody hates their kid's teacher." His eyes glittered. She didn't doubt that he'd got what he wanted.

The next day she bumped into him at the town supermarket. Its chain name was in smaller letters, that's how you could tell you were going to pay yuppie prices, he informed her later.

"Andy," he said, which she knew meant he had no idea what her name was. "I was wondering how I was ever going to—" and he whipped up the air between them. He was serious. But how else, other than serious, would an intelligent person act in the face of his own infidelity?

In the face of her imagination. Her stomach felt like it was made out of parachute material. She could hear the rustle.

His wife was away on a tour of seven cities. He didn't say "my wife," he said her name, which was rare and formidable. She was a dancer. She must have worn her clothes as seamlessly as skin. It was his wife's company: she made up the steps and chose the music.

"I'd like to meet her," said Taylor.

He raised his eyebrows. She'd be on tour for two weeks, then she'd be back for three days, then a brief residency at a small college.

"Come on over and keep us company." He and his daughter. "Do you eat dinner?"

Taylor glanced at her shopping cart and they both laughed because there was just the water bag of baby carrots.

He cast them both as outsiders in such a town: he was the right age but the wrong spirit, she—what was she doing here? He affected being baffled. He flattered her by implying she belonged someplace better. It was true, though: the only other twenty-somethings were soda-logged computer folk from the Middle Earth of their parents' basements. Boys of men, with loose lips and barber haircuts; one had spied her in the municipal park in the summer and asked her to go for ice cream.

Andy laughed for a long time. His daughter was glued to a video. He brushed Taylor's hair out of her eyes when she was drying the dishes.

"So?" he said finally, smugly, as if he already knew the answer. She didn't understand him.

"What flavor?"

"I—" she started.

"Cruel!" He shook his head. "I figured."

Actually, despite her terror, she *had* gone with the laundry-and-rec-room creature. She couldn't remember what flavor. His body had seemed shapeless, like sheets over furniture. Gallantly he'd held the door of the Daily Scoops for her and then they were stranded together on the sidewalk.

Taylor's junior-year roommate had tried to interest her in ball-room dancing. Chunni was big-boned, forceful, Korean. She kept

a crock pot like a cauldron in their room that smelled unremit-
tingly of reheated soup. Lined up across her desk were vials of
homemade sauces.

"Dancing will make you more coordinated, Tayloh!" Taylor
was unmoved; Chunni was stubbornly disappointed.

In fact Chunni was Taylor's favorite roommate, with her stoic
good nature, and finally Taylor relented. She would prove to Chunni
once and for all that she was not, constitutionally or spiritually, social.

One Thursday night in early spring Taylor found herself Chunni's guest in a cavernous hall with thirty or so other Korean students, all dressed as if for church in the early 1960s. Somehow
Chunni had overlooked Taylor's blue jeans and sweatshirt, and it
was as if Taylor were the only female with legs. She begged to sit
out, she promised to watch, but Chunni kept pushing her ahead
like a broken wheelbarrow.

It wasn't Chunni's fault; Chunni may have been insensitive, but she
wasn't malicious. And there seemed to be plenty of affable young men
who genuinely wanted to hold her hands, coach her through the foot-
work. As Chunni stood by, Taylor rejected them one after another.

The sense of public pressure mounted until the air turned hot
and fleshy. All at once Taylor couldn't catch her breath and, suf-
focating, she passed out gently across a couple of vacant folding
chairs. When she came to Chunni was squatting alongside her
like a midwife, alarmed, holding her shoulders. The boys who had
asked her to dance looked askance, not wanting to be blamed for
anything. Chunni released her reluctantly, making her promise to
return straight to their dorm room.

The other park in town his daughter called Stone Ladies. There
were two statues, he called them platitudes of kneeling. "Of genu-
flection," he added, eyeing her. "Are you Catholic?"

Seagulls fell across the park on guy wires. Taylor shook her head, but he continued to look at her as if she would revise her answer. The stone ladies were naked. Their eyes were closed, their noses aquiline. The left breast on each lady was fuller.

There was a little bit of a vista, the sky stacked up on the horizon. A steeple half a mile away was blurred by permanent haze at the edges.

They gravitated toward the small pond. They found out he was twenty years older. He said, "Why is it always exactly by decades?"

She was quiet.

He said, "Did you know there are different culling periods for men and women?"

His daughter seemed to have something going on under a cedar tree. "She's kind of a water baby," he boasted. "She fell in that pond once." Taylor could see her as a nyad. She had a distractibility that made Taylor uneasy.

They sat side by side watching loose snowflakes mesh and dissolve in water. Taylor had to concentrate to keep her teeth from clattering. "This time last year it wasn't half as warm," he said accusingly, as if it stood in for a deeper truth. He said she couldn't keep avoiding the question of where she was from. She took everything he said as a kind of compliment. "Nobody's from nowhere," he chided. He cocked his head. "Unless they're an angel." He squinted and rolled an imaginary movie camera at her. "You're a Wim Wenders angel!"

She hadn't seen any of the movies. He said he hated when people said film instead of movie. He liked how she dressed too. He looked at her, appraising. "So where *did* the lovely Taylor spend her childhood?"

She didn't want to force him to comment on the rain, Kurt Cobain, Bruce Lee, or coffee.

"Mystery child!" As if she were driving him slightly crazy. Taylor was freezing, laughing.

"Come on," he said, holding out a hand to her. Slightly sexually crazy.

He bought a cone for his daughter and one for himself at one end of Elm Street. Soon his daughter was busy with her dripping chocolate. "I'm getting messy," she warned them, and there was something messy overall about her. Taylor had pocketed a whole ream of napkins. She stopped to hand them over. "But I'm sticky!" his daughter protested. Taylor could see. Around the wrists, in the armpits of her fingers.

His daughter was half a block ahead of them, licking her wrists, looking at the toy store display window. Taylor watched her drop the used napkins on the sidewalk.

He told her his daughter was slow to read and write. "But super creative." He shrugged. From working at the school, Taylor had the sense that diagnoses came in waves, as if the diagnoses themselves were contagious. She herself had always felt safer in class with the smarter kids, those with subtler language capabilities. Although she didn't manage to make friends. She closed her eyes for a moment. Differently sized girls from the same age group swinging on the bars, high knees like carousel ponies, revolving in mill circles, the perfume of the thuddy woodchip carpet.

In her senior year of high school, one Advanced Placement track had been folded into another, and suddenly Taylor had all her classes with a girl named Morgan. Two girls with boy names, and Morgan soon uncovered the fact that they were both only children whose parents had divorced when they were eleven. They even looked alike, with their plain brown hair unfashionably barretted, their slightly protruding, oily foreheads. They both had such long

legs that Morgan said ominously, "We have the proportions of cru-
cifixes." Her mother was Born Again. Morgan said she never would
have been born at all if she'd known it involved the inanity of high
school. Both girls were thinking of going out of state for college.

Morgan's father lived in Seattle. Taylor concealed her admiration. He had a dollhouse bungalow, said Morgan, in one of the
Lake Washington neighborhoods, Madrona, and he had given
Morgan a pickup truck so she could visit him independent of her
mother. Morgan invited Taylor to come along one weekend and
they left straight from school on Friday.

They listened to Morgan's music on the freeway. Morgan sang
along and Taylor found herself blushing. "I never know what to
listen to," she ventured.

There was heavy traffic. Taylor liked surveying it from the el-
evated cab; she had never ridden in a pickup truck.

"We brought this upon ourselves," announced Morgan, and it
took Taylor a minute. "We invented cars," Morgan elaborated.

Taylor looked out again: a sheet of traffic, nine or ten lanes across,
stretching back and forward, manmade infinity. She tried blaming
herself for it, but it seemed like a force of nature. Maybe Morgan was
into the environment? It was impossible to just ask a question.

A couple of helicopters hung in the sky ahead, reflecting the
cold sunset. Morgan had to duck a little to look out the windshield
and up. She said, "An accident?"

"Yeah," Taylor heard herself saying.

There was a big splash of metal and metallic lights flashing on
the upcoming exit ramp. It looked like a seven-car pileup. Taylor
didn't know how Morgan could count the mashed cars so efficiently. After they passed it they talked about having no friends in
childhood, without knowing if they would be friends.

Saturday morning Morgan packed two watercolor paint sets. They could easily walk to the lake beach from her father's bungalow. All they had to do was fall down a series of staircases like chutes, narrow city holdings. Taylor caught glimpses of fanciful bohemian dwellings with floating decks, treehouse platforms behind thick bangs of foliage. She had no idea if it was a safe neighborhood but she felt a sense of romantic abandonment.

The sky was mixed, and Morgan dipped glass jars in the lake water. Taylor saw a transparent, flickering creature caught in one jar but Morgan didn't seem to notice. They set up in the grass looking over a crescent of sand and across the water. Morgan provided sporadic instruction but didn't seem moved by the fact that Taylor had never before painted.

The sky had a collar of tumbled clouds. A water bird came in for a ski landing. It made perfect sense that water was the basis for everything, thought Taylor.

Morgan pointed out the Microsoft city across the lake. "My dad calls it the military-industrial complex." She was showing off a little bit, thought Taylor. They both put it in their paintings when the sun hit it: the towers beamed out and made the water look like oil. They painted the floating bridges that looked like dams, motorboats, sailboats, a U-shaped swallow.

Morgan laughed when Taylor said she thought it was one of life's miracles that people knew how to get other people out of the water.

She stopped laughing. "Wait a minute," she said. "You can't swim?"

Was it possible Taylor had never been so happy? It wasn't that she was good at painting. She was obviously terrible. Morgan leaned back to assess her own painting. "Well," she said, "this is what I would look like if I were a lake instead of a Morgan."

Taylor produced an unbecoming cry of surprise before she could stop herself. But it was true. Her seemingly secret Taylor-ness was laid bare in the amateur landscape. She had no technique to save herself from drowning but she felt emboldened. She could swim, she could paint: how many other things could she do simply by trying?

The clouds got darker over Microsoft and there were rain lines and a flashbulb of lightning. Morgan made no move to pack up. Suddenly she cried, "It's a double!" It was. Two of each color, at first bleary, then sharper, as if—said Morgan condescendingly—God adjusted the binoculars. The colors intensified, and then suddenly the rainbow was heavy enough to lay its tracks across the water.

It was strange: Taylor found she couldn't keep her eyes on it. She watched a crow spear the soft bank and haul out a worm. She wished she could say that beauty was demanding.

But Morgan must have felt the same. "I can't stand it any longer," she said, and she began dumping the jars of used water.

The girls were cold when they got back and Morgan said they would take turns showering. Morgan went first and Taylor was alone in the bedroom. The eaves were stoopingly low and the walls were a shade of purple that reminded Taylor of roll-down maps in a social studies classroom. Morgan's jeans lay over the pillow on her bed. Taylor went completely still and quiet before she lifted them; the risk seemed dizzyingly fateful, and even as she unzipped her own jeans and struggled damply out of them she knew it wasn't worth it. Still. She wanted to know Morgan.

Morgan's jeans were damp too, and now, over the vaguely shoe-store smell of Morgan's bedroom, there was the unmistakable odor of pee like heated pineapple. Taylor's nose seemed to whistle so she breathed shallowly through her mouth and she tasted the sweet-and-sour. Just as she was pulling the waist around her waist there was a knock on the bedroom door. She stopped breathing.

Morgan's father must have stopped breathing too, she imagined, in order to listen. But she had to think. What was her best bet? Would he go away if she didn't answer, or would silence be his cue to enter? It wasn't like she was in the bathroom. Then, "Is one of you in there?"

"Just a moment," said Taylor. She needed an hour. An eternity of him not coming in the bedroom. Should she try to get out of Morgan's jeans and back into her own? Had he even heard her? Would he barge in when she was naked? She focused on the strip of light at the bottom of the door. She could hear herself in her own ears.

He said, "Morgnificent?"

Taylor held still. The door began to open.

It seemed as if he didn't see her at first. Then he was staring at her openly. She found she had pinned herself against the closet door. Was he incapable of hiding his true feelings? Grownups were more childish than teenagers. She knew she wouldn't scream or fight. She was a rag doll, she was Morgan in Morgan's jeans. She waited.

"You and Morg could have been separated at birth," he said finally.

"There you are!" Morgan exclaimed when she returned from the shower. She looked at Taylor strangely. "I thought you might have been making friends with my dad or something."

When it was Taylor's turn she took all of her clothes into the bathroom with her.

Morgan's father had a showpiece coffee machine that looked like the prototype for an elaborate steampunk engine. He said it had cost more than Morgan's pickup. Morgan handled the seething invention while he bragged about it. Taylor received a mug fit for a giant. She didn't say she had never had a "latte."

"Are you trying to keep her up all night?" laughed Morgan's father. Morgan sucked hers down, keeping one eye on Taylor.

Taylor thought she would get better at fashioning trees, interpreting shadow, expressing those grounded, native (said Morgan) runt berries along the lakeshore. Better at painting the sky drinking up the water.

But back at school, in their AP classes, there was no obvious ending. Just the slightly discomfiting feeling that there had been no beginning, either.

And later, when Taylor went over it, she was unsettled that Morgan made the coffee. Like a young wife to her father. Her long plain hair in two barrettes, braided belt around the waist of those blue jeans.

Between each ring of the phone Taylor said to herself, I don't know if it's him yet. Swiftly she pulled on a pair of clean white pants. He said she was like a colt, the off-center gait, persistent girlishness. A navy sweater, she'd looked better in the green one, known she would never have the strength to wear it. She twisted her hair up.

She cleared her throat. She wished she'd had a drink of water instead of pulling on her pants—she could've answered naked. Too late now. Six rings and people would think she'd been in the bathroom. He'd think—he'd see her streaming out of the bathroom before she'd even flushed the toilet.

People opened up or closed up with other people. They never stayed the same.

Emily with the bra straps, Adina who would be a lawyer, Chunni the ballroom dancer, they all thought she stayed the same. It was the opposite.

The phone kept ringing. The last thing was shoes. Boots. He liked it when she ran around the park with his daughter.

Through courtship, marriage, and divorce, Taylor's parents had taught at the same large, suburban blue-collar high school. When Taylor left for college (her guidance counselor leered about West Coast quotas, but it was unclear to Taylor who was being taken advantage of), her parents promptly, if separately, retired from teaching. There was the little harbor of their pensions. All on her own, Taylor's mother opened a florist shop in an under-subscribed strip mall. When Taylor came home for Christmas her mother's house was filled with flowers that smelled like frozen peas and formaldehyde. The camellia bloomed in the front yard and Taylor cut a stem with four strawberry-pink flowers and put it in a juice glass on the kitchen table. Later the same day her mother had already tossed it. It was disconcerting that Taylor had had no idea her mother wanted to be a florist. Suddenly there was the possibility that even boring lives were secret.

Taylor's sophomore year of college her mother hired a land-scaping company to exhume the camellia and put in a matching pair of inky Japanese maples. Her eyes twinkled when she told Taylor the neighbors took note, that certain neighbors were now looking into their own landscape accents. Otherwise it was a sub-dued development of nine-hundred-square-foot ranches with their driveways on the left and a welcome bush to the right of their walkways. Taylor's parents had sacrificed, long ago, to live in a better school district. Her mother had bought out her father.

Light lurked in the sky until ten o'clock at night in the summer, when Taylor was home working with her mother. There was a miraculous small-business loan for menopausal (her mother joked) single women business owners, and Taylor's mother had bought a

van with a refrigerated chamber. One afternoon they were picking
through peaked corsages, saving baby thickets of baby's breath,
when an order came in from Seattle. "Well, well," said Taylor's
mother. "You just have to stick to your guns. Your dreams." She
was brisk with pride. In less than an hour they were on the road,
bearing the delivery.

Riding in the passenger seat of the van was like bouncing on a
trampoline, even more so as they ticked off the Seattle exits below Northgate where the heavy commuter stretch was grooved
and rutted. There was traffic. Taylor's mother kept stuttering the
brakes, which she claimed made them last longer. Taylor watched
a seaplane scud down on Lake Union as they waited in the long
line on the freeway bridge facing the city towers.

Taylor read the directions out loud once they took their exit,
and soon they were twirled along park-like, lakeshore streets with
no grid logic. Suddenly Taylor said, "Is this Madrona?"

Then she was embarrassed. As if she thought she had some
claim to it. They passed gaudy deck-and-glass numbers, enhanced
stucco remodels of older Craftsmans. She felt something wasn't
quite right, what should have been the same was different.

They overshot the address and had to find a place to turn
around. Retracing the route more carefully, Taylor spotted the
numbers engraved in old brick, shrouded in laurel, at the head of
a long, obscured driveway. They pulled through giant wrought-
iron gates tipped with lances and stamped with red and gold es-
cutcheons. These Japanese maples were like weeping willows at
midnight.

They parked as quietly and inconspicuously as possible, and
Taylor's mother set out to find the foreman. The brick mansion
and flanking carriage houses blocked the view of the lake and
the mountains. The driveway was forested with red cedars and a

flotilla of hydrangeas so constantly gardened, Taylor imagined, it never quit producing blossom heads of Aegean blue and antique indigo.

Quiet fell. Maybe wealth was quiet—or at least it didn't speak to those who didn't have it. Taylor undid her seatbelt and turned toward the van's compartment. She could not remember a single instance in her childhood when either of her parents had patronized a florist. It seemed for a moment that she could not remember anything about her childhood, and she wondered if she was, in fact, still a child, and going to college out east was a dream she would wake from, shake off.

She forced herself out of her reverie. The refrigerated chamber behind her was sealed with a dwarf door, the stainless-steel handle like some kind of ancient folk weapon. It was cold to the touch. Her mother would return any moment and Taylor would have the flowers unloaded and ready.

Almost at the same moment she opened the refrigerator door, the van began to tremble. Taylor pressed herself back in her seat as if she'd been chastened. Outside, the black drive was crumbling around the van like pie crust. She felt the front wheels buckle. She felt the earth—as if the whole thing were a muscle—seize and shudder. She was falling down, over edges and false edges of earth, rocks fell with her, clumps of sod, sprays of acid-tasting soil. She managed to catch herself on the rung of a root. Still the contents of the earth rained down around her.

She must have blacked out. It seemed like a long time later that she heard the van's alarm bleating from far, far above her.

She lay in the underground darkness. She could smell packed wet earth and the kind of mold that finds its way into the molecular structure of concrete. Mold that looks like the man in the moon on a basement wall.

Her mother had set up the laundry area in the basement as a guest room. "Your summer suite," she'd shown Taylor. She'd seemed a little bit embarrassed to have kicked Taylor out of her old bedroom. A little bit resentful that Taylor was grown up, moved away, but knowing she shouldn't be. Taylor's bedroom she now used as an office.

Almost before Taylor woke she realized it was the wrong dream. A florist had nothing to do with earth, everything to do with water. The earthquake dream—she'd never told anyone. Not her mother. Her decision to remain out east had tapered into private silence. Her mother didn't know if she could keep the shop open. Two nail salons had popped up and then vanished in the same strip mall, a music and movies store had gone into foreclosure, the liquor store had tried both reducing and increasing its hours. "I'm going to do more balloons," her mother promised. There was the gap opening, widening, until there was more gap than earth between her and her mother.

She grabbed the phone as if she were jumping off a bridge.

"Are you at the library?"

He laughed. But it sounded too smooth, someone else was in the room with him. His wife would be stretching on the floor at his feet. Taylor could see her rolling up, vertebra by vertebra, hollowing her abdomen, ready now to begin marking steps and poses.

Was he an official liar who told run-on stories that didn't end until he, the liar, believed every ornate detail? Were his excuses baroque, frosted with rosettes and angels? He'd called her an angel.

He wondered if she could come for dinner on Friday. "En famille," he said, in a brighter register than usual. "And you can't bring anything at all but your lovely self, Miss Taylor." She tried to breathe normally.

His house was on a residential connector street. The first time she was over he'd called it "our shelter house," which he'd had to explain was a reference to a certain kind of glossy magazine, of which she was totally ignorant. In fact he'd said, "You had to be there," and it stung her.

"Do you feel ridiculous following the winding walkway?" he'd said cleverly, possibly making it up to her. Taylor had laughed, turning left and right and left again behind him.

That first time she was surprised his house was so modest. The entry had a coat closet with a thin tri-fold door and loose handles. He was not the kind of man who would fix handles on the weekends. There was a single futon sofa in the living room and unframed dance posters thumb-tacked into sheetrock marrow. He'd bent to turn on a lamp, but it was the middle of the day, and it made the room feel like a school or a hospital.

He hadn't seemed to care what she thought of his house. She felt like one of his daughter's friends, mute but hungry for after-school cookies.

Now, carving across the front yard in order to follow the walk-way, Taylor wondered if the house would have changed with his wife inside it. Was it really her house? The front door was ever-green plastic. He had opened it before, so Taylor hadn't noticed. He had taken her coat before. She had shed her skin with her coat so he would hold it.

She pressed the bell. She could hear it like a fire alarm inside. She was in two places at once, the flimsiness between worlds. She wished she had knocked instead. She could have been the new babysitter.

She hadn't really noticed the landscaping tufts before. She looked sideways and traced the artificial rock facing that formed a low wall between the yard and the sunken driveway. Last time, his daughter had walked along the top of that wall rather than fall into line on the walkway.

Taylor heard rapid footsteps. She took a step backward.

"It's Taylor!" cried his wife, throwing the door open.

She was stringy, hollow-eyed, with an enormous bony mouth that suggested her skeleton. No makeup. They faced each other. Her eyes skittered down the full length of Taylor.

"You found us okay?" She had stringy hair, too, that she pulled to the side and then wove into its own knotlet. "That weird *bear left* under the highway?" she persisted.

Taylor nodded. It wasn't a lie.

Taylor folded her coat over her arm. The other times she'd been here, she'd taken off her shoes like he did. His wife had bare feet. She didn't ask Taylor to take her shoes off and so Taylor didn't.

His wife seemed flat-footed, or ostentatiously tired, for a dancer. Her hair was inching its way out of the knot against her shoulder. She urged Taylor onto the futon sofa. She sighed. "It's totally Andy to remember the beer and forget the salad."

"Oh, I could have—" Taylor started. But his wife wasn't apologizing for his absence.

Taylor found herself looking across the room at one of the dance posters. An extraordinarily long-limbed black woman swept in a snow-white sundress. The skirt made a half circle. One long leg seemed to hang from a hook in the sky. Her arms were endless, bare and gleaming.

They all drank beer with the rice casserole, and the salad was dotted with pomegranate seeds his wife had wrested from pomegranate tissue. His daughter picked out the rubies and then erected a tent of spinach leaves. She dropped her fork. Without thinking, it appeared to Taylor, his wife leaned down and retrieved it.

There was no feeling in his look, neither intimacy nor animosity. Some packaged cookies for dessert, and Taylor excused herself. She was tipsy, compromised, she never should have come. She drank water from her hands in the bathroom. She sat down on the burgundy bathmat, it had a weird, tinsel-like texture.

When she returned to the table he got up and began clearing.

"May I help?" said Taylor.

"No way," he and his wife said together.

His wife opened the green door for her. "Where's your coat?" she said. Taylor took it off her arm, where it had weighted her down the entire evening.

He called her from the library. He was doing research, he really needed to come up with a big idea, he couldn't go on like this, creatively he was impoverished, hand to mouth, he needed to talk to her, now did she see how hard it could be to live with a self-fulfilled artist like his wife? Did she want to meet at Stone Ladies?

She was self-aware enough to know she was depressed. How could it not be obvious that she was cold, insignificant?

But he came up behind her. "Hey, lovely lady." He wore cowboy Levi's, the kind that make men look saddle-sore and bandy-legged. The thighs were faded to gauze bandage material.

He led her to the stone steps that terraced toward the pond. He motioned for her to sit beside him. She knew she'd freeze. She avoided the dried curl of an earthworm.

"I'm going to give you my little speech about love, Taylor." He knocked her knee with his knee and kept it there. "Ready?"

"About a week before my wedding, I decided to call up my ex-girlfriend." He rubbed his hands together. It was cold. He didn't wear a wedding ring, Taylor had already noticed.

"I told myself I was the big man to apologize for not inviting her." He squinted toward the pond. "Because that's what we do now," he said. "We're so *open*." He tapped her once on her coat on her breastbone.

"My ex-girlfriend picked up the phone and I said, 'Sweetheart.'" He paused theatrically. "It just slipped out!" He smiled at himself in wonder. "Then I had to tell her I was getting married." He slid farther out along his thighs until the heads of his elbows were on his kneecaps. He seemed to need to look out into the middle distance. "I told her that all love was part of the same big love. That marrying my wife wasn't as much about my wife as it was about being part of this big love."

He leaned back again abruptly. "So there you have it." He turned toward her and she was sure he was going to kiss her.

But he stood up instead, and the sudden change in level made her almost seasick. Was she supposed to feel rejected? He took out the silver cigarette lighter and toyed with it. Her spirit was like an MRI. The metal hurt, everything went haywire in the echo chamber.

He refitted himself beside her, even closer this time, as if they'd suddenly been through something together. "Do you see what I'm saying?"

It seemed like the park was a painting of a park. There was a gray filminess about it. Nipples of light from the houses below, suddenly it was evening.

"Are you there?" he said. But he wasn't used to listening.

She stayed where she was. The sky had a black eye, silver seams, seagulls coasted in on air bikes. He said he'd offer to walk her home but she looked like she was feeling pretty pensive.

What was there to go back to? Morgan's disappearance? Her mother losing the florist shop? In both instances Taylor had been useless. Chunni had invited Taylor to her wedding just last fall and Taylor had never responded. There was always the demarcation of herself and the outside world. The park darkened like a theater.

It had seemed almost sacrilegious to turn her back on a double rainbow, but Morgan was the leader. They climbed back up the staircases, vertical tunnels of dark and glossy laurel. This jungle was all steep-bank waterfront, Morgan informed Taylor. The cement stairs were eroded by moss and Taylor had to concentrate to avoid slipping. Without turning Morgan said, "It would be the perfect place to get abducted."

Taylor felt a quick stab of guilt for picturing Morgan's father. He was so kind and so cool and here she was, nearly mute, monstrously shy, descending on them for the entire weekend. Morgan halted suddenly and Taylor ran straight into her and cried out in surprise before she could help it. Morgan had a low, almost manly chuckle.

Morgan quit school two weeks before graduation.

The AP English teacher informed them, and the socially deft students in the front row, commandeered by two brilliant Indian girls, speculated gothically before the teacher hushed them. Taylor cultivated indifference toward her classmates as a matter of survival, but it was terrifying the way Anjali and Enid could zoom in on someone, their psychoanalysis in high resolution.

As the class period dwindled, Anjali suddenly whipped around and fixated on Taylor. "You knew Morgan," she demanded. The room fell silent.

Taylor's vision, her hearing, even the taste in her mouth pinholed. Her skin was a sheer sundress, everyone could see through it. Somewhere far away the teacher might have said something in her defense but Taylor's ears were plugged with raw earth, her mouth was filled with dirt, it was packed in around her and she could only breathe through the prick of light at the far, far end of the tunnel.

CHARM CIRCLE

1

From the sea, the pub would be a barnacle on the wall of the cliff, thought Sara. She had flown, of course, Seattle to London over the top of the globe, and the seasick coach tour to Cornwall. She wasn't romantic.

The rowboat looked orthotic. The pub owner had proposed the excursion and Sara had replied that she was not at all into boating. He had looked at her even more searchingly for her refusal.

The pub was an ancient stone house, a wall rising from the narrow road, there was hardly a curb, not to mention a sidewalk. It was marked by a single, charmless streetlight. No great stretch of the imagination to see the drinkers like jowly insects drawn to the glow. Faintly green, as if the lens had moss in the corners.

The road wound inland through salt-and-pepper plots marked by herringbone stone walls like calligraphy. Hectares and hectares, one of their obscure words, before you heard the main road, then you saw it, with a tourist center at the junction where the farm road had crossed the main road for centuries.

Centuries. So the pub owner told her. She had finally relented. The water was choppier than it appeared from land, from the cliff top. Afterward he drove her to the pit stop, as she told him it would be called in America, and he bought the tourist center lunch (he had no clue that "pit stop" was derogatory, but he didn't adopt it) and stared at her across the table, cuddling his jaw in his hands. If he tried to draw her out she squinted up at the television mounted over the bar, green with constant football. Soccer. Just getting along with someone was sentimental.

Her mother had insisted she put together a travel address book. Her mother was under the impression that Sara's dyslexia tutor had taken a special interest in Sara. Every so often the little book with the gold stair-step letters, A—XYZ, would make its way to the top of Sara's jumbled luggage and she would become as nauseated by the sight of it as she'd been on the turbulent flight. The pilot had touted the polar route and it had seemed to Sara that they were buffeted by glaciers. The postcards to choose from were sheep hunched over their pasture, a taciturn pitchfork.

Secretly she considered her dyslexia a form of civil disobedience. Apparently she needed glasses. It was the very evening she and her mother were driving home from the eye doctor's appointment that Sara had decided she would travel. As they merged onto the rush-hour interstate Sara's eyes had stung with tears. To the west, the clouds were shredded over the mountains. She had made a small scene, refusing glasses.

Her mother was trapped in the slow lane. Far to the left, male drivers were slewing northward. There was the moon, even. The sky was like white laundry. Her mother had got that look of a mother animal that Sara hated. As if she longed to feed her baby bird her own vomit.

In her mind's eye her mother was waving goodbye, nobody waved anymore, her mother looked like she thought she was in a hat, too. In a postcard with deckled edges. The thing about eighteen was that you only knew you were doing the right thing when it felt wrong, somehow.

The room she rented over the pub was wallpapered in parakeet-blue stripes studded with cameos of a slim-necked bundle-haired lady. Sara looked like her, like a nineteenth-century locket: tapered nose, budded mouth, a great deal of fresh slippery hair to twist up and take down several times over the course of an evening. She appeared more sullen than she felt, when she caught herself in the mirror over the fireplace, but it didn't seem to stop the pub owner.

Her room had two windows looking over the tenacious road, no wider than one of her parents' matching sofas, and across a field to the teal ocean. But the room itself was nothing more than a hammocky bed and a bare light bulb. Were those shower curtains on the windows? No pretense, the streetlight shown right through them. At least the door locked. That was how the pub owner was able to charge rent for it.

Sara used the pub owner's bathroom. She used the payphone under the streetlight to call her parents once, as they said here, a fortnight. Like pop psychology, she was nine years old again every time she talked to her mother. If it were a family vacation, her mother would have voted for a stop at the very same tourist center. Her father was Mr. Tourist Arrangements, her brother had hated her since the moment she uncribbed him.

She'd insisted she didn't know if she would go to college. It wasn't a given to do what her parents—although she never pretended there was anything wrong with her parents. The last half of senior year other girls made speeches, how their mothers had been there for them, I'd-like-to-give-a-shout-out-to-my-amazing-mother, how they would be forced, in college, to spend exorbitant sums on Girl Scout cookies, in Samoa season, ponyish fourth-graders trotting their stacks of boxes out in front of their own mothers. They pantomimed daggers to hearts behind their blouses.

The pub owner begged her, "Have a drink with me, Sara?"

Beer was served warm over here like a form of porridge.

She left after seven months—in self-defense, mostly.

She went to Portugal.

She met a travel-thin girl named Meegan whose tawny eyebrows were too high up her forehead. Meegan of the diaspora of Antioch College. That was sort of the point of Antioch, said Meegan, if Antioch succeeded. "I'm pro-life." Her eyebrows strangely suspended. "In Life v. College."

She acted as if she had nothing to protect, though. She never bothered sleeping unless sex was a part of it. She pointed out Britishly (she was from California) that it was a very decent way to organize your lodgings.

Neo-hippy again, she said she had a relosophy about barter, and her offering was just her sweet positive self in the world.

She looked at Sara. "Religion and philosophy?"

All her clothes reminded Sara of old blankets.

One night they found themselves staring up at a white ship steep as an iceberg. There were four red letters on its flank, CCCP. Meegan said it was a Soviet tanker. They were barefoot in a little grassy park between docks. They couldn't have been very drunk because they found themselves standing. The dark grass went down to the dark water. Sara's feet were cold, and she noticed she was carrying a plastic market bag with her shoes inside it.

They didn't know how they got there or how to get back to the apartment where they weren't sleeping but where another diasporan had indicated a corner where fifteen or twenty backpacks were already huddled, dropped off like preschoolers.

They didn't know if they'd arrived quietly or made some crucial disturbance. The water was worse than a hole it was so un-seeable. It seemed to Sara that the dark was slowly bending. From behind the bend of a boat came the shadows of dancers. Sinuous young men in small sweaters and high-waisted pants leapt around them. Meegan fell to her knees, laughing and praying. Sara stared out at the four red letters and the piers on stilts and the lapping water. Fear made her body light and tingly.

It seemed that the young men were trying to herd the girls away from the water, toward the blackish clumps of houses and thready streets above them. Meegan half rose and began to do a Sufi dance, maybe it was Cossack. Then one of the men—they were slender as snakes, thought Sara—showed a knife and Meegan dropped to the ground and rolled out of their charm circle. She ran barefoot toward the water and the men stood amazed, watching. Sara watched too, until the dark form of a dinghy began to rock on what must have been water. They could hear the oars splashing.

The young men, now Sara's head was clear enough to count three of them, shook their heads and dropped their voices.

"Bus?" she said.

She didn't even bother with the Portuguese. If they were. She wasn't trying to impress them. They shook their heads again but they pointed toward the neighborhood. She walked off knowing there were no buses at this hour but she was safe because—this was how it was—Meegan wasn't.

The summer that Sara was seven they visited her grandmother in Connecticut. The first and last visit; she still wasn't sure of the spelling.

There was a dogpatch yard beneath a hangnail of a front porch, Sara was shocked but she would not show it. Tarps and disintegrating straw beach mats looked like scarecrows. The front rooms of her grandmother's house were so dark that the rugs and furniture seemed unreliable; landmines of filched postal crates, garbage bags of old clothes studded with expired canned goods. Sara's brother said it was a pit, and their parents didn't protest.

Her mother never stopped weaving between rooms, sighing extravagantly. They would pay the dump fees, she pleaded, it was a firetrap, and weren't those asbestos shingles?

There was a squawking sound from the mechanical voicebox in her grandmother's neck—Sara could see the outline.

One afternoon Sara's parents decamped to Hartford. Her brother promptly disappeared in the basement, where all four of them were sleeping on army cots beneath low fluorescent tubes jerry-rigged by their grandmother.

The house fell quiet. Her mother had discovered caches of droppings in the living room, but Sara was far less afraid of bats (her grandmother's claim, to spite her mother) or ghosts (she had overheard her mother say once that she, Sara, was simply not an imaginative child) than she was wary of her grandmother. Heeled-down cardboard boxes of old magazines took up the sofa but Sara couldn't read yet. She didn't really even like to look at pictures; she had reason to believe she was the only one in her family who suffered boredom. Almost a year had passed since a certain Sunday morning, thinking she was alone, she'd opened a book and spoken gibberish. Too late she'd heard the bathroom door creak open, and there was her gaping, over-grinning brother.

She'd pushed past him to shut herself in the same bathroom he'd just abandoned; his own book was lying face down on the tile. In his excitement to out her he'd failed to flush the toilet. She might not be imaginative, but she could bear a grudge like no one else in her family.

She heard her grandmother grunt without using the voicebox and her grandmother's shape was in the doorway.

Her mother said her grandmother had smoker's wrinkles. Some dogs had wrinkles too; folds, even, thought Sara. She watched her grandmother take two kinds of cookies and a jar of peanut butter down from an unpainted kitchen cabinet. Her grandmother used the same glass all day. "Vodka kills germs," Sara had heard the voicebox growl.

They sat at the kitchen table spreading peanut butter on Lorna Doones and Ladyfingers.

It seemed she was allowed to pour as much of the sweet, perfumey tea as she liked, take as many cookies. She thought of her clever brother starving in the basement. Soon the teapot was empty. A strange feeling: her whole chest seemed to be getting faster and faster.

Her grandmother asked her if she put herself to bed and she had to admit she didn't. Her grandmother said she could fall asleep upstairs but Sara had never felt less tired. She had the feeling that her heart was many new baby hearts squirming like an earthworm chopped up by the lawnmower. That's what she had lied once, when she had, herself, hacked apart an earthworm with a knife of slate from the shedding patio.

The sheets on her grandmother's bed were tangy and the bed swallowed her in the middle. She tried not to fight the deep pillow. She thought of the voicebox resting on the pillow like the miniature treasure chest she had recently been given for the tooth fairy. It had locks like buckles.

The streetlight slammed across her grandmother's dresser. There was a picture of Sara's mother with a round face, a strange and pretty child. Each minute banged into the next one. Sara's arms and legs kicked of their own accord. She couldn't hold onto her thoughts, but she couldn't stop thinking. She got up and went to the dresser in bare feet—the floor was gritty.

She walked around the bed, a dark peninsula. Light fell in the doorway and met the light from the streetlight. She didn't want to touch anything. There was a deep channel between bed and dresser. Her lungs were tight, her heart, or hearts, like coursing water.

What was going on here?

Her parents had come back after midnight.

"Seizures!" cried her grandmother, catching them at the door, trembling herself, almost in ruins.

But her mother had coldly inquired what they'd had for dinner. "Caffeine, Mother?"

She pretended not to speak English when a missionary-looking American in silky slacks approached her on the train to Paris. It was the short-sleeved button-down that gave him away, thought Sara. Meegan had bragged about a cheap youth hostel in Paris and Sara knew the museums from a trip with her parents. She could have spoken high school French if she weren't so shy. Self-protective.

She had a bottom bunk in the hostel that was as good as a mansion. Impossible to fall asleep before two in the morning, but during the day the large tiled dorm was empty except for a few Asian girls dropping their film off.

She never thought about the pub owner. She never thought about Meegan. She never thought about her friends from high school. She saw her mother pulling out of the driveway, swiveling backward, like a mature Barbie with her chin wrapped around her shoulders and her hard-packed tits in a sports outfit. Then the driveway pulling out from under the car, resuming itself at the mouth of the garage, now automatically closing.

She bought packaged French groceries in the supermarché; she didn't even like pastries. She ate on her bed, which was what she meant by a mansion. How many other girls had also?

Once she jumped a turnstile and she was promptly pulled out of the crowd and ticketed. She started to feel sick and then she went out of the metro and dropped the ticket in a can on the street and an hour later jumped another turnstile at a different station. She heard the bureaucrat in the kiosk rioting through the bullet-proof glass.

Nobody stopped her.

The hostel bunks were metal painted crimson. Was it supposed to give the auditorium-sized room an alpine feel? She knew she had no right to hate her mother but it was a free country. She supposed France was also, or was it deceptively socialist? Something her brother would accuse her of misunderstanding. At least hating her mother was better than missing her. More pop psychology. The lights in the hostel went out at 1 a.m. but girls still tramped back and forth to the bathrooms. The only way to get to sleep was to think about her own abduction.

She had fantasies. Just not her mother's year-round Christmas-carol idea of imagination.

The girl above her seemed to find a good position. Cheerily she had said she was from that prison colony. Sara had looked at her blankly. She had an Australian accent and a wide sandy face with crow's feet.

The perfect form of escape, abduction.

Sara put her hand out to make sure of her flashlight. Her wallet was smooth in her pocket.

She spread her mind over the breast of it. It could happen here, in Paris. It could happen any day now, tomorrow. She wouldn't even know it was happening. She would be chloroformed, hypnotized, charmed, captured. There was an island where she would be sustained on wine coolers. The ultimate privacy: no one would speak English.

There would be nothing to do on the island except drink the wine coolers. She could wander off into the hospitable jungle— there were no animals, there had never been any land bridges or evolutionary swimming rodents—but there were guards on all the beaches. They never talked and she never talked to any of them.

The girl in the top bunk turned over.

Sara waited a moment.

There would be, in fact, a group of girls who were prisoners on the island, who would someday be able to vouch for each other. And there was the occasional rumor—screw language, thought Sara—that one of them would be chosen as the High Priest's new sexual favorite.

It didn't embarrass her.

Everything she had ever said out loud or written for school embarrassed her. Her mother had been an English major. Her mother taught British literature at the community college, her mother got a glad-eyed voice when she recommended a book to

someone, when she loaned out one of her books she presented it
with two hands as if it were a fruitcake.

Not literally a priest, not literally an island. Sara despised fairy
tales. European history. British literature. Her mother's affectations.

Something she wanted to tell someone, at some point, was that
a model had lived next door to her. Their neighbors were families
finishing their basements, families heaving lacrosse balls up and
down alleys, families contagious with Halloween and Fourth of
July parties. And then there was the model, Debra Nederlander.
Her affiliation with a family—she was, unbelievably, the wife and
mother—was redeemed by her beauty.

It was as if she knew exactly what she was doing with her
teeth and her gums, cue her heart, when she smiled. She was
slender without being starving or athletic like the other skinny
mothers. She was taller than most of the dads, taller than her
own husband. Her hair and her shoes. For years, when Sara was
upset she would calm herself by thinking of Debra Nederlander's
hair and shoes.

The Nederlanders moved in and suddenly the neighborhood
mothers lingered in their front yards, chatted louder and longer
on the sidewalk. Sara caught her mother reading a novel on the
front steps as if she were a teenager, and she saw how it was the un-
beautiful, actually, who wanted to be beheld by the beauty.

There was her mother wiping down counters, fanning out
cookies. "Oh, but do you eat—?" said her mother, and Debra hung
back, obviously she didn't, but Sara's mother swam up and around
her as Sara watched in horror. Finally Debra shrugged sort of helplessly and made a small secretive wave toward Sara.

That was the story. That was the whole true story of her childhood, thought Sara.

Two months in Paris and she was running out of money.

She cut out the laundromat, the cardboard orange juice with her meals, and she wondered if she could sleep in the day in a park and walk around at night to save on the youth hostel. Sooner or later she would have to face the open roundtrip ticket her parents had generously funded. She would have to take the metro to Charles de Gaulle and find a more-or-less English-speaking window and make a reservation. She could stay at the airport until her flight. Even if it were a day or two or a week, she imagined washing, as she had seen other women travelers do, in the long and mirrored airport bathrooms.

What if she called her parents? Send money. The sound of her voice in her head was what stopped her. She couldn't imagine breaking her silence.

She took her pack out of the day locker and left the hostel. She owed three nights. That was a flaw in their French system. She had just enough left for a metro token.

She had a sense, now, with no money, of needing to conserve her energy and emotion. It would cost her to worry, cost her to stand as the train lurched into motion. She found a seat and she sat her pack beside her. She listened to the sound of the stops, place names, the mild burbling of a conversation on the opposite benches. Her underpants and bra were hand-washed but her jeans and sweater were silky-dirty. She did not feel like she had nothing left to lose; she felt like she must be even quieter, with no money.

At the next stop the conversers got off and a young man in a hood took their spot opposite Sara. She unzipped the top of her pack. What she had left were two fruit-filled biscuits.

The train was a sewing machine making a long seam out of the station. Her mother used to love to sew. She'd get quiet and hummy, and Sara would also. Her mother liked quaint cotton prints, and Sara suddenly remembered the "rhubarb dress" with the red zipper that squeezed her up the side and into her left armpit. If she ever saw her mother again she'd have to remind her.

She raised her eyes to the advertisements above the windows. If she ever saw her mother? Taking her whole life into account, that's right. She could hear herself saying she'd already seen a lot of her mother. She thought of the playfields that seemed to have cropped up nearly every day of her childhood. She'd been gone ten months. Not a year. Ten years would have annihilated her. Ten years would have been full of admiration.

She let her eyes fall to the sweatshirt hood beneath the strip of advertisements. A handsome boy with shadowy eyes and aquiline features. Carrying nothing. Middle Eastern? How was it boys could get away with carrying nothing? Did they know themselves that well? He was her age or older. Good-looking boys were always older. Meegan had got very serious when Sara told her she wasn't into sleeping with people.

"Did something happen?" Meegan had asked her.

No, not that she knew of. And then they'd both laughed because didn't things happen to them all the time with no idea what those things would mean in the future? Meegan, pro-present.

After a while Meegan had offered that she'd never had sex with a girl before and Sara knew she was meant to say if she had or hadn't. Meegan shrugged and said she thought it must be all fingers.

Then she had backed off kindly. Sara knew that she hated sex because she hated—well, she did. That's what Portugal was for, she realized. It wasn't just her mother but humankind she hated. She'd said it. Her stupid heart was racing. And there wasn't any easy out for her, she wasn't adopted or abused or mentally ill that she knew of, she had absolutely no corner on misery, but she was now and forever—she was smiling—Sara Who Hated People.

The hood looked up and across the aisle.

Dark and delicate. Painfully handsome.

Painful because she wasn't him. She would have traded places in a second.

The train slowed in the dark between stations. He wasn't afraid to stare right past her out the blank window.

Just then, the train blew out its air and stopped completely.

The mid-tunnel stop was longer than it should have been, long enough to claim a part of the day, and the mood, and a few of the riders began to get restless. A bony fair-haired man with white rabbit eyelashes kept a lookout up and down the aisle. He turned to the dark mirror window and before he could help himself he rapped on the glass—it wasn't glass, it must have been plastic. He saw that Sara had seen and he tried to smile at his let-me-out antics, but Sara fidgeted instead of returning the smile.

A black woman with enormous marble eyes sighed and shifted her shopping bag from one side of her body to the other.

The boy in the hood leaned over his long legs with his hand extended. Sara watched, mesmerized, as his eyes opened on her at the last possible moment.

What was going on here?

Without any warning at all Sara felt she was in the land of the living. Here, underground, the land of the living.

His arm was still extended. He was waiting. She thought he was going to pull her, up and out of a body of water she was only just aware of. How long had she been drowning? She saw herself in the window behind him, the reflection was colorless, her chin and jaw like loose bones in a sock. Her hair was pulled back too severely.

He had her hand now. "It's pleased to meet you."

"What?" said Sara.

He withdrew his hand, smiling but disappointed. He said, "My name is Christophe."

Take it or leave it, he seemed to be saying.

She said her name. She had to speak louder than she was comfortable speaking. She said, "How did you know I spoke English?"

He pointed to the tag on her backpack. Return address, like Paddington, one of the many bear stories she had endured as a child.

"Do you think?" he said, as he rose and crossed and sat beside her. The hood fell backward and bareheaded he was older. Do you mind, he must have meant. His English. Sara was glad she was so thin, as if it signified strength of character. She thought he was one of those effortlessly controlled people whose body was a temple, who, being a boy, burned such a hot, clean fire inside he could turn anything into a few airborne ashes. Could turn an encounter with a stranger—

"Where are you?"

"Going?" said Sara.

"Of course," he said, brushing off the English.

"The airport." It sounded wrong. Deadening.

"I thinked—the airport."

"You?"

"The same, of course," said Christophe with a French style of mild exasperation.

What could she possibly say to him?

"So we have time." He showed her time between his hands. "But not forever." With a sad half smile.

"Last year, when I was in high school"—had she really said that? It had been so long since she'd spoken.

"I understand you," he said simply.

"I know the French system is different. High school goes to thirteenth grade?" said Sara.

Christophe shrugged.

She was mortified, unbearable, sitting still stumbling wildly.

He took her hand again. She felt as if she were the victim of truth. Not an equal partner. But maybe that was the truth, that truth was always greater.

The train rolled backward, and then it shook resolutely into forward motion. Slowly at first, quietly, then picking up speed, as if to make up for lost time, almost whirring through the dark batting. The man with those eyelashes, they were not made of the usual eyelash material, sat back tersely. Another man down the row tucked his paperback in his leather jacket with a very precise arrogance.

Christophe held up their hands, the interlocking hub of fingers. Necky wrists. Onion dome of fingers. Here is the church, here is the steeple—moist, creased interior, drenched lint in the divots.

2

When the phone rings I hear myself playing it back already, *the phone rang,* as if I'm playing house, or writing a novel.

I hear myself saying, *she ran to get it,* and I find I really am running.

Ten thirty. The day is still cool and tender.

Here I go again, *phone cords weren't made like umbilical cords by accident.*

Although when was the last time anyone used a phone that was attached to anything? Just air, evidently. Crowded with feelings.

I know it's her. She calls at the same time every morning.

I can hear the baby banging in the background.

"How's the baby?"

No answer.

Still no answer.

"Sara?"

"I didn't even mean to call you," she snarls.

She's taken to blaming me for every grievance.

I'm a sorrow sponge, she squeezes me out then holds me up for the overcharge on her phone bill.

She blames me for the cars that splash mud puddles into the stroller. For the walks I take with friends when I could be volunteering in a soup kitchen. When I could be drinking her thin soup of sadness. She calls me when she's bored with the baby. She calls me later, when she's drinking.

Motherhood is how it looks on other people. It doesn't become us, me and my Sara.

She hangs up on me, and I imagine the baby with the only pot they have, the pot I brought over, it's not even a kitchen but a sticky little closet. I brought over a toaster oven that had been in the garage since the last time an elementary school had a tag sale, and a mini fridge she unplugs when she's out of milk, to save on electric.

Of course I bought a crib for Christopher. I would have bought a thousand.

The phone rings again and I throw myself upon it. "Sara!"

Silence.

"It's Carolyn." Beads slide together. Like an abacus, counting against me. One of the old moms. The moms from the old days, when we were moms all day every day, like actors in a living history museum.

"It's been too long again, sweetie!"

Carolyn's voice is all tosses.

I go upstairs to change. Carolyn always dresses for walks, and I'm as susceptible as any woman over fifty to exercise outfits. The one time we get to wear the same clothing as our daughters.

There's a window seat in my bedroom with cushions I made on my sewing machine, years and years ago, when I used to glow late into the night in the nook I set up for myself in the basement. I still like the fabric, even though I don't know what it means anymore. Cabbage roses. You never know what's on the other side of the lovely cabbage rose garden.

You never know if that sound you hear in the middle of the night is the onset of an ax murder or just the old radiator popping. You don't believe in destiny or hocus-pocus but you still have to admit you don't know much of anything about your children.

It comforts me to say it.

Sara went to Europe because she thought no one else had ever. She never read a single book; she thought her feelings against me meant she had invented psychology.

I always wondered, did she want to be different because she *was* different?

What I mean is, was she trying to be herself, or was she trying to be different? It would help me to know. I could never ask her.

She'd been home two weeks when my husband said reasonably, conversationally, that he felt we should separate. I felt it was either an enormous thing of him to say, or a very, very small thing. He rented a condo with housekeeping and room service. Linguine with manila clams, their shells like the rhythm instruments found in every preschool classroom. When I used his bathroom I found my hand hovering over the eternally extra box of soap, smaller than any lay soap, I thought, which made it seem precious.

Sara was shocked, affronted. "I'm never speaking to him again!" and so on.

Poor green soul. She looked more like a pear than ever, pregnant. And her face so fat in spite of her bare-bones anguish.

There were all the different categories and subcategories of government assistance she could get, she and her tiny lamb, bleating and peeing through the night beside her.

I can live without Carolyn coming inside. A few calf stretches on the porch steps. I suppose I'm acting like Sara, who makes it a habit to keep me at bay in the parking lot of the apartment complex. Section 8 Housing, she corrects me. Carolyn's still talking on her phone as she approaches, but she sees me and makes an enthusiastic show of hurrying the call to closure. She still has a son at home. He still troops down from his bedroom and the three of them sit down for dinner. The thought catches me off guard and my throat tightens.

I let her head us off in the direction she chooses. Her steps are short and feisty. Her philosophy is that everything is a weight loss opportunity. She says it again: "I miss you, sweetie!"

"I know," I say, and I do know I miss her too.

I ask after her two older sons.

Jason has a salvage store in an undiscovered neighborhood of an undiscovered city. Would Carolyn please stop calling it an antiques store? says Jason.

"He's growing one of these," Carolyn says, scrubbing her big chin to show me.

"And Noah," she sighs. "Is buried." She pauses. "His girlfriend *Dimitra* is buried with him."

She laughs, taking those tiny punchy steps, and I remember her telling everybody on the sidelines of a drizzling soccer game that she could not, repeat *could*n't, get Noah to stop drawing. We all wanted our children to do one thing so prodigiously that we'd never have to try another new sport or lesson. We all wanted our children to raise themselves on their genius so we could just sit down and yabber—rest, finally—and Noah, she'd allowed him to wait out the game in the car with the window cracked so he could continue his intricate lace of aircraft carriers. It felt all right to hate someone for it, although it wasn't quite Carolyn.

As if to trick me into talking, she keeps her pace steady: "Tell me about Sara."

We turn into the little park-side dog-leg where all the houses look like they have enchanted gardens. I've lived in this neighborhood for thirty years and I've never met a single one of the inhabitants. Maybe I wouldn't want to know they were just another set of bottled-water-drinking walking partners.

Still, the fig trees.

I used to push the stroller through this arbor. I used to think I could set a whole novel among these bungalows. All I needed was a day. A day to myself, a day was a novel.

I wanted to write—*some*thing. It hardly distinguishes me from anyone else who hoped to elevate her inchoate sadness.

My husband said, "Sadness?"

I must have looked wary.

"Not boredom?" he persisted.

I'd put my own mother in my novel, that disturbed creature. I'd write a chapter for the ex-model, Debra Nederlander, who lived down the street, our street, and drove us all crazy.

"So, Sara?" says Carolyn.

"Sara O'Sara." As my husband used to call her.

Of all the children from their group and all the groups their group overlapped with, schools and camps and sports and piano, neighborhoods and buses and somebody's cousins: I lie awake at night and remember entire rosters of third-grade classes. I remember leafy flowery names on phone trees. Children's names that, at first, seemed to belong to their parents. Always somebody going out on a limb—Solveig, Seven—somebody hyphenating, somebody going with a Jr.

Look at me. I staved off the "h" in Sara.

"Boo," says Carolyn.

Our walk takes us past their first preschool. Carolyn's Noah, my Charlie. Later, Sara.

"Sorry."

I force an up-tempo. "So does he think research or teaching?"

"Dimitra is research," says Carolyn, sighing.

The jealous mother of boys, always.

"I always think of him drawing." I pause generously. "And drawing," I smile. He's ended up in marine biology.

I see him throwing handfuls of the driveway gravel. Noah. I see his elastic-waist corduroys. I see him simulating a Tonka crash with Charlie. I see Miss Anne, the teacher, in her snack apron, the preschool whore, my husband called her. Awful husbands in those days. In this mood, I miss them.

"I think about Sara."

"That's sweet," I manage. My compression tank is riding up under my fitted T-shirt.

"How much time today?" She treads on the balls of her feet to keep her heart rate, looking in two possible directions. "An hour? If we go around Montlake?"

There's a loop around the playfields. The good city was always providing. There were so many things to do, so much for Sara—

When she was six months old her eyes were completely clear and knowing. The dark hair on her head was as fine as the hair on my thighs where I'd never shaved them. It's what you always think, but it overwhelmed me with Sara: what would happen if I ever lost her?

I felt like I had invented death in the form of my baby.

Sleepless became fretful became neurotic. My scalp seemed to release its hold on my hair, and I pulled out birds' nests of it with my fingers. Charlie was against the new baby, my husband was working constantly, up for a promotion. It got so I believed in it completely, the fear of losing Sara.

One morning I took her on a long walk through the arboretum. I found a bench half in sun and I took her out of the carriage. Her legs were stiff and her arms were woodenly perpendicular. She could sit up, a recent development, with her new stiffness, but I thought she was like a tiny chair that floated. She could sit, but there was all this space around her.

I propped her beside me on the park bench. It was the middle of the morning. Charlie might have been at school, he might even have been at Carolyn's. We shared a babysitter for a while.

Each moment was endless. That's what I remember clearly.

There was no time, in fact, so that my fear for Sara never lessened, was never halved and halved again by "moments."

When she went over it was all in one piece like a tiny tree. "Tim-ber," I whispered. I pushed her up against me. We sat there with our four eyes regarding the separate world. Honey grass. Big blooms of trees. Late September.

I got up from the park bench, and Sara fell sideways, softly, behind me. She didn't say anything.

I stood with my back to the bench looking into the trees with yellow-brown edges cut into the cloudless blue universe. Sara never made a sound. As if she understood the whole thing already.

When I finally turned back, the sun was fully on the park bench.

It must have been because of the sun that I didn't see her.

The bench was empty. I know it doesn't make sense, but I felt for half a second as if I could start all over.

And then my whole body turned to water. I was wearing tights and so the urine was forced around my legs, all the way down to my ankles.

When I looked again Sara was lying sideways, just as I had left her.

"Boo again, sweetie," says Carolyn.

Were we talking about Noah? Funny, I think now. I never liked him. He never seemed very innocent. The corduroy trousers like a little boy costume.

It seems unfair to dislike a child, but it happens. What I'd never do is hurt Carolyn's love for him.

"I said I saw Sara."

What?

I feel the heat prickle below my collarbone where I'm newly old and dented. Carolyn is the mistress of the steady pace, though.

Can love be loftier than the person upon whom it's lavished? I don't want to know what she saw when she saw Sara, or where, or if the baby.

"Last week," starts Carolyn.

I cover my ears and duck my head a little. The way Sara used to.

Carolyn has to stop talking.

She laughs to give herself time to decide whether or not to be offended.

It was my own mother's position that she had paid her dues. Some people still owed the world their struggle—not my mother.

She would not separate newspapers and cans, she would not turn off the lights when she went out, and she would never take a multivitamin. She found such cultural nods to suffering and hardship disgusting. She found cans and newspapers some kind of cruel parody of herself as a skinny child in a skinny dress pulling a wagon along the curtain-colored sidewalk looking for scrap between buildings and underneath the paper blown up against fences.

I'd picture her at the kitchen table with her jar of peanut butter and her tumbler of clear liquid. My husband laughed when we first met and I said that. Her fat brassy curls like a doll's wig, breasts like a massive overbite.

My husband would decide I was maudlin about her. Actually what he would say was that there seemed to be some competition, between East Coast people, about who came from the lowliest circumstances. He insisted he didn't think her wreck of a life was anything special.

In the home—we moved her across the country to be closer to us—in the diapers, seeds of hair on her shoulders, she relished saying she had sold her soul to bitterness when she was a babe without a cradle. My husband thought she must have read it somewhere. She was a great consumer of dime-store novels.

I can never decide which way she would have gone about her great-grandson, Christopher.

He looks like her. Sara pointed it out to me. "He's grumpy too," she laughed on the phone, almost warmly.

"Yoohoo, my *good*ness," says Carolyn. I try to catch her last words but it seems I was still listening to the baby banging the pot in the kitchen. The pot I brought over.

We're on the homeward side of the loop now. This September

has been crackly, the sky a sparkling blue, bright nervy lines in the leaves and branches. Suddenly I fall back and sit down on the long, low retaining wall of concrete.

"I'm so sorry, Caro. I just can't keep your pace today. You go ahead. I'll call you."

Carolyn stands there astonished, hands on hips, all the trim and determined vanished. She has even momentarily forgotten to lift her shoulders off her breasts, something we all must do now. Her tight green sports top shows dark sweat shadows like egg-plants. Her chin is like a doorknob, all these years I've studied its odd shape and only in this moment.

"Seriously," I say. "Go on without me."

The sun is a lump of clay at the top of the noon hour. We both know the walk hasn't gone *smash*ingly, we both know I won't talk about Sara. We both suspect we wouldn't have lingered for lunch at one of our places afterward—but who eats lunch now, anyway? Lunch went out with the last crusts of a child's cheese sandwich.

The baby's screaming in the background. "How could you do this?" rages Sara, and it has so many meanings. The baby has lobbed the plastic cup of juice off the table.

How could I have brought her into this world?

Would I have chosen pain and bitterness for her? If I'd known it would go hand in hand with everything else the world had to offer?

Suddenly I remember her face when she waved to us one last time, off to Cornwall, Cornball, my husband called it, why did she want to go there? Eighteen, behind a bar, I don't think so, O'Sara. It's restocking and stuff, she'd told him. When she waved, in the airport, her face was like a locket of itself, a memory already.

"I have a completely free day and I'm coming over."

"I'm drinking," says Sara.

I wail, "How's the baby?"

I'm still sitting on the cement wall, Carolyn's still standing over me. The wet yarn of my guts, choose a tree, any tree, hard and bright with September, you'll see it hung with gooey insides.

"Leave me alone, Carolyn," I say. Finally. She winces.

Driven to it, she says coldly, "Well I hope you're all right, then."

It occurs to me I'm acting out Sara. My own mother. Carolyn will have to go half an hour with no one to yabber. Love to Jason and Noah. Love to William, still at home, carrying his homework in his soft mouth like a dog with the Sunday paper. She has the fat below her bra straps. Who doesn't. Who told you you look good in light green, *sweetie*?

She's stalling a little, she still hopes I'll come up behind her, breathlessly apologetic.

A car passes, shining brightly. The sky is snapping blue, the sky should be a car color.

So she's drinking.

I'm afraid to say anything compared to her suffering. I'm the only one in the world who has a spare key to her apartment. She knows very well the power is all hers in giving it to me. She can change the lock like a change of heart. The moment is hers, any moment.

I whisper over the phone, "Is the baby napping?"

The baby is no longer a baby. Christopher is two, but still a baby to me because I see him so rarely. He has big dark eyes, like his father, presumably. Secretly I think of him as a fairy tale. I only know one of Sara's secrets.

She was pregnant in Paris. The father worked as a porter at Charles de Gaulle airport. They lived with his mother on the far side of the airport, the outskirts, says Sara. Yes, he spoke English. Some English. They went boating one Sunday. They rented a boat at a public launch and they set out with their picnic for some duck-covered island. Sara was seven months pregnant. It was only a lake. Not an ocean. Halfway out he was fooling around. He stood up for some reason, says Sara. It was like the boat shrugged him over. I picture a flat-bottomed rowboat. It was, says Sara. He couldn't swim. She didn't know he couldn't swim—couldn't conceive of it, had never met anyone—and she laughed as she circled him in the boat, as he drowned, blowing bubbles, thinking he was trying to get her laughing.

GREEN

This morning, before your arrival, a blond boy with red knees called out to me imperiously, "Your feeder's empty, Mevrouw Bon! You should fill it!"

I tamped my loose hair—the color of a speckled egg, I have observed lately. A proper gardener, I thought to myself, sits to lunch with wine, silver, and fresh cucumbers after her toils. Now which boy was this? I beckoned and he leapt across the street with no heed for traffic. A rather quiet suburb, it's true. Some distance— as you know—from the city.

I held him up to unhook the feeder from a branch in the pear tree. On the back of his neck there was a raised freckle. They used to tell us to catalogue our children. The boy poured the black seeds in the plastic tube quite capably. Bravo, I told him. But I thought to myself it was a sound like wind in heavy grasses.

The garden reaches around my house in a profligate embrace. My neighbors call it a jungle. You must have heard the morning uproar of birds, Naomi, for you arrived, suddenly, in the morning.

This cacophony also shocks my neighbors. There goes Anna Vong, they say, the *old colonist*. Dripping water from a can with the throat of an insect.

My house is like me, isn't it? Tall and narrow. Vong was not my husband's name, but one he composed, his pentatonic ear, from our separate histories. This new name would hide his heroism in Indonesia—not his modesty but his desire to forget war altogether—and my van de *Something*, my whiteness. He kept Wayan, which only meant firstborn. I kept Anna.

I laugh at myself in your company: as a young woman my skin, too, was pearled abalone. Of course I appear quite an old woman now, who shares the tics and habits of all elderly. We sleep poorly, like cats. At night we scavenge memory, in the day we doze in armchairs. We cannot remember yesterday, but a given day sixty years ago is a cool oasis. I must apologize for my faded complexion—as they say, colorless. When I reach up to touch my face I am reminded of the stucco sheath of a house: my own house, one of many identical houses in the development.

You see my forearms mottled with scaly sunspots from years of exposure, long straight bones from knee to ankle. I do not belong to a generation with calf muscles.

I confess. I no longer find it necessary to wash upon waking. But perhaps you believe, as I do, that age is only a veil, a curtain.

Before I could speak to the boy who had attended to my bird feeder, his father was bearing down upon us dressed for a city office. A puppy with a shampooed fleece followed and the boy dropped and tumbled away with it. I thought to myself, I know the boy's father. He bathes in the morning. In winter the steam rises off his northerly seal head as he strides to the commuter station.

You do not have to know the East Indies to fall under the spell of light filtered through chlorophyll stars, tentacles of green like dragon tails. These Dutch are children who follow their noses, A to B, even before they know their alphabet. But I have seen for many years now how they can't help slowing when they pass my garden. I do not, Naomi, see light in children unequivocally. Or goodness. I see light—but it's a science!—in leaves, and flowers. One day my knees will simply give way as I hoist a neighbor child to a berry in my bushes.

Across the street you see Mevrouw Van Daale's garden and its centerpiece, a tidy, skirted windmill. No one lets on it looks like that same little boy, about to be whipped for trying on his sister's dresses. Their concern is great for the male progeny. They would not look kindly on you and your female companion, Naomi. Keep her to yourself. There you lie so sweetly against her clothed shoulder, your hair an aureole—if radiance can be dark. Of course you've kept your shirts on. For my sake, isn't it? I'm an old woman, you've considered. What if I were to look in on you? But you've whispered deliciously to each other in my presence, even held hands, because of course you're also children, and want me to notice.

No doubt you have told your Krista that as a child, for that singular year of your father's sabbatical, the outskirts of Amsterdam, this very street, how estranged you were, how homesick. So that when you return—today! Is it still?—you are surprised the street is not like the view one has from an airplane. Of farmland, for example, patchwork greens and browns, made abstract by distance. You are surprised that the child's bicycle stitched carefully in the grass in front of Verdaasdonk's—the exact house your family rented—is not, to scale, a dragonfly.

Perhaps it is not what you wanted, that the street appears so *cozy*, that I am still here, in fact waiting for you at the gate of my garden. But here you are asleep in my spare bedroom. I've folded fresh towels in the bathroom: did I forget to tell you?

The hollyhocks bend over the fence in front. Living alone has its own order. Why bother returning the garden shears to a crooked nail? There, the scent from the row of potted jasmine. It transports me. And to prod behind it with the fork of my hand for the small green cucumbers like crisp caterpillars.

I will confess my aptitude for drink, which is well known as a comfort for heartbreak, a balm for loneliness. You can see it on my face if you come closer: the flared pores, bone swelling. Oh it's not so terrible, is it? A single distraction?

I was never trained in the art of cooking—*the colonist*. To Wayan, all food was paste in this European country. Anna, please do not affect Frau Housewife. He used the German. He waved his hands. He could bend his hands backward like a dancer. Give me what you've prepared for the baby. He did not understand that mashed carrots, for instance, did not flow from my body. This same kitchen, so narrow.

Of course I remember you, Naomi! You were a shy girl of seven with long brown hair the color of brown skin in my native country. You were a precocious reader. You had made a pact with yourself not to smile. You arrived in autumn, your father's academic calendar, and you reminded me of an autumn firefly, brave and chilly. I said, Can you read those bright signals? I remember your brother too. But he was at ease with the children from the American school who moved like a herd of antelope.

Naomi Lee! How glad I am to see you! Your mother was white and your father, as they say, Asian American.

But I confess I dreamed someone else returning. In the same manner. I belong to a generation for whom the ring of the telephone is jarring. And the voice *on the other end*, as they say, is tentative. Is that you? Either too colloquial or too formal for the wires.

The hour arrives and I am at the gate. I step into the street— witness! Black eyes, a certain freckle...

Are every mother's senses so particular? His skin was wrinkled like a cocooned leaf, damp, and so soft as to be almost furry. The lines around his eyes reminded us of a pouchy grandfather. His scalp smelled of cream and curry which is a smell of new earth in a garden. If he was in my arms he would search out Wayan with his eyes and smile with the unflinching love we call innocence. I prefer to call it joy.

I have been here all along, waiting.

You look down, embarrassed and delighted. I say, You must be twenty! Imagine! Come in, and your companion! Hello, Krista. Ah, the hollyhocks need a heavy glass. Tell me in English, is it pitcher? My kitchen, excuse me, a dim aisle. The wallpaper of auburn willow trees is stained with oil and shadow. My windows are screened by the trees of my garden. I don't bother pruning. Look how the leaves cover the glass like a living petticoat, suffuse the house with green. I have replaced doors with bamboo curtains. These are Hindu thangkas hanging in layers, depicting the sexual exploits of gods and goddesses. My rugs are worn dark and shiny. I wear my slippers in the garden.

The neighborhood was first a development for returning colonials. Wayan had wanted to go farther, perhaps America, but I was entitled to a brand-new dwelling in the country of my ancestors. There were parties every evening. We could not believe we owned these houses. We threw them open with their electric, empty rooms, bald windows. Indonesians—we couldn't be choosy, whether from Bali, Java, even old servants from Borneo, Timor—were sneaked in to cook with hot peppers and coconut. We former colonials, we had the digestive systems of conquerors. And we missed the native dishes of our nurseries. Wayan and I were at the center. His languages were impeccable and I was haughty, pearl-toned, broad-shouldered.

I learned not to speak of my loss. Wayan's loss was greater. I was twenty-four and he was an old man, forty. He said I have lost my country, everything.

My father, mother, two sisters were dead. Our little son Marcus...but I could not, in my heart of hearts, claim to have lost *everything*.

At first, I sustained Wayan with my youth and my belief—girlish, he called it—we might someday recover. But my husband's soul was frail: he could not ward off daily disenchantment. He could not will himself to fit in this country where his spidery fingers, like a scholar-prince, palms as dry as paper, were suddenly womanish. Where he was a shadow. He became infuriated by my patronizing, demonstrative generosity—With me, Anna! he shouted—from growing up with baboes. He began to call me a missionary to spite me. My family had a charmed life, yes, deep verandas, but political, intellectual, never *missionary*.

The streets of our new development were wide—too wide, a survey error—although it is hard to imagine the Dutch careless with their small bequest, or generous with their country. One could become lost in crossing, we joked, we expatriates in our own country. Of course, we were lost already.

Wayan and I would make love in reconciliation, it didn't matter where in the house, none of the rooms were furnished. He came to hate the expat parties. He did not drink. I have no constitution for your liquor, he spat. He pulled me home and flooded me night after night until I conceived a child.

But we had all weathered the loss of dignity. Our former lives had been starved out of us. The expat parties began to dwindle. To live snug against Germany was sickening. The Netherlands opens to the North Sea. Or people took jet planes back toward former colonies, South Africa, Argentina.

I was eighteen with the first, now lost, child. Wayan, almost twice my age, projected a certain *immaculacy* in these matters. We used to think of him as all spirit, in his white linen Punjabis and candle-bright eyes. No doubt we flattered him.

In the mornings we walked in my parents' garden like storybook lovers. This was my confinement while my parents decided what to do with me. They were gentle, life-affirming, as a rule with their three daughters. They did not want me to fall accidentally into marriage. And it would be a difficult marriage, between races. But I insisted: it would be a new world order! The child was warm inside me, a hearth in a hot country. Wayan, for all his extraterrestrial purity, never flinched from my light eyes, the color and consistency of poor-quality jade, he joked, imitating a street hawker's catcall.

Indeed Marcus came out in a rush of warm water. Eyes like glossy beetles, face as round as a moon low on the horizon...

Here, in the suburb, my new, postwar pregnancy was the jewel of the whole development. My skin turned from ivory to pink and I smelled of cherries. I began to work a garden. I leveled and raked our plot, which was mounded with the construction debris of the settlement. By six months I was a sow! Might it be twins? My back seized into a small burning bunion and I simpered and whined delectably until Wayan was shamed out of doors to help me, squinting, almond skin gone chalky. I lay on my left side upon a blanket and called out orders. It was the first time Wayan had worn short sleeves in the new country.

But the baby looked like neither of his parents. He was his own uncharted island, a terrible light-red collusion, a member of a tribe with no leader. Wayan jumped from a bridge before his second birthday.

And I was never able to forget the exact source of sadness. That moon, of the East Indies.

Do you see the sixty-year-old shade trees along our grid, Naomi? It is no longer a *development*...very civilized, very Dutch. My garden, with roots that net and pry through the earth toward Indonesia.

Regular folk replaced expatriates—malarial, trilingual expatriates who had mourned and thrown opiate parties. Walls were knocked out to conjoin the galley kitchens with dining and living rooms. New, larger, freer rooms in hues of white and beige, spare, bright, continental.

The kitchens, Naomi, smell of plastic and burbling coffee. I attend to the quotidian rites of my garden.

Imagine! Little Naomi! A world traveler! *Out of the blue*—the English delights me!

Who is your protector? Krista, a sheen of sweat, a long peasant skirt greasy with travel. Your colossal backpacks rise behind your heads like ancient sea turtles. What is it your dark shapes remind me of?

Once, long after I had settled in this country, I traveled to England. It was a tour group, all of us over sixty, widows and widowers whose *better halves*—again, the English—had been averse to travel. My travel fellows were befuddled, spending more time changing kroners into pounds than sightseeing. I was aloof and self-consciously capable. We arrived at the silhouettes of Stonehenge in the late afternoon with not much time before closing. Despite myself I was moved. Of course, the old stones were animate, like the statues of Hindu gods of my girlhood.

I pull out chairs with a view to the vase of hollyhocks. I pour a small cut glass of sweet wine for Krista. You shake your head no, thank you. Your cropped, tousled hair is surprising, lovely, like dark grass. You think you are utterly private.

I drink my tea and wine together. I ferry bread and butter upon a tray. From the corner of my eye I see a pile of stiffly curling photographs...

A white girl in a sari, prone on the grass beneath bougainvillea and palm fronds.

I'll have to leave you tonight, I warn. I regret, I say in English. There is a yearly supper I have always attended. I shall take the rail to Amsterdam myself after I have fed you.

I clap my hands. Some wine, Naomi! Ah, there you are. Don't worry about it! I wave my long, fan-boned hands to interrupt and open a second bottle.

We'll move to the garden! It is still light outside like a benediction.

You must really visit the Anne Frank House, girls, while in Amsterdam, I might have said, *effusively*. Why do I tell you, instead, my story? 1941, I say. Indonesia. A tour guide of my own heart. In sensible walking shoes.

Girls, I say. We sit with our early supper in my garden. Please imagine. A concrete yard hastily stamped on the outskirts of an Indonesian village. A barracks with thatched roof, a holding place for women and children. We were all there: my mother, my two sisters, me and my little son, Marcus. He was two. He carried himself taut belly first, a prosperous little grandfather. We teased him, called him Opa, and kissed his eyelids. He loved best to watch the birds as they rose steeply from the prison yard to clear the chain link. They dropped into the abandoned, bolting gardens on the other side of the fence. What a persistent, mustardy fragrance! At noon there was a bowl of rice and some peas, water that turned our stomachs to jelly. The children sucked on their

sleeves and cried, I'm sure, but it's strange; I remember their complaints like beautiful singing.

Of course, we left our pram behind; we left our jewelry and
our grandmothers' jewelry; our books embossed in gold, soft
leather covers; necessarily, our grand carved furniture. But for
little Marcus, free to roam between us, not one of us breezing off
to a lawn party at a neighboring farm and leaving him with a host
of baboes, the camp was a heaven. There were crawlers in the
dirt and snakes in the cool corners of the bunkers. He was a baby
naturalist, our father had said. Our mother had a heavy body but a
light heart that delighted in her only grandchild.

The wife of a guard had demonstrated how to wrap the child up
in a length of cloth so he could ride against the body of the imprisoned mother. I tied my son to me. You look like a heathen! cried
my mother, doubled with laughter, mocking our lost pram and the
other imprisoned mothers who refused the native instruction.

Those other mothers watched us warily. Some were mission-
aries. Some were privy to our family history: not just the way the
three daughters waited on their mother, but that Marcus was out
of wedlock, that the liberal views of my family had sustained it until a proper wedding could be arranged one year later. Of course,
such women tried to cover the drumbeats of fear with idle gossip.
They discussed how the three sisters shared Marcus, as if we were
a harem, allowed his fine dark hair to grow long with curls. They
made note his eyes were black and the shape of willow leaves in
dark green water.

One day it was brought to my attention that Marcus had wan-
dered with his ration of rice into the yard of the prison. In an
instant, birds gathered about him.

As I watched my son feed the indifferent blackbirds, the other
mothers bared their teeth around me—the tea-stained teeth of all

colonialists. At least Marcus might share his rice with *their* children if he was not hungry. The birds were free to come and go! The boy must learn to take care of himself before he feeds birds for sport as if he were in the Tuileries of Paris!

My mother had no other home than this country, although her white skin, snow-pale eyes, and solid build were wrong for it. She was accustomed to being fanned and shaded. She had cataracts and could not tolerate the glare in the concrete yard: she had not once left the barracks since our "arrest" four months previous.

My sisters and I relished bringing tales back to her: birds that fed from Marcus's hands, the outrage of the other women prisoners. How the sense of moral limbo entertained our mother! She was known for her school for the children of servants: ethics, and the natural sciences. She had a dry laugh, full of dust and moth wings. But we were all exotic animals in our zoo-like compounds...

What a coincidence, then, of morality, when our father arrived at the camp for women and children.

He had arranged for our release, a boat to America. Perhaps he had traded something; he had never been against Independence. We were to meet him at a port on the unoccupied tip of Java. In one week, a miracle! Everyone in the camp wished she had fed the birds herself, like my Marcus.

A week passed. We were treated as if our good fortune were palpable, to be inherited upon our departure.

The day came and we clustered like hens at the guard's vestibule, the five of us, my mother shaded with a turban. Each one of us was secretly saying to herself, Of course. All our lives we have been lucky. Which is perhaps why, at the last possible moment, they detained me.

Just me. Not my mother, my two sisters.

They handed Marcus to my sister Marina. What could she do but take him? I hated her for an instant.

My cry as they left had an awful quality of being presaged—tinny—like a recurring dream, losing a child.

Sometime later the end of the story reached me. A skirmish had broken out as they reached the free zone. A gang fight, looting. Nothing to do with the war, they assured me, as if this was important in the final reckoning. My mother was killed, and Marina. My other sister, Dara, could not be accounted for. Marcus, my son, was seen standing beneath a pier in water to his nostrils. *Seen?* I cried. No—no one saw him go under, but neither did anyone recount a rescue.

My father reached the meeting point. I was told he died there, in a hotel foyer, of heartbreak.

But what does it mean, *to the nostrils?* Was it an expression? It seemed to me my little son would tilt his head up to the sky to watch morning birds circle for fish in the harbor.

Ah. You remind me of my sisters, Naomi, Krista. They too slept together, for comfort. I slept curled around Marcus.

The train to the city is almost empty. I choose a seat by a window. Suddenly, I am very tired.

I am eighty-four years old. I have not worked a day in my life. My—how shall I say it?—my Dutch child manages my pension. He comes out to my suburb once a quarter, he calls it, with an allowance. He is broad-shouldered like I am. He keeps his black hair too short and he performs one hundred pushups after lunch and dinner. His dark eyes are Wayan's. They seem incongruous with his blue suit, conventionally nasal accent—but of course all of Asia now wears blue suits. He betrays no history. Perhaps he knows no history, and that is my fault entirely.

I would not recognize him in a crowd.

High summer green streaks by like yardage of cloth for new saris for all the servants. The train slows and I watch a flock of blackbirds lift off a field.

The bread in the shopping bag on my lap is like a starchy baby. The prisoner of war supper is a potluck. Dutch dishes, if one knows how to prepare them, for we are too old to make our particular claims to one island or another, no longer colonies, names shuffled or dropped altogether.

Here on the train I am old, invisible. Not even my own son comes to see me. Wayan's son. Distant as his father.

Naomi and Krista. I imagine you there, close to dusk, in the garden...

The air is close in the hall with the other veterans, their medicinal, geranium smell, skin powdered with orange rouge or dandruff. How they bore me! They have listened to all the new recordings of Bach and Beethoven, American orchestras. I was the governor's daughter! Broad-shouldered, ivory-toned, haughty. I draw an old metal chair against the wall and sit upon it justly. I rest my hands on the lip of my waist. I close my eyes for a moment.

When I look up there is a young man standing over me. Not young—in his sixties, but too young to be here. I begin to rise and he protests, suddenly flustered and deferential. He pounces upon another metal chair and lifts it over. There is something green, nascent about him.

Well who can you be? I inquire.

I take his hand between my hands instead of shaking it, partly, I admit, for balance. But is it my imagination that makes it suddenly small and trusting like a child's? His eyes have something of the narrow shape of willow leaves, his skin the finish of a full moon low on the horizon. He is taller than me by a few inches.

It is as if I can see the sound. Television static, chain link, the blur from a train window. The green water of that Javanese harbor. I wake deep inside with the sense of hoarding a dream, an inner angle. The sun is burning behind a white gauze veil.

You're sleeping well, Naomi.

I am glad my house comforts you.

If you did wake suddenly, you would think I was a ghost wafting in the doorway. You would think I was the scent of jasmine.

You would think I was a dream, as if I could take you out of town, on a train, across the flat fields of our small country...

Some are green, purple, brown, and gold, for it happens to be a fertile season.

When we reach the border we'll get off the train and walk for a while.

We'll walk into the hills.

What is this? you'll cry. We're still in Europe—all these palm trees, bougainvillea, birds like kites, flashing and dipping, a sweetness in the air—is it jasmine?

I'll be too far ahead to hear you, Naomi. You'll go on for half a mile, you and your Krista, thinking you see my white shirt, white hair, just there, through the dense foliage. But your eyes aren't accustomed to this green, a million shades of it, and the color of light here is green also. You'll slow your pace. As your breathing quiets, you'll grow tired. The jungle will close around you.

That's where memory awaits us.

After a bit you'll wake up—where are you? In an old woman's spare bedroom, a suburb of the city of Amsterdam...

I won't stand here longer. He's waiting for me in the garden. Is it so surprising that such a reunion occurs on the day I have told the story?

The garden never grows entirely dark, I say to my son Marcus. Green absorbs light, I say, and holds it.

STILL LIFE

At six o'clock the morning is a light sleeve.

Heather drops her key into one of her son's sneakers on the porch and shakes it toward the toe. What a sneaker. It's been tenderized, like a cheap steak. Garrett is nine and his feet are sort of the point of his whole body.

Down the steps. She notices the damage to the braided bricks again as she does every morning. The sidewalk chipped and scraped from shoveling.

It's summer.

When she pointed out the vivid flesh of the brick to her husband he said with that oblique good humor he uses to deflect her, "Wealth can afford to be impractical." As if it were a proverb. Brick rather than old WPO concrete.

She looks up at her house. Are they wealthy? Heather and Matthew: once they were post-college sweeties with a collection of plastic cutlery in a shoebox.

Who is she talking to?

The ghost streams down the sidewalk trailing a floor-length cashmere sweater. Big dark glasses, expensive shoes. Then there's the after-ghost of pure oxygen.

She has to suck hard to get her breath back, then she's lightheaded. When she looks for her house there's only a bright, blank pulse.

They're not as wealthy as the original owners of the houses in the historic registry neighborhood; Matthew is in academia. The whole thing is coded and proportional.

In fact they bought their house from the university: under market value, but they must sell it back to the university when they're finished with it. Matthew said once that she didn't need to tell people, and she'd felt, first, falsely accused, then startled to realize he was ashamed of the situation. Of course she told Gilda, and Gilda was electrified, suddenly ravenous.

"But you guys!" protested Heather. "In finance!"

"We save nothing," said Gilda darkly.

Heather, Protestant, fell silent.

It's true the university is as much a pillar of civilization as the trades—bricklaying—in Providence. It's fashionable to be sort of self-conscious about their little city; or maybe not so little: just last night Heather's daughter, Persia, fourteen, discovered online that it ranked as a "global metropolis."

Who knew?

Then Garrett crowded his sister at the desktop and Persia cried out that "Alpha ++" cities were in blood red while "sufficiency cities," like Providence, Ciudad Juarez, and Kaohsiung, were in anorexic yellow.

"Anemic," Heather had murmured.

In the east the sky is translucent.

A dog and owner pair materialize before her and she hates to greet them, but they're not forthcoming either, and no word is exchanged as the parties meet and separate. She can't help thinking that Gilda would have loved the fact that a psychologist couldn't choke out hello in the neighbory morning.

The ghost moves swiftly down the block ahead of her. It's five two, the sweater becomes a caftan, Heather suspects it's been looking in all the neighbors' windows.

Sometimes Gilda made up her eyes so heavily they seemed recessed. The mask was primitive and ageless.

The ghost vaporizes around the corner. Gilda admitted to belittling the other school moms out of insecurity. And in the neighbors, muted New Englanders who raised indoor children, hired yard work but not gardeners, she diagnosed a self-deprecation that had nothing to do with self-knowledge.

Heather trips over a joint in the sidewalk ruptured by the roots of a big old linden. A hairy beast of a tree holding onto its dried wings and potato-smelling flowers.

Neurosis or ritual that she walks past Gilda's house every morning? Icicle chandeliers circa 1875, nautilus staircases, stained glass and deep wood paneling. Wrought iron, slate, cornstarch plaster. Gilda in dismay: "Our house isn't fancy anymore with us in it."

Heather's own house holds the heat in summer and the cold in winter and with wall cavities full of old knob and tube it's impossible to insulate.

But of course they've corrupted their houses. Bundles of alarm wires, smoke detectors, shapeless family rooms.

A pair of young professionals live in Gilda's house now, commuting to Boston, nesting on weekends like shy storks. There's a sense of stewardship, as Matthew says, when you live in a house built two centuries ago. But also of passing through. Ghost-like.

She pauses at the bottom of the steep granite stairs. She can see Gilda at the top, all four kids arrayed around her, Maggie, Rachel, the little twins Ben and Lila. A precarious glass of white wine somewhere in the picture.

She sees Gilda descending with her small hand trailing behind on the iron railing. She imagines tight black garbage bags of Gilda's clothes bouncing down the same stairs, abandoned at the donation bay behind the Salvation Army.

She would have looked through every pocket, every fold, to find some message. It's a cliché but so is death: some meaning.

Giant showerheads of dill poke up out of the community garden in the hollow of the playing fields. Two years Heather was on the waiting list. The in-crowd strutting bristles of parsley, photogenic cherry tomatoes. Bourgeoisie, as Gilda said, but who knew the neighbors could conjure those bright yellow and orange daisies Heather had just learned were calendula?

A couple of off-leash dogs zoom around the split-rail fence, a congregation of captive humans in the faded baseball diamond. How do dog owners have so much to say to each other? Is it going to be as hot as yesterday? The day is still poised, undecided. Pink mist rises from the bean teepees and sunflowers. Heather looks up.

There's a channel of blue sky through the clouds.

A long, shirred contrail.

Once Gilda showed up at a dinner party wearing a belted kimono. Nothing underneath—she flashed Heather coming out of the bathroom. It would have been the Scheidels', there would have been gossip about the head of lower school, bearded, corpulent, marinated in coffee, how he said mothers in this community would do well to check some of their parking lot chitchat, how it was war now between him and the mothers.

Gilda's cold, dry hand was suddenly on top of hers. In a low voice, "I want to get out of here." She didn't look at Heather directly. They both let it settle.

The Scheidels' dining room was over-lit, the table bald as a mirror between dishes and paper napkins. Females with forced hair, glad-handing males had nothing to say that they hadn't said already. Tracy Donlon, on Heather's other side, was red-nosed and chafed from Shiraz—her son cried when he didn't get one hundred percent on his spelling, Garrett reported, then petitioned for a retake, and the teacher obliged because she thought she was supposed to reward self-advocacy.

"Come with me?" said Gilda. Heather looked around. She had not uttered a full sentence all evening. The Scheidels' daughter had scampered down the stairs in her ballet slippers to practice taking their coats in port de bras, Joe Scheidel received the bottle of wine apologetically, Julia Scheidel's long hands flew up in surprise at the chocolates.

Heather poked at her pesto chicken, her spiral pasta pesto. Otis Redding atmospherizing from the air-conditioning ducts in the ceiling.

"I used to lust after getting invited to these parties," whispered Gilda. "Back in the 1950s."

Heather laughed belatedly.

"What's so funny down there," called Julia. Tracy Donlon pretended she'd been part of Heather and Gilda's conversation but Heather and Gilda were more or less a bottleneck of close friendship.

Now the heat is stirring. Every summer gets hotter but it's not called global warming, Garrett admonishes her.

She and Gilda agreed they'd never gut their houses for central
air, like the Scheidels, though. In retrospect, natural enough for
heliotropic Gilda, who tanned to walnut, donned those goddess
dresses with straps that slipped as she shouldered bags, children.
Heather's feet get thick in the heat. She never had the arms, even
before the yoga standard, for sundresses.

She catches the ghost out of the corner of her eye walking Gilda's three-legged dog, forced to zigzag awkwardly behind him.
The ghost's sundress brushes the ground.

Heather stumbles on a seam again and stops, shaken. What was
it, in light of Gilda's death, that was false about Gilda's life? Gilda,
you liar. Betrayer of the pact between the living to keep living.

But every time she fake-talks to Gilda she ends up feeling defeated. The self-help canon would have a field day with her, as
would her pastor, who's lately affected "mindfulness" as the anti-
dote to all "reactivity."

Curriculum night, the terrarium brightness, Gilda performing
for the school moms: "You'd think I had PTSD," re: the difficulty
of recovering from the front lines of childrearing.

Heather had laughed along, but really she was more alarmed
that her kids spent their days cooped up in such a classroom, stuffy
with hamster, while she was so well-suited to her position as a
three-quarter-time administrator, telling anyone who asked how
she adored her colleagues and the folks she served through the
mission-driven hospital.

Gilda had never worked "outside the home," she'd say, evoking
mid-century mystique. Then, ominously, "I work inside the loony
bin," and everyone would be won over. Heather would call her
midday in good weather, walk breaks replaced smoke breaks in
the progressive workplace culture, and Gilda would answer her

phone anywhere, any time. Even if the conversation was potholed by the twins, Ben and Lila, or she was dawdling in the presence of the earth-shatteringly beautiful Latina girl who slaved away at the Chinese cleaners (they found it incomprehensible that the girl hadn't been discovered), Gilda was also, always, listening. If Heather didn't know it then, she knows it now: she felt unconditionally loved when Gilda was listening.

Come on! Heather wants to shake her. She'd shake the corpse till everything that was loose fell out, teeth and toenails. Couldn't you have gotten fat, gotten drunk, stayed drunk, stayed in bed all day, before you *killed* yourself, Gilda?

A jogger comes up behind her, his dog after him, busy with the smells under holly hedges, the stains at dog height on the slender street trees. Why did Gilda do it, but also why did she think she did it? Heather overtakes the dog squatting irritably in someone's blighted little flower patch. There's no solution. The jogger up ahead, unaware, the street suddenly in full daylight, Gilda had that scurrying walk, furtive almost—the dog keens as the ghost passes.

She's late returning from her morning walk, and Matthew's already hollering, "Out the door!" as the kids flail and whiz around her. Persia has a babysitting job for the neighbors, and this is Garrett's fifth consecutive week at soccer camp, a.k.a., as he says, paradise, which Persia has noted makes him sound like a jihadist. What a cliché, effortlessly adapted by her brainpan. There's a round of goodbyes and then the house is abruptly silent.

Heather stands back from the front door as if struck, immobilized.

The house seems enormous in its quiet, a dark forest, her floors are oak, fir, and maple. It's more than her share, she knows this deeply. In fact, who does she think she is? There it is again: she has always tried to live in some kind of reasonable proportion. Fuel-efficient cars; she's let Japanese knotweed take over her yard rather than water a hobnob of little boxwoods from Home Depot; and if Matthew bemoans the fact that two thousand kids pass through Econ—that's two-thirds of the undergraduate population—and he has to woo and bribe to keep classes half full in History, he can still walk to the university.

Who is she talking to? Her life in proportion to what?

Lemons softening in her favorite glass bowl. What had she imagined a family of four would do with a bowl of lemons? Not even Garrett had seen lemonade in them. She suspects she'll find blue fur on their slack bellies.

She looks around her forest. Garrett's unreasonably long and damp soccer socks deposited like bunched cocoons; Persia's food journal in which all the mothers and daughters are supposed to write positive things about body image; Garrett's empty firefly jar—the last firefly was caught in 1971 in Providence.

She sees Garrett dribbling the soccer ball crablike in the full sun. His new cleats remind her of the bean pods from their locust tree. She sees Persia, flat-chested but with a green-apple puberty headache, her new argyles pulled up over her knotted knees in a long tradition of trampy schoolgirls, reading *The Hungry Caterpillar* to the neighbor's three-year-old.

The kitchen smells like a lemon grove.

She quit work six weeks after Gilda died. More than a year later she's still home with herself as if she were an infant. She's read that children raised by working moms are more resilient, have higher self-esteem, attend more prestigious colleges.

She's met with unapologetic darkness at the first turn in the basement stairs. Why does she always forget to turn the light on?

So, laundry before breakfast dishes, before getting a job to impress her children. The cement floor is cool on her bare feet. She bats around for the chain on the light bulb. Brown paper bags of giveaway clothes stand at attention. She sees the concrete loading dock at the Salvation Army again, sees herself heaving the bags up to the recovering addict with haunches so melted by heroin he wears children's blue jeans—

She supposes she thought of Gilda as a fellow working mom, and Gilda considered her a sort of honorary stay-home mother. What did Gilda do all day, though? Besides laundry? She'd get bored of sororitizing and begin toying with the moms who bragged about their kids whizzing through some series: "But can I count you in for my *Harry Potter* book-burning party?"

Matthew laughed fully when Heather told him, he had to suffer college kids playing that broomstick game out in the open, on the quad. She didn't tell him that Gilda believed Harry Potter was underwritten by Big Pharma using an algorithm designed to promote Attention Deficit Disorder.

Besides laundry, Gilda emailed writers of novels. Once she insisted Heather read a story by Doris Lessing that one of her writers had sent her, in a manila envelope, and here was the marked-up Xerox, the writer's code of checks and circles and question marks in an off-putting green pencil, and Gilda's descant in ballpoint.

"To Room Nineteen." Heather thought it was one of the most galling things she'd ever read, but when she leveled the accusation Gilda seemed pleased. "So tell me about it."

Briefly Heather wondered if it was a trap, but the story had in fact offended her, and she felt righteous. "Well," said Heather, trying to match Gilda's tone. "First of all," she faltered.

"The domain of vested privilege," Gilda readily interrupted. "English gardens, lovely river behind the manor, faithful husband and four adorable children." She paused with satisfaction. "Do we have a happy housewife?" Gilda shook her head no as if prompting kindergarteners.

At first Heather had assumed the protagonist was a proxy for Doris Lessing. "Rookie mistake," said Gilda.

"Call it anomie, call it existential," Gilda smiled, "but our poor housewife wants solitude."

Secretly Heather found it pretentious to talk about literature. The gas fireplace that requires a shilling in the hotel room in London where the housewife seeks her isolation wasn't real; Heather could not feel the heat from it.

But she could feel Doris Lessing's nastiness, even cruelty, as she chases her protagonist further and further from center.

The story ends with the housewife gassing herself in the hotel room, Room Nineteen—unreasonably, unjustifiably, with no sympathy from Lessing, no psychological intervention either.

"What is she trying to say?" said Heather. "You want solitude, I'll give you solitude?"

To Heather's irritation, Gilda had declared easily, "The insolubility of the modern woman.

"Or maybe," she'd added, "the suicide only proves that the protagonist is unreliable, like any other woman."

Heather leaves the giveaway bags behind and heads upstairs, promptly skidding on a T-shirt, banging her shin badly. "Fucking T-shirt." She remembers how in the early days she had thought she herself discovered the genre of housekeeping complaints, transgressive. But then the fiber-optic lines were choked with racy female protest and it was revealed by blog, etc. that all the moms were cynical about laundry. Heather turns and nudges the T-shirt back down the basement stairs ahead of her. In fact it's Persia's favorite, and it would be unconscionable not to wash it.

Facing the paper bags again, she has to admit some of the give-away clothes are so badly stained and torn not even the Salvation Army would want them. The reel picks up right where she left off: the sinewy smoker ("Human beef jerky!" said Garrett once, not unkindly) reaches down from the loading dock to receive her round-bottomed bags with their fragile paper handles. Another admission: she's too cheap to use the heavy plastic garbage bags she buys for her own garbage. Garrett pointed out to her recently that you can read the name of the person who made the paper bag if you look at the base where it's folded. The kids' school has an annual yard sale fundraiser and she's always being nabbed to donate. To be honest, she said to Matthew, she's a little freaked out by all that privilege going round and round. But really she's embarrassed. She's sure nobody else holds onto the junk she holds onto. There's the cord of an old clock radio, its simple two-prong plug, a piteous relic. Her heart is a battered woman who will pick through "household goods" down the food chain, so to speak, in order to set up the tiny post-restraining-order efficiency, courtesy of the Salvation Army. A cutting board—but was she supposed to just toss it? It's maple. Is it?—the shape of a fish, a houseguest present—it's true, she has made use of it, it has probably been christened with runnels of meat juice, and she burns with shame as the battered woman holds the fish shape out with two hands for a long unsure moment.

How does she get to feel sorry for herself as she feels sorry for the battered woman? How is it a twofer?

She sits down on a cooler. Her eyes pass over a tower of nested yogurt tubs. Empty shoeboxes. So many brown paper bags they're like a species. Suddenly she remembers Gilda saying, "So many people can't even have children, how can I complain that mine don't pick up their socks?" And there's that shockingly blunt instrument, grief. She has to stand up, she has to hug the washing machine for counter-pressure.

Every day since Gilda's death (she hears herself saying this), she has asked herself how much suffering tips a life over. When she reads in the paper that recent fiscal austerity has caused "great suffering," she's repulsed, and fear of the Afghanistan kind—those barren moon shots—the Holocaust kind, of course, grips her. How much pain? How high did the water have to rise to sweep Gilda away from her? Is suffering indigenous to motherhood or is it our modern condition? And is she exhibiting signs of the condition by living with a running commentary, a comparison to non-modern times when breakfast dishes and laundry and socks on the floor weren't so freighted? Were women at peace as they moved barefoot about the fire pit with their papooses? I'm talking to you, Gilda.

Hi Gilda, (She has a recurring dream that Gilda's name appears in her inbox and when she opens the email it's not a message but a whole scene, colorful trees and firm sky, clouds like sifted flour.)

I had a total breakdown the other morning, in the middle of the whole feeding and readying hustle, when I discovered that someone had left the freezer door open. Overnight!!

A surge of ill will had overtaken her and bodied forth: for once in her life she wanted to name names. Cast blame. Just haul off and take someone to task, no more of this earnest disappointment: "Oooh, shoot, guys. It looks like the freezer door got left open." Or as if she had a scientific interest in the big mess: "Wow! How about all this water on the floor, guys!" Or (she's on a roll) an admiring curiosity: "All twenty-four organic ice cream sandwiches are liquefied in their packages." Enough! Who did this? There's ground beef, by God, in beautiful waxed-paper packages. Think of the poignant cows. The woolly lambs, the piglets with their quivering sawed-off noses. And clean it up while begging forgiveness!

Later in the day she had remembered quite clearly that she herself had opened the freezer after everyone else retired for the evening; she'd been impatient for her tea to cool and wanted an ice cube. She was awash in relief then. Her own carelessness she could bear. With an upwelling of gratitude she knew that she would sacrifice herself in a minute for Matthew and the children.

Last weekend, driving Garrett to a play date in a suburb to the south, she'd gotten trapped on one of those raucous strips of Toyota-Scion-Lexus, malls anchored by a Sam's Club or a Circuit City. "Here a Trader Joe's, there a swimming pool supply store," she sang menacingly, and Garrett, in the backseat, his new haircut squeezing his head, did not comment.

They arrived late, Heather wound up and Garrett disapproving, and she wondered why, if everyone hated play dates (they said they did), they kept performing the ritual. She made her way up the walk staunchly, and there was the mom already at the door, cheep, cheep, cheep, "So shall we say two thirty?"

Heather didn't have to look at her watch to know she had less than two hours. It might take her forty-five minutes to drive back home through all that traffic. She swallowed her dismay. Of course she didn't expect the other mom to keep Garrett all day, of course Garrett couldn't teleport.

She retreated back down the flagstones. A spacious development bracketed by woods, each house was new but different. Lawns maintained by professionals who rolled new lawns out every spring; otherwise, she knew from her own failings, it was a full-time job of aeration, seeding, fertilizing, weeding, and water. Suddenly she had this crazy idea: what if the other mom hadn't clocked her arrival? What if—contrary to school mom protocol—the other mom had not taken a peek outside in order to ascertain Heather's husband's income, vehicularly reflected? Heather felt a rush of truancy. Weird as it may have been, outlying, really, she walked right past her car (a base-model Honda with decent mileage that reflected nothing but her and Matthew's disinterest in it) where it was parked against that nap of green, and kept walking.

Where the hell was she?

The question expanded. She felt invisible. The sky shifted and grumbled and she tipped her head to look. She knew her zoology was off, but it seemed like it should have been the lizard brain that couldn't help imagining the airplane dropping, the lobe of the sky falling. Although lizards, with their eyes like side-view mirrors, weren't exactly in the business of looking up toward the heavens. She had reached the main road. No houses now, no sidewalk, and she felt repelled by the maple and pine forest, the vining exuberance of blackberry and poison ivy. In fact it was no place to walk, and after the first car swept past her at sixty miles an hour her ears began to buzz, lizard-like, signaling danger.

After a while the road T'd at a bigger road. She turned left and walked a few tentative yards on the shoulder until a truck passed and nearly sucked her into its wind tunnel. She was about to turn around when she saw a break in the thickety woods just ahead, a pull-off. Her body propelled her, suddenly she was jogging, and in a moment she reached the simple rail gate across the entrance to an old carriage road. A wooden sign with that funny wormhole calligraphy: TOWN FOREST.

She felt auspiciously welcomed. The wide pine-needle path was soft and clean and the forest here was light and airy. There was a time when she would have been afraid walking alone; now she thought that the loss of fear of men was perhaps the single substantial perk of getting older. In her day, suburban woods were a free-for-all of crime and litter. Like the ocean. Even good girls like her considered cigarette butts compost. But here in the Town Forest there was not a single wrapper.

By and by she noticed that she was walking through a plantation of blueberries. The bushes were almost lacy, two or three feet high, and dangling with deeply colored berries. Was there some enchantment at large? Let this path go on forever! Let it be her life, the way the sun scrambled through the twigs and branches, the unselfconscious birds, the cars silenced—

She finds herself standing in the middle of the kitchen.

Nothing needs to happen.

Still life with breakfast dishes, with wild blueberry bushes. Her inner life is as big as the Big Bang, in modern times it's heavy on the bass, on the studio reverb. If a man were to jump her in the Town Forest, if a car were to hit her on a blind curve on the hot and disappointing walk back to the house in the new development—no vulgar plot for her, thanks. It's all she can do to go back down to the basement with the dishtowels she is always forgetting and eject the ball of them into the barrel. The load's not full but she's going to run it anyway. Who is she talking to? What is it about the basement that reminds her of a church? Just its cool and quiet? Small, high windows? At Gilda's service she was seated so that she had a crotch shot of the 3-D cross that hung from the tiled dome in the center. There was a startling intimacy of skulls around her, she had wondered before she lost it, and Matthew did not merely put his arms around her but locked her to him. Her crying felt like breathing underwater if you could, miraculously, but you were untrained and awkward. She had seen Christine Jones shaking in the pew in front of her, she had seen the tall man in a barn coat come up the aisle, he carried himself like a banker, but that was cheating. She knew who he was immediately, and if she'd had any doubt about Gilda's ability to pull it off, with gifts of jewelry, etc., now she didn't and neither did she care to crane around for Dan, Gilda's husband.

Where does this leave her? She's not in a detective story, but she always thinks: Gilda who didn't mean to die, as if it set Gilda apart from all the people who didn't mean to die by lightning strike, cancer, car accident. Yesterday morning, walking Garrett to soccer camp, passing the windows of the consignment shop where Gilda was a regular treasure hunter, she thought how dying had nothing to do with death and everything to do with life, for Gilda.

Is that the doorbell?

Her train of thought jumps the rails and rolls longwise down the embankment and bursts into flame. The ghost in the cashmere smoke, Gilda with the hood of her Burberry raincoat obscuring not just her face but her entire body, picking her way out of the accident, through the rubble, up the hill toward Heather.

She hurries upstairs. She can see through the sidelights that it's the cat-lady type who lives on the corner in the baggy Victorian. She fumbles with the alarm, looking up intermittently, apologetically, until finally she manages, and the neighbor, dressed in old gardening jeans and a grown son's sweatshirt, sidles in, keeping a wary eye on the blinking keypad. Heather doesn't think they've ever properly introduced themselves, but before she can begin, the neighbor produces a letter. "I got your mail?"

Heather sees immediately that it's not for her but for another neighbor, a woman about her age and stage of life up the
block whom she's on friendly terms with. Obviously, it's too
late now for introductions, and she feels desperate to abort the
encounter before the cat-lady discovers her blunder. "Thank
you so much!" she cries as she plows her back out through the
dark hallway.

Her heart is pounding. She is distressed more than is warranted—
derailed, as if she has failed a life-or-death test of her humanity.
Finally (how did she get upstairs?) she pitches herself across Garrett's twin bed. Her shirt catches on the edge and rides up and she
sees her bare stomach. It looks like a cadaver. She knows the flesh
is numb and she resists the temptation to pinch it.

She rolls onto her back and there's the cracked ceiling. Plastic gold team trophies poke out of the clothes piled on top of the
dresser; Garrett is still in the long middle of the years of trophies
like party favors. All the boys still examine the trophies at other
boys' houses. There's the poster of the frilled lizard he chose from
National Geographic when Persia toured him through the website,
otherwise the walls are bare, painted watery white in a bygone
decade, scuffed and streaked, indifferent to the lizard's flat eye
and the sunlight that wobbles across them.

Gilda once blurted that Garrett's room was a cell. By accident?
Then she'd shuffled out backward like a disgraced geisha.

Another time they were sitting at the top of Gilda's granite
stairs drinking white wine, looking out through the linden onto
the street, and Gilda said dangerously, "Do you think I should
join the Junior League, Heather?" Maggie, the oldest, Gilda's shadow, preferred to sit with them rather than mix with the younger
children, and she listened to every word they said, twisting the
ends of her hair in that intense way she had just before puberty.

Gilda took a long swallow. She glanced at Maggie. "All tennis and violin and interior decorating?"

But suddenly she dropped her hair in her face, and she looked small and crazy. Reaching for her wine glass she missed and knocked it down the stone stairs in an explosion of crystals.

Heather follows the light bobbing up the wall of her son's bedroom. Garrett is a tight weave. She doesn't know anything about weaving, but his warp and his weft are in balance. His ups and downs and crosswises make a durable but supple fabric, Gilda.

Gilda confessed to drugging herself before dinner parties. At first Heather had to work hard to pretend she wasn't shocked. If there's anything to help you through you should help yourself, she knows she said once, tightly.

Matthew said Gilda's dinner parties were *Alice in Wonderland*, surreal, hysterical, sugar in the saltshaker. There was this air of childish wreckage, as if Gilda set her house up to be toppled. The last Christnukkah party (Gilda punished the holidays by putting them together. One year she called it an Abraham party, but then, after 9/11, she had to admit—everyone had to—she didn't know anything about Islam) she'd been crazier, to use an inexact word, more off center than usual. Her hair was in a new shag cut and she'd worn a lot of sunset-blue eye shadow, falsies, and a transvestite tutu. She'd corralled and goaded the women to drink her "rowdy rum" punch and the men had caught the spirit and followed heedlessly. Heather herself had thrown up in the third-floor bathroom, efficiently and discreetly, and returned to the scrum with a directive to rescue Gilda. She'd found her practically grinding with Joe Scheidel in the kitchen. Dinner had not been served yet.

Now she wonders if she was enabling when she took over and redirected the party to the table. Was Gilda trying to signal that something more than her inner hostess was off-kilter? Was it Gilda's fault the evening turned stupid? The men and women like oil and water, the salad dressing painful with vinegar. At some point she had realized that Dan, to whom no one had directed a single question all evening, was drunkenly disassembling Gilda's parents.

"We put them up at the Westin and they stole the toilet paper. Maggie found four rolls in her grandmother's bag with the Westin seal still on them."

Heather knew Maggie would never betray Gilda. She saw very clearly how Dan had rummaged in his mother-in-law's belongings. Even through the pills and wine, Heather had seen Gilda's hurt and confusion.

When Heather tiptoed upstairs later, she found Gilda asleep under the bedside lamp beside Lila. Lila's room was all white, there were little white pompoms on the curtains. On the mantel above the original marble fireplace Gilda and Lila together had arranged small white objects: a German polar bear, a die, a pyramid of white sewing thread.

Gilda's mouth was draped oddly over her chin and her closed eyes were hollows, as if the eyeballs had sunk to the bottom. Heather leaned closer as she used to do when she was checking her babies. Of course Gilda was breathing. But still, the body was vacated. Gilda was so small when she wasn't in motion. Heather kept watch for a few moments. When she finally snuck out of Lila's bedroom and back downstairs she was almost relieved to see that Dan was not in the kitchen; she would be left in peace to do Gilda's dishes.

Where is she?

Still in Garrett's bedroom. She fights the cadaver to death quickly. Matthew is faintly offended by her description of her stomach. "I loved it when you were pregnant," he says. She tugs Garrett's quilt straight. She saw Gilda asleep but not dead. Everyone is cremated now, but still, you imagine them lying on their backs in corpse pose in their dusky coffins. Mouths slack, but if their eyes were open you'd be able to see they were smiling knowingly. She's not gothic. But there's a body to account for. There's her own body despite herself, slightly slouched all the time now, she's holding the railing as she takes the stairs, if you took the total population, the seven and a half billion, she'd probably come out in an upper quartile, and in her group of First World females between childbearing and menopause in a third-tier (fourth?) city in the coastal Northeast, she may feel like an outsider but she's right in the middle. She's tinkered unadventurously with her hair and settled on a tempered blond; she has a large nose, narrow face, an uncertain voice, and much to her chagrin, because it's such a stretch it's a non sequitur, she's been told she looks like Helen Mirren. What kind of brain tumor—as Persia would say—makes people say you look like an actress? Oh, she knows she fits in, roughly. She knows grief is nothing special.

If she leaves the house now she'll have time to stop at the community garden before meeting Christine Jones for coffee. Of course she should have taken the tiny detour on her walk this morning to water her tomatoes. But there's a pall over the garden, she's avoided it since last week, since what she's come to think of as *the encounter*.

She was weeding out crabgrass and amaranth when she realized that the teenage boys in her peripheral vision were stalking the perimeter. She had only a minute to register them before, as if cued by her unease, they hitched up their clothes and took ironic running starts to vault over the split-rail.

She'd let go of the hose and summoned attitude. "You know there's a gate?" There was a combination lock. They swiveled obediently to look at it. Then they went up and down the rows, sampling a leaf here, a bean there, all artful insouciance. When they arrived at her row she said as coolly as she could manage, "Hey, just steer clear of *my* tomatoes."

They nodded solemnly. They continued their subtle pillage, and she kept on watering, her fist cramped around the trigger, until her plot became soup, with stray basil leaves floating on the surface.

Finally, albeit with less brio than their breach, the boys climbed back out over the fence and Heather watched them amble across the playing fields. She tried to tell herself that her stolid presence had at least put a damper on their adventure, but mostly she felt exposed, outstripped, and exhausted.

The day Gilda died Heather had spent too much time with the morning paper and, late for work, she scooted out past Matthew with a last word over her shoulder, "Did you see there were babies?" Plague, war, tsunami—a moment later she realized she'd said it with a kind of easy horror. She'd called Gilda on her first walk break. The sun was still a little green in April but there were daffodils waving in the wind from the industrial fans behind the hospital cafeteria. There was no answer. She left a message. She called Gilda again on her way home from work and left another message, about half an hour after, she would learn, Gilda had passed out in a "Standard" room at the Westin. As is often the case with pills and vodka, Gilda didn't die instantly—Heather always gives the facts, like she's the newspaper. She won't color people's judgment with her sadness, her sadness is not the story, her sadness is not on trial, it's Gilda's death that may be deemed unacceptable. A beautiful young mother of four does not commit suicide. See, Gilda?

So no, she's not up for policing the community garden, and actually, she never feels like another cup of coffee at eleven o'clock in the morning. But she'll break the sound barrier of the depressed housewife, she'll do it for Gilda. Shoe, other shoe, purse, package, keys—she feels around the likely surfaces like a blind person, resigned but confident.

She'd barely known Christine before Gilda died, when Christine was Gilda's mysterious older friend, out of Heather's league in the hierarchy of school moms. (Cool moms. Very sweetly Persia insisted Heather was one.) Gilda had told Heather that she and Christine went out drinking, a few times they'd ended up dancing at a strip club, and Heather had been intimidated, knowing she didn't have that kind of imagination.

Suddenly she misses Matthew. Should she stop by his office? He'll ask her why she's having coffee with Christine in the first place, and, avoiding the topic of Gilda, she'll tell him it's because Persia has a crush on Christine's son, Jordan, and he'll look baffled, and she'll describe Jordan Jones, a beady-eyed sixteen-year-old with a quiff of blond hair like the front man in a boy band.

She'll perch on Matthew's desk, feeling more alive for a moment, because even though Jordan has never spoken a word to young Persia, do not, she'll tell her husband, underestimate our daughter's power of attraction. Sure, she'll continue, hectically now, boys can be white men and date rapists, but girls these days take their supremacy for granted. Hillary Clinton is going to seem like such a try-hard when Persia and her friends grow up to be presidents!

Matthew will laugh appreciatively before shooing her out and again she'll wonder, how could Gilda check out before she got to witness the full force of Maggie and Rachel and Lila?

Why hadn't she been brave enough to suggest to Christine that they meet somewhere else, in a park, like when the kids were babies?

Where she met Gilda in the very beginning.

The first week of September, the trees were desiccated, their leaves rattled. There was dust in the air, even in the dew, and Persia was still too little to go to preschool. Oh, those gaping weekday mornings when Heather was working half time, leaving more room for post-partum depression; she didn't make the same mistake twice, Garrett graduated straight from maternity leave to daycare.

She'd noticed Gilda right away, hunched on a park bench: red clogs, black and blond hair extra streaky, very thin (she would learn that Gilda had dramatic cycles), watching a girl a couple of years older than Persia curled in the mouth of the tube slide— Maggie. Persia had already wriggled from the stroller—all of their strollers strewn and abandoned where the young passengers tipped themselves out before their caregivers had even parked them—so that Heather had been forced to approach Gilda without cover.

Gilda had taken one look at her and narrowed her eyes, but Heather sat down anyway. Just then they caught sight of the self-appointed squirrel watch—Natalie? Valerie?—a near-emaciated former lawyer with purple adult acne, famous for her raw contempt of those who left Ziplocs of Cheerios or Craisins on the seats of strollers. Heather and Gilda had peeked at each other at the same moment and then fallen together in unfiltered, cathartic laughter.

Valerie Marshall, Heather thinks now, who let it be known she was aching to get back to lawyering, and the other moms agreed—the moms who made fun of themselves for their own former lives as women—that she had surely been a formidable woman lawyer. The squirrels bugged and twitched around her as if she were St. Francis.

No, Heather would rather die than spend an hour at a baby park now, the way the music of the ice cream truck wavers and goes flat in the distance.

She leans on the door of the coffee shop to open it and waves to Christine and immediately feels flustered. She's never sure about the whole order of greeting her friend, buying her coffee, doctoring her coffee, and the mild shame, in front of Christine, of soy milk. Should she sort of sign language to Christine from her place in line, or look straight ahead at the coffee-bean-porn poster? Today, the added embarrassment of decaf—her heart is already shattering, and frankly even the smell of coffee is making her a little nauseous.

But there is no virtue in anxiety, she chides herself. What's the worst that can happen? The awkward moment of silence when she sits down. She latches onto her straw and pulls up on the poison.

She eyes Christine's mug of tea with its green cast, teabag ballooned on the surface like a dead body. Christine catches her looking and pushes it away.

A beat and a half goes by, or maybe it's half an hour. Christine says, "I don't know how people drink this veggie water."

Heather tries to laugh but it's out of sync. Suddenly she realizes that somewhere along the way her mind has been swept clean of conversation. It's a new level of loneliness; she has zero curiosity.

That new song comes on the radio, or Pandora, "La-dy, running down to the riptide..." and Heather knows it's not meant for
their demographic but still, here's a song Gilda will never hear.
How could Gilda have done it, knowing pop songs would go on
without her? She will never know that Hamas fought Israel in Gaza
all summer! Gilda, a secular Jew whose memorial service was held
in a congregational church—what would she say about Israel? That
the birthright nation fought terrorists?

She won't get the news that people are once again wearying of
Facebook (but still posting rows of hearts on Gilda's wall, I miss
yous), that Dan moved to a different state to get away from all the
co-mothers. Heather's grandmother died September 10, 2001, un-
suspecting, slipping out with a whole era; for that matter, Persia
was born and named in 1999, light-years before 9/11. What tears
Heather apart is that the dead become innocents so quickly.

"Well, you picked the wrong person to reach out to," Christine
says tiredly. For a moment Heather is too surprised to process.
Then—she knows it's not meant as a rebuke or a rejection, but it
lands that way—she stares at Christine dumbly. Christine, usually
polished and elegant with her auburn hair and pale skin, has traces of sunblock on her cheeks this morning. The person Heather
wants to talk to about Gilda's death is Gilda.

"Heather?"

She draws herself up. She has to go. She has to water her
tomatoes in the community garden. The acid-soil smell of coffee! The rocks caught in the coffee grinder! She really has to go.
The moment is suddenly unbearable, yet it bears her up, and
she has a view of another school mom entering the coffee shop,
all brokered up for her workday, deep in conversation with a
male colleague. With superhuman effort she turns to Christine
in parting.

She knows she's afraid to discover a "reason" for Gilda's suicide. Why? Because it might be banal. It might just be life getting in the way of death. What if she found Gilda's reason was no better than anything she herself could come up with?

Outside, the air is still as if it's been trapped under a hat for days. There's the pungent smell of burning asphalt, summer roadwork on the surface streets in the university neighborhood, and the long rattle of a jackhammer. Her jeans are sticking to her thighs; who wears jeans in this weather? She doesn't believe grown women should wear shorts though. The word "unseemly" lights up in her circuits but she's not going to preach to the choir of herself right now, she's not crazy. Not crazy? Do the math, as Persia says lately, because if she's crazy, then everybody is crazy. If everybody has days they talk to themselves a little too constantly, loudly, days they can't handle a simple coffee, why had Gilda been singled out?

Her loose sandals snap the sidewalk. She turns into her own neighborhood, the houses themselves like neighbors. She passes her own house. She should stop to change her clothes but she can't afford to lose her momentum.

Gilda turned her nose up at the community garden. What really got her, she said, were burghers pretending to be hipsters, copping to be all down with zukes and compost. But then she accepted a plastic newspaper sleeve of herbs with uncensored delight, a handful of cherry tomatoes with reverence.

A month after Gilda died there was a heat wave and it felt like high summer in May, like Heather had flown somewhere far away for vacation. Her light skirts and tank tops seemed foreign, and it was in this dislocated state that she found herself descending the hill toward the Westin one morning.

She was always ashamed of her shock at downtown Providence; it surprised her that such a small city could sustain so many home-less people. Sustain? Or people who looked homeless, waiting for buses or friends or a cigarette, eyeing her with interest. She didn't know if she should look back at them, as if to bear witness, or train her gaze on the horizon of office buildings, signaling her ease with manifold humanity. That morning was no different.

She had never been inside the Westin, and pushing through the revolving doors she couldn't help but feel she was passing into a netherworld. The shadowed lobby was refrigerated and she felt suddenly naked. Of course it was like any hotel in any city though, and she had the sense again of having traveled—taken a flight in a half daze—and that this was the first surreal hour of some half-dreamed vacation. There was a reception table in the center of the room with an enormous, formal, funeral-worthy arrangement of fresh flowers. Then Gilda passed her on the other side of the lilies and roses. She wore her full-length fake fur coat and dark glasses. There she was bunched at the desk, checking in, ready to die or not at all ready?

She really just misses Gilda. It's not fancy. She's hardwired, she supposes, to be shocked and repulsed by death, and she is. But faced with it, with death, she finds she believes in everything. Ghosts, resurrection, wrinkles in time, miracles.

Despite the heat she charges down the grass hill now, suddenly every minute matters in terms of her tomatoes. She rotates the dial on the lock to get the right combination of numbers, one, two, three, four: Persia had regarded her with disbelief when Heather inducted her, Persia who is mistress of a thousand and one night skies of passwords, each constellation an intricate admixture of caps and signs and numbers. The garden is at a midday droop, not so much listless as waiting, but already she feels better. She remembers her walk this morning and she looks up to find the sky again. Clouds like parchment.

Her tomatoes could have used her attention yesterday, but the Velcro leaves are still green, and she turns her water cannon on them. The surface soil runs off the edges of the raised bed and she pauses to let the water soak deeper. Those weightless white pellets stay on top now. Are they Styrofoam? She lets the plants rest while she showers the fragrant tent of green beans, basil and nasturtium in the undergrowth.

She gazes over the garden and catches motion. A figure in a long tunic, harem pants, and a floral patterned headscarf is passing suspiciously close along the outside of the split-rail. Heather steps to one side of her jungle to see better. The figure drops to a crouch behind a screen of pea vines. Heather is suddenly aware that she's breathing loudly through her mouth and she tries to calm herself. There's a rustle in her own ears—it looks like the stranger is weaving her hand through the rabbit fence to get at someone's bounty.

Heather hears a voice: "Please don't pick those tomatoes." It's her voice. Proprietary. Also supercilious. She sees the big cherry tomato plant shiver. She drops the hose on the ground.

"No," she says very clearly, striding across the garden.

The stranger stands up on the other side of the fence. She's heavy, swarthy, dirty, with striking dark-lashed green eyes. She's holding a ball of used plastic shopping bags in one hand. She looks, improbably, like a gypsy, like the hardened older sister of the Afghan refugee girl from the *National Geographic* cover. Heather was twelve when that photograph came out, the same age, purportedly, as the refugee.

Heather finds she can't maintain eye contact. She takes in the plastic sandals, bare toes black with dirt. "No," she says again, before she can stop herself.

"No English," replies the woman, staring straight at Heather. She holds up her hands and her plastic bags and backs away, but not so far that she isn't still connected to the harvest. Is that a smile?

A chasm opens up between them. Heather's been wronged, she tells herself, but she feels unmoored rather than indignant. She doesn't believe the woman has no English: the look in her eyes is of roaring intelligence.

She hears herself babbling shrilly now, and finally the woman shrugs and moves off, obviously unashamed and unimpressed with Heather.

Heather goes back to her plot and collects a few basil tips, a fallen tomato. She feels watched. She loops the heavy hose around its dock. She has to concentrate on not fleeing. She locks the gate behind her. She imagines the stranger already doubling back to the garden. She thinks of the *National Geographic* girl in her loose red hijab like a painting of the Virgin Mary. The longing Heather had, as a girl herself, to save her. By which she really meant befriend her.

The neighborhood seems altered. She's drawn toward the narrow passage behind one of the university gym buildings: an entire alley for the HVAC. She's walked this way countless times but for the first time she notices the tough, shade-resistant plantings in gravel, the gigantic air-cycling roar, and the smokestacks. She feels cold and floaty. She sees the whole university athletic complex as a crematorium, she remembers reading recently that German prosecutors were beginning to use 3-D imaging of the death camps to recreate the vantage points of individual guards, in order to indict them.

At that moment she sees the woman slipping around the hockey rink, a giant scallop shell of painted metal. Before she can think it through she starts after her. Come back! In her heart she's relinquishing the whole garden. She too would have been a top-notch gatherer if she came from a stealer-gatherer society. She would have prowled the neighborhood in her rags, her plastic bags, unmoved by someone like herself. She begins to walk faster and then to run. Please! Let me open the gate for you! She can hear her own breathing with the HVAC. She'll scale walls, drop and roll on the landscaping gravel if she has to. But she comes out the other end of the athletic complex and the woman has vanished.

It's too hot to run like this. She's been left behind, the way the dead leave the living. The way Gilda alone knows her mystery. There's some shade under a row of serviceberry trees and she stumbles into it.

QUETZAL

1

In a vanished time (dinosaurs, thinks Marguerite), Marguerite and her mother lived in a one-room cottage between the landlord's sea-captain Colonial and an overshadowing, porchy Victorian. 18½ Maple Street was hardly bigger than a child's playhouse, but Marguerite's mother was the beneficiary of the landlord's particular New England philanthropy.

Philanthropy, sure, but who could resist her mother, Diana? The beautiful young widow, natural mother of a child who looked nothing like her, gentle, presumably hopeful yet ravishing Diana, making a go of it in a forbidding climate, making sacrifices for her daughter, overqualified for her work at the library, known to take solitary winter walks along Newport's public beaches. The wind salted and swept seaweed into giant nests for bird bones, as if some pterosaur had collapsed after its flight across the Atlantic.

Mr. Goff, the philanthropist-landlord, was in his sixties, tall, with a high forehead and faded eyebrows, a drinker of gin in table-spoon measures, a pronouncer of long a's, as in h*ah*f and tom*ah*to. Mrs. Goff had a 1950s waist and wore circle skirts to accentuate it. Her hand-loomed sashes and folky silver brooches were unique in Newport; the couple had lived in Guatemala. They had one child and he had died there. Perhaps sorrow had made them broadmin-ded. Indeed it was because of the Goffs that Marguerite was under the impression that young single mothers like her mother were rare, and precious.

Mr. Goff had renovated the cottage for Diana. There was a perfunctory kitchen along one wall, a prefabricated shower stall in the bathroom, and a fixed ladder to the open loft "bedroom." His generosity was somewhat austere: Marguerite's mattress was separated by a narrow aisle of bare floor from her mother's. The small skylight seemed muffled, as if a large gray cat, harangued by tireless seagulls, lay across it.

The neighborhood was rundown but historic. There were raw patches on every street where the blacktop had worn or potholed to reveal the original cobbles. Eighteenth and nineteenth-century houses in muted stone and sand and seagull colors, the occasional drab olive or deep cranberry, lined the streets, small windows divided into small panes, no shutters, no front yards, the sidewalks lapping up (frozen) against them. There were a few overextended, trammeled-looking Victorians, which Diana called haunted houses.

Even in the winter Diana liked to sit on the Goffs' granite steps, the navy-blue Rhode Island flag snapping at the sky's rib-cage. The cold burned Marguerite's skin through her blue jeans. "You don't have to stay," Diana started, and Marguerite could nev-er quite tell if it was motherly empathy or a secret hope that her daughter would leave her to a sunset that was invariably lost in the mattress of clouds and early darkness.

The view was territorial: Andrade's Liquor across the street, dun-painted cinderblock, bars on the windows. The store was tended severely, funereally by the Andrade family, but there was a stand of peach trees in the back. "Just think," Mr. Goff regaled Diana, with self-satisfied admiration for both his subject and his audience, "Tony Andrade chipped out the loading dock by hand for an orchard!"

When Mr. Goff crossed the street for a bottle of Gordon's he'd often add, for Marguerite, one of the register-side baglets of cocktail peanuts, and when Mrs. Goff sent her for milk, Marguerite entered the lemon-smelling shade almost holy with her errand.

At the library, Diana Webb re-shelved in flat shoes; secretly Marguerite held in high regard the fact that her mother had never had her ears pierced. "You're to go to Mrs. Goff in an emergency," Diana told her carefully. On days her mother worked late Marguerite spent hours imagining what sort of event might release her from solitude to the care of the landlady.

Mr. Goff was an avid hobbiest. He brandished a cheerful, layman's philosophy: "The brain, Diana, is marvelous, and it craves new information." Marguerite never conflated her disinterest in dinosaurs (for they were the object of his hobby) with being a girl, possibly because her mother could be engaged on the subject for hours. There were weekend afternoons Diana spent wholly with Mr. Goff, touring his amateur collection of replica fossils and low-resolution photos of dig sites and open display cases. Marguerite had noticed that her mother looked even more beautiful than usual when she was rapt—and wrapped up in someone else's life altogether.

One afternoon Mr. Goff staged a backyard scavenger hunt. It was March, and Marguerite was nearly eleven—too old for Easter egg hunts, which was distinctly what it felt like—old enough to know it wouldn't be polite to refuse the landlord.

The flowerbeds were soft and bare except for a few pale snow-drops, and with a quick scan Marguerite could see the places where Mr. Goff had been active, and how he'd patted the dirt for her benefit. Come to think of it she'd been half-listening to the sound the back of the trowel made when it hit a rock for what seemed like hours. She stood a bit apart from the three adults, and, now that her ears were trained, she could hear the ice bash around in their cocktails. Her prize, if she completed the treasure hunt, was to be a children's dinosaur encyclopedia.

Dutifully she rummaged through the garden borders. She could feel Mrs Goff watching, her features as small and tense as a mouse's, through her cat glasses. The landlady called out a couple of times, "Please, the bulbs, Marguerite," and Marguerite heard her scold her husband for putting daffodils and tulips in danger.

Mrs. Goff needn't have worried. Marguerite was constrained by the vague sense of shame the endeavor caused her—her lack of heart and Mr. Goff's whinnying eagerness to please her mother.

She paced herself. She had a sense of how long Mr. Goff thought it should take her, and in the end, with no surprise, she came up with all the ivory-stained resin bones he had planted. He puzzled them together himself, a sketch of a skeleton. Marguerite couldn't help noticing that his deft fingers were the same color, and that her mother had lost interest.

Mr. Goff wiped his hands and then folded the towel devoutly, as if to preserve prehistoric bone dust. Marguerite held the encyclopedia out like a serving platter.

"Well, tell us what it is!" her mother cried rather too forcefully, as if she were yanking herself back to the present. But Mr. Goff regarded Diana with almost fairytale adoration. He gathered them

close and paged through the encyclopedia until he found it. The
wings of the Quetzalcoatlus were webbed forearms and fingers.

Marguerite takes a dinosaur-sized swallow of vodka. In the
fearsome illustrations the monsters are all gradations of the same
potato color.

There is not enough light to grant much depth of field; in fact
it's as if the light were already being dismantled. Still, there are
a few sulfuric weeds in the foreground. They look like shallots.
And a quadruped, its dusky, granular hide loose in the leg pits, its
forehead collapsed, its eyes crystaled with cataracts.

She's teaching in fifteen minutes. It won't take her that long
to get to campus, and she pours again, just enough to wet the ice
cubes. She stands looking down over the encyclopedia. It suddenly
amuses her to speculate that the earth was still flat, in the time of
the dinosaurs.

She finds herself crossing the quad in near darkness. Early December, the trees are baskets, leaves extinct, bony branches. Her
gait feels stiff and tapping. She's angular but not athletic, not yet
thirty, not yet drunk, her head feels like hardware with which to
assemble a headache.

She charts her diagonal for the side entrance of a certain
eponymous building. Brick and mortar and beard strings of ivy,
broader than twenty trees, she still has two minutes. The double doors at ground level are smoky shatterproof glass-stuff. Even
Webb Hall has succumbed to fire codes and handicapped access.
Stairs and marble have undergone top-to-bottom demystification,
there's been a frank rearrangement of restrooms. The doors have
a bodyish suctioning quality she hasn't anticipated.

When was the last time she taught aboveground? Her classroom is dark and her eyes feel muddy, stirred up from the bottom.

She gropes for the head of the horseshoe of tables; she may as well be hammering out that horseshoe with her headache.

In a moment she'll hit the light switch. Her headache. In the dark she can better picture her students on their own quad-crossing courses. Jonathan Hughes, racing for a last-minute coffee, salty dew between his narrow, plucky shoulders. She can see him rifling through his backpack, determined to produce his university ID card and reap the fifteen-percent discount. She can even hear the cashier, a local girl wearing doll's eyelashes, blinking.

To be fair, she has no reason to think Jonathan Hughes is penurious. But it's perversely pleasing to imagine him stymied by a few pennies. Her schoolgirl crush makes her feel alliterative and necessarily cynical. And combative. She imagines the coffee sloshing over, scalding the roots of his fingers.

Her eyes adjust and she picks a tiny cloud of lint off her black sweater. What is going on around the neck? Something "romantic," the reason the sweater was on sale, and she grabs the knitted scruff and tries to stretch it away from her headache. She's pretty sure that psychogarble points to unbecoming neuroses rather than elegant intelligence, but still, she can solve herself backward from where she is now, caught in an academic eddy, the same beach garbage and coleslaw of seaweed drowning and repurposing, insoluble, tidal, endless...from where she is now, right back to her mother's disappearance. The spring she was eleven, the same spring as the dinosaur encyclopedia.

As a long-suffering graduate student she can't take herself seriously using a word like "endless;" she can't really touch any words anymore without turning them into jargon. But even before her mother left her, Marguerite had set herself the private task of beheading love, of undoing love from its original, maternal referent. Once, at the beach club, when she was six or seven, Marguerite watched her mother stagger, laughing and disheveled, from the water. Oh! Her mother had been ploughed into the seabed by a rogue wave, and now she had a sand suit under her bathing suit. Marguerite watched in horror as her mother reached into the stretchy fabric and pulled out the matted sand cakes veined with seaweed.

The classroom clock, ka-chunk, ka-chunk, seems to be clocking her rather than vice versa. She has a love-hate relationship with her teaching persona. It keeps her real, and nervous, and it makes her unreal, a total faker.

They're all late, every single one of her students. They don't fear her: she slums her well-bred vowels, she's one of them, she completely understands their problems.

Then the lights come on, and Jonathan Hughes is smiling at her curiously from the doorway. "Hey," he says, and she feels instantly flattered. He has poreless skin any girl would die for, freckles like cocoa powder, dark brown eyes with liquid centers—that's her crush talking. He comes bearing coffee, and wow, he's holding a paper cup out to his professor. He must have crossed the quad double-fisted. Look at you, she wants to say. His back is straight and he reminds her of a prescient five-year-old, pretending his bathrobe is an overcoat.

"It's b-black," he apologizes. Prescient because she knows him now, in the future of his childhood? "And b-b-bad." He smiles. That bit of a stutter must have charmed his mother.

He's also a graduate student—in creative writing. She knows his work for her class does double duty, and she finds his writing sort of unmanned. *Undisciplined* would be a more politic description. But she can't actually fail another grad student. They share the same birth year, she and Jonathan. He takes his shoes off as a condition of being seated, and she has, on several occasions, run into his empty shoes under the table. He's a month older.

Despite herself her spirits lift in his presence. The rest of the students stagger in and it's Jonathan who greets them. He is brimming with emotional intelligence, he flirts out of the goodness of his heart, he really does make people feel better. She watches him slip out of his ponytail. She's WASPy about the long hair. The elastic band hangs off his narrow wrist and suddenly it startles her to imagine him choosing a packet from the beauty aisle.

She crosses the quad again, now in total darkness. The trees are marionettes of the dark sky, sloe-eyed, possibly bulky with blood, and Marguerite forces herself not to panic. She's an inveterate interleaver of nature descriptions, afraid of the dark, and it's true that seasons matter as much as countries, even continents, in New England. Lines drawn in the sand, lines—prints, maybe—in the snow, the life-organizing principle of her mother's disappearance.

A different season: a bloom of an evening.

Petal-colored light, chambray surf, Marguerite's skin, and her mother's, sticky with saltwater.

There she goes, she's eleven, up the beach toward the clambake, red-faced clubbies in bleach-white trousers, her mother, she presumes, watching.

In Marguerite's mind's eye there's a sailboat with spiderweb lines, its boom rolled like a rug, rotting inevitably in the rocking water. There's her aunt Margaret—wading among clubhounds, rectangular head like a woodcutter icon, deep lines around her mouth, she already knows why her niece and namesake's eyes are a little wild.

Honeysuckle, beach plum, purple loosestrife. Horsetail full of ground glass that it pulled from somewhere. Was the air full of shards? Was the soil? Mr. Goff was just beginning to develop a stoop at the time her mother left her.

The lights are blazing in the vestibule of the department office. Two lean grad students are stooping into their mailboxes, and Marguerite slips in to clear hers of proliferating memos.

Ridiculous to drive, since her apartment is barely two miles off campus, but she really hates walking at night. She resents the inherent melodrama of it. Her car is as cold as a meat locker. She's not sure whether it's a good thing she'll be home before the heat comes on, before the car even registers it's being driven. She pulls into the large gravel parking lot behind her building, a staging area for student beaters and a couple of rust-hewn dumpsters. The recycling bins are lacy with mini plastic water bottles. Before the windshield fogs up she can see the moon disc sliding between clouds like dirt clods, the blue flame of the moon pushing tree silhouettes out of their velvet boxes. She locks the car behind her—she hates the few moments between locked car and locked apartment.

But no one is waiting to slit her throat at the dark door of her building, and she almost laughs out loud, imagining a kind of dinosaur rapist. She turns on the overhead light in her kitchen and smells coffee. Who's the idiot. More than half a cup, the milk on the surface like albino algae. No wonder she felt short-changed all day. Now she splashes it against stainless steel. Time for a vodka, thank you very much; she cracks a couple of ice cubes, the other half of a lemon. She doesn't mind the seeds. Sometimes they serve as her dinner. She sits down with her drink and the dinosaur encyclopedia. Wasn't this where she left herself less than three hours ago? How about that. Another deep pour. It really is sort of an amazing story. The way her mother—she turns a page over. Precursor life forms locked in rocks that were once the mud banks of a foul-smelling organ of water.

She was disappointed by the encyclopedia, and ashamed of her disappointment. The book wasn't even new, she noted. Her mother had leaned in and ruffled the pages, but Marguerite immediately disdained the expressiveness in the dinosaurs' pointy faces, heads too small for the engorged, epic bodies. The way her mother—she finishes the thought—disappeared on her. Another drink and she imagines time as a number line and the dinosaurs abandoning the zero and marching left, into the negative numbers.

2

But it would be sentimental to say that the Goffs were like grandparents. She had her own, on her father's side, who regularly sent a driver to fetch her. Mr. Bucci, Grandfather Webb's driver, lived in Middletown with his wife and three grown children. Marguerite knew their names, but she had never met them. The back of Mr. Bucci's neck was creased in diamonds and she used to wonder if there was a snake that had the same markings.

Her father died in the blur of her infant weeks (not her own blur, but her mother's), and Marguerite had always believed her mother's reticence on the subject was her way of preserving sadness. Marguerite was told she cried for him; how awful it would have been if she hadn't.

"You cried for everything," her grandmother added, a great fan of her own dry humor.

Her grandparents' sadness at the death of their son was expressed formally, unflaggingly, and, from the moment Marguerite was out of diapers (Grandmother Webb claimed never to have changed one), in the organization of Saturday excursions.

Tradition was an exercise. Mr. Bucci would squire Marguerite to her grandparents'; from there, Grandfather Webb manned the wheel. The pride he took in stocking the boot of the car with plaid wool blankets and "utility sweaters," milk chocolate bars and canned seltzer!

"Chin up, Marguerite," Grandfather Webb would say, handing out an old green V-neck. (He himself had a long chin, and a jaw like a drawbridge.) The sweater came with elbow patches, and the sandwiches were skinny. Marguerite had yet to classify the kind of frugality that redeemed the embarrassment of riches. But she was indeed a child respectful out of embarrassment. She would admit neither her breast buds, when they finally fleshed, nor her hunger for another sandwich.

The excursions took them to the Webbs' alma mater, all sheltering elms, fresh lawn, and contemporary sculptures on loan from major museums. Marguerite watched her grandmother turn stiffly away when faculty toddlers were lifted up to the stone saddles. Or to the beach club, where her grandfather would gin up while her grandmother peacocked the premises and Marguerite was let loose among cousins. Even then, Marguerite thought of herself as half Newport mansion, and slightly tainted by the other half. Her "good grandparents," as they used to wryly call themselves, were patronizingly cheerful about it.

Once or twice a year the three of them took the toy train to Green Animals and lunched beneath an arbor: the boxwood giraffe resembled a small dinosaur, with a path trod bare around it. Her mother always looked slightly different when they returned, as if a season had changed their absence...

She was seven or eight when her grandmother caught her delivering a certain premeditated line to a playmate; she must have been allowed to bring a friend along on one of the excursions.

"My father," declared Marguerite, "was the father I never had." Where had she learned to be grandiose—and maudlin? No sooner were the words out than she was aware of Grandmother Webb behind her. It was a bracing and blowy winter day; they were out on the boardwalk at the beach club. Marguerite felt, in a flicker of self-defense, that she had been carried away by the weather.

And all at once she understood that she was equally inconstant. Offering up her father's ashes! They would blow away, she imagined her grandmother saying, and then Marguerite would be doubly fatherless.

Friendless was what she'd be when her grandmother finished with her. What distress already, as if there'd been a betrayal, when her playmate discovered they were getting in the car with grandparents. You had to speak up, everyone older than mothers was deaf, but it was also necessary to maintain a deathly quiet. A little girl at either end of a backseat so long and plungingly soft it could have accommodated ten of them, even punched as they were into stiff winter jackets: Marguerite's friend braved the earsplitting rustle of her parka when she crawled all the way across to whisper acutely, "Where's your mother?"

But in the treacherous moment that followed Marguerite's declaration, Grandmother Webb surprised her. She let the playmate wither under her gaze before she divulged, ever so evenly, "Your father, Mah-gret, died in Bermuda." The queen of the commanding pause. "They had separated," she added. She seemed utterly unmoved by the information. Marguerite waited for more but her grandmother simply turned and pointed herself toward the clubhouse.

They changed drivers at Marguerite's grandparents'. Mr. Bucci was well versed in waiting. They dropped Marguerite's playmate off in Jamestown and the little girl's father strolled out, poorly concealing his lust for the old Bentley. Mr. Bucci was always obliging.

The girl's mother invited Marguerite in and pulled out a chair for her in the over-lit kitchen. Even the curtains were too bright, like angel wings in a crèche scene in a church parking lot.

Angel wings. Marguerite cringes.

She knows she would have declined the hot chocolate, although she longed to watch the tiny marshmallows dissolving. She was never a familiar child.

She starts again, with a mandate to be terse, but then verging on sententious: There is no such monster as a normal family; even a normal family is a monster. A la Tolstoy.

Marguerite's "ground-floor rear" is a one-bedroom peninsula in the parking lot. The building is a cabbage patch of eleven un-gainly, irregular apartments. The doors are oyster shells of old paint, the windowsills have hundred-year-old dirt under their fin-gernails. There's a variation on a theme of rooflines: dormers, a turret, a couple of additions, and a clutch of cement chimneys. The street is wide and treeless, a chute to the traffic lights and shopping center at the bottom. Marguerite always seems to leave and return on the downhill, traveling in a circle.

There's a funeral home and a YMCA and a laundromat and Chinese takeout, but no pedestrian bustle. The landlords are an old Portuguese couple who live in an urban-agrarian oasis in North Providence. One year they invited Marguerite for the grape harvest.

Of the inside of her apartment, suffice to say that the bathtub is criminally shallow, or else manufactured for renters, who are somehow always smaller in spirit.

Saturday, she's been reading and taking notes all day and she feels at once jumpy and fallow. The last time she looked up, she could see the gold and platinum trees in the unbuilt lot behind her building. Now, a dirty window, and behind it another glass plate of darkness. She's in sweatpants and two gray sweaters.

Just last week, walking down her block in the early evening, a couple of boys had risen up out of nowhere. They faced off against her, laughing soundlessly at her—she was so afraid her ears stopped working. She unshoveled her wallet before they even asked her, or, as she imagined, gunned her down for it.

In fact, she'd hurled the wallet to the moon-white sidewalk. Seen stars before one of them lunged at her, playing to her fears, playacting. His fists flew around her face and she could feel the air drum they created.

She tells herself this is the reason she's been going a little heavy on a certain fire water. She pours again and drinks between the ice cubes. She has another problem, which is that she's not rushing to get to her grandmother's Christmas party. Every year, her ritual of attending includes baroque contemplation of breaking with tradition. If she charted it, she'd find that every year she arrives a quarter hour later. She closes her eyes. She sees her grandmother, the Christmas party bully, statuesque out of sheer haughtiness, mouth twisted to greet a pair of lesser mortals. She can almost touch her grandmother's bouffant of chestnut hair, as if she, Marguerite, were the professional who sets it once a week, charged with making sure it adds to Mrs. Webb's already intimidating height another two inches.

She can hear her grandmother's greeting voice like one of those stock-market graphs, jagged with exorbitant wealth or shoeless poverty. Grandmother Webb, commandeering the dark and twinkling drive, "Has my granddaughter..." She has always scorned the French version in favor of her very own Mah-gret. She survived cancer in her early forties and has refused dessert since the day she received her diagnosis. Suddenly it occurs to

Marguerite that her grandmother has never disclosed the body part afflicted.

But she'll be more than fifteen minutes off from last year if she doesn't hurry. Another tipple, slug, whatever, Grandfather Webb calls it spring water. A cranberry silk blouse with cloth-covered buttons, and rather droopy black velvet trousers. She may resemble a medieval prince in pajamas.

Despite Grandmother Webb's character of restraint, she would adore it if Marguerite arrived early—say, for lunch—with a cocktail dress in plastic. If Marguerite freshened up in one of the boudoirs, borrowed a necklace. Grandmother Webb is perennially appalled that Marguerite drives in her "assemblage." She isn't at all embarrassed to use fake French. She finds the French ridiculous.

In her mind's eye Marguerite sees a photo her grandmother keeps on the mantel of one antechamber or another. Grandmother-phalanges on her head, grandmother-mouth pinched in distaste, as if Marguerite's hair were oily. Marguerite is baring her teeth to show that she's recently lost one. Maybe it's only that—the drippy, blood-scented gap—that makes Grandmother Webb queasy.

In less than an hour Marguerite is on the Newport Bridge, then traveling quickly overland. Deep, dark Jamestown. What was it like when there were Indians? The truth is she never really bothers to conceive it. She feels a swallow of guilt left over from childhood, from when her grandfather used to ask that question and it would fail to spark her imagination.

It's a wet night and the carriage lights dance in slicks in her grandparents' jet driveway. They've engaged a valet service. Here comes the hollow-cheeked, wind-breakered teenager: Marguerite gives up her keys and is satisfied to see his disappointment with the crummy little Mazda.

The coat check is an older woman with a wiry smoker's body and long, varicolored hair who offers to pin Marguerite's corsage of mistletoe. Her hands work above Marguerite's heart for a few seconds. "You'll get a hole in your blouse, dear." Marguerite should have worn a jacket.

An old geezer, curved like a shrimp, is handing out snowflake goblets.

"Thanks," Marguerite murmurs.

Already there's enough collective, alcoholic heat to warm the cavernous miscellany of rooms otherwise known as one of their fair state's most prominent piles. Marguerite wanders between drink stations with little cast-lit lamps among silent, penguin caterers.

There's a prevailing sense of time and space in the great first-floor galleries. Time: quite effortlessly Marguerite can feel herself decked out in one of a succession of stiff red dresses that made her look, as a little girl, like a grocery-store poinsettia and never quite matched the sleek, fire-engine red of her grandmother's sheath and spill of pearls. Marguerite was the one who felt too pink, or maroon, or orange, and it occurs to her now that Grandmother Webb's social graces are informed by a bracing, innate gracelessness.

Space: she always came alone, without her mother. Suddenly she remembers a rather decaying cousin cornering her, sometime in the boarding school era. "Someone under the age of thirty!" Was it supposed to be a stage whisper? Marguerite knew who she was: Nancy Webb who had changed her name to Naima.

The cousin had hissed, "I'm looking to archive my correspondence with Betty Friedan."

"You are?" Marguerite had managed. Nancy-Naima was so close Marguerite couldn't help staring at the puffy peppered skin where the rest of the eyebrow had been before she picked it.

"We were extraordinarily close." The cousin twitched furtively. "Our letters are extraordinary."

Her eyes were the same yellow as her teeth. In fact, Nancy-Naima had a strange, collaged face, like a Picasso.

"In my day," her face was in Marguerite's face now, and Marguerite breathed shallowly, "feminists were girls who preferred typing and answering phones to raising children." She ended on a furious note and Marguerite took a step backward.

Of course, there were cousins who, according to Marguerite's grandmother, had "garden-variety" mental debilitations, but mostly, said Grandmother Webb dryly, they simply adored their cocktails. Indeed it was with witchy glee that her grandmother composed a punch by dumping out the year's end of the liquor cabinet.

Nancy-Naima seemed to hold her highball in her fingernails.

Marguerite had excused herself abruptly, swiping a beaded glass of white wine from a side table. As she turned back for a guilty half second, it seemed that her cousin had two sad fish eyes on one side of her profile.

She can't say she didn't used to wonder about her father. Was her grandmother implicating him when she said "garden variety"? Marguerite had no reason to think so. Still. She used to imagine him wandering among lush, chest-high sunflowers, leeks, tomatoes. But she was never a prying child.

Now she lifts her neat little vodka. She rounds a paneled corner. There's her grandmother's long spine in that siren color. Her immobile upsweep: for a second Marguerite thinks she has grown even taller. There's her throttle of laughter. It will never do to be caught skulking around corners. Grandmother Webb no longer has her guests announced, but she'd certainly prefer it.

Suddenly there's a light touch between Marguerite's shoulders. She jumps, sparking. She whips around before she can censor her electrical anticipation.

It's a tuxedoed caterer, steering her off a collision course with the punch bowl.

A weakness of character that she can't imagine the Indians, can't even remember if they were Wampanoag or Narragansett. She's seen their tools and replica dwellings. So why, then, does she keep imagining her mother?

3

Six out of nine students present, variously propped around the U of tables in the otherwise barren basement classroom. Webb Hall. Marguerite's own lineage. Not even a map on the wall or a second-rate portrait of a third-rate university president. Jonathan Hughes with his cheeks in his hands, his lips a moribund colorless gelatin color, there really is something rubbery about his comfort level. The delphic incest of him bringing her coffee.

Her lecture is the new non-lecture lecture. It's full of inviting pauses, collegial ellipses, and pop culture references. The idea is to get the students to think they play a part in their really very contemporary educations. Why? At least, answers her advisor, the new non-answer answer, this must be the posture of perennial PhD-candidate pseudo-professors like you, Marguerite. Why are her lecture notes wrinkled and damp like bed sheets after passing out on a bender?

The self-proclaimed logger's son from the state of Washington is paring his nails. Jonathan is fiddling with a paperclip. The same way a paperclip gets metal fatigue and loses its squeezingness, so there's love-of-life fatigue, and in Marguerite's case it's called a hangover. She is the paperclip, she has completely lost form and function.

Full disclosure? She's been a graduate student for fourteen semesters. She knows how to spin her lecture, all sophistry, like cotton candy. All of a sudden the clever bit of metal comes spinning across the table. She stops talking and Jonathan blushes.

She has a requisite appointment with her advisor after class, before he heads off for his Parisian sabbatical cycle. His wife is a translator of considerable repute; and Swedish. She scoops up all the prizes.

Their last sabbatical—Marguerite has heard her advisor call it their "tour of duty"—Marguerite was the protégé-housesitter, as if her youth would rub off on their sheets and towels. They had decimated their party stash of ten-dollar-a-bottle cases, but left, of course, the library: rather famously, there were bookshelves built into every room of the otherwise neighborhoody, gambrel-roofed residence. Lintel bookshelves, bathroom bookshelves, and where the cheap wine should have been, bookshelves in the basement. Marguerite was charged with emptying the dehumidifier, a three-gallon trough of chilly water daily diverted from those garment-like pages. She dumped it in the front yard, and by the end of that year she'd drowned the massed periwinkle.

Now Marguerite spies some pages of hers on her advisor's desk, his heavy hand upon them like a book weight. She braces herself for the well-worn quips regarding the duration of her "process;" beneath her advisor's eyes are shadows like standing water.

"I've got the Faculty Club in seven minutes," says her advisor. She closes her ears and opens her eyes to the monkey-brown hairs on the back of his hand and the wide, horned thumbnail.

She imagines him eating whole fish in Paris—lifting the feathery spine from the white flesh, or his wife doing it for him. In profile, her advisor's Adam's apple is almost greater than his chin. Marguerite smiles grimly. She sees inside the mind-chamber. Tall, white-robed sentinels of thought. As tall as boxwood giraffes. As tall as those steel-plated creatures in Mr. Goff's dinosaur encyclopedia. Suddenly it's terribly vivid. Their cruel eyes and cauliflowered noses...

The earth was immeasurable. It stopped where the herd of Brachiosaurs stopped. Smooth earless heads and Mona Lisa smiles.

It stopped only in their imaginations.

Where was Quetzalcoatlus flying?

Was it more of the same or was it different?

In the artists' renditions they always appear to be enjoying their ignorance.

When they lay down on their sides their bellies must have poured out around them.

It's dark again and she pulls the blinds on the blank side yard of her building. She'll get the blinds in the back, on the parking lot, later.

The dinosaur encyclopedia cracks and out falls a purple mimeographed handout, some teacher's ovoid handwriting. Out falls a feather-colored leaf, out falls a snapshot. Marguerite and her mother with bare legs, bare toes dug into the sand, the slant of the sand down to saltwater. They're both wearing shorts hardly bigger than underwear. They're looking straight into the future. Primitive, two-dimensional, as if their shared code of self-consciousness has been shattered.

Marguerite pours herself a vodka. What's new. She disembowels a drawer for hidden—from herself—cigarettes. Conversely, Grandfather Webb likes to call water vodka.

She pours again. She's as heavy-handed as a dinosaur. There's a lot of ice-yellow callus. Like topaz. In fact, this dinosaur thing serves all her purposes.

Fifty to one hundred and forty-five million years ago huge bones clanked and thudded over huge earth. Like prisoners in chains. Not much has changed. She's still chained to her vision of the past: its terrible innocence.

She has the foresight to dump the ice and vodka mixture into a promotional gas station travel mug that is so ugly no one would imagine it held such a beautiful liquid. A private joke. She drinks it down and then replenishes it before she lurches out of her apartment. The night is as cold as a reptile. She means cold-blooded. There's a surging sound in her ears—imagine if a single ocean wave could sustain itself like a highway. She fits herself behind the wheel of the self-deprecating little Mazda—95 South. The exits burst on the scene only to evaporate. Atwells, Thurber, she possibly blacks out around the airport. Did she mention the darkness? The ground falls away and the muddy air presses closer.

Up and over Jamestown. Up over the threshold to Newport. The off ramp curves around the dark cemetery. The streetlights are unto themselves, car headlights are mixed with an equal part of darkness, there's a dense fog that could turn to snow at any moment. Marguerite turns onto Maple Street. The house and the cottage are dark. It's still Christmas party season. She pulls into what used to be Andrade's Liquor. She asks herself if she thinks she's some secret agent of autobiography.

She has a hard time attributing the car in the single gravel parking spot to Mr. Goff, although she can barely see it. The dark seems to bleed up the house seamlessly from the sidewalk. The harder she stares the less she can see. There's no Rhody flag flying its single wing off the ledge of granite. But come on, Marguerite. In this darkness, the gold anchor would be invisible.

Her mother's maiden name was Dinah Holly. She changed both names when she married. Diana, as she now called herself, may have come from humble people—remarked Grandmother Webb, blinking her bald eyes rhetorically—but her beauty was extravagant. Diana's mother was a dark German. Her father had fought the Germans at the age of forty, taken a German bride at forty-five, and failed to teach her English. Diana said once that her father was an early environmentalist. At least a preservationist; a Californian, ravaged and scarred by cancerous sunspots. Marguerite imagined that if you'd seen the three Hollys together you'd have thought trolls had kidnapped a baby goddess.

At seventeen Dinah received a scholarship to an East Coast university. Did that university—Marguerite's grandparents' alma mater, Marguerite's too, several times over if she ever finishes—know, somehow, that Marguerite's mother's hair was the lustrous black of a polished plum in an expensive Christmas box? That her lips scrolled like the prow of a friendly ship when she smiled?

Of course they didn't. Dinah Holly was summarily brilliant, and she had written in her application that she wanted to be an economist.

Her father drove her across the country in his landscaping truck with an army blanket laid across the bench seat. The repressed environmentalist. Marguerite pictures him both pained and proud when California earth blew out of the bed of the truck in every state they passed through.

When they reached the college—*university*, Dinah corrected her father softly—the green quads like a chain of lakes were teeming with young people, pink and silver. The trees, elms and maples, ginkgos and magnolias, were crowned with gold where they touched the polished sky. Their shadows were cool and moist, mushrooms made fairy rings where the day before students had flopped down with their notebooks. There was a buoyant mist that smelled faintly of the bays of the Atlantic and the shallow salt river that, Dinah's ogling roommate informed her, was as moody as a dorm full of coeds.

Dinah watched her fellow students veering away from their parents. She didn't miss her own, but she had a strange sense of missing herself, as if for her parents...as if, even before her daughter came along, Dinah Holly knew what it felt like to be a lost parent.

Some of the college girls twirled the ends of their hair in class or took off their glasses and put their cool fingers over their eyelids. All the girls crossed their legs, and, despite her parents— they must have, indeed, missed her—Dinah followed. Her hair had magnificent reddish highlights under a lamp or in the sun and other girls commented, even crowed over it, as if beauty were collective. She had dark freckles and narrow eyes that sparkled when she was nervous or happy.

In the first few weeks of that first semester a young man caught Dinah's notice. He was tall with broad shoulders and a lantern jaw, but Dinah thought he probably wouldn't be a sportsman. He had light, flickering eyes: she couldn't see him at the dull repetitions of a ballgame. Besides, there was something loose in the way he held his body that simultaneously repulsed and thrilled her. He had a despotic mouth that turned down at the corners when he smiled.

He seemed oddly old-fashioned in his starched shirts, but then he would turn, say, after tucking his pendulous necktie between the buttons, and his eyes were phosphorus.

He had no compunction about rising and interrupting the lecture. No doubt he was far beyond the callow shrugs of his compatriots. The professor was a small man with flaps of skin for eyelids who addressed him by name, as if he were someone famous. Indeed he had the same name as the hall, Webb Hall, the same name as the horse-faced men in the dark, greasy portraits in the foyer.

Dinah wouldn't have breathed a word of her interest. She had no idea that such a whisper would draw other girls closer. Neither did she send any loose-lipped letters to California.

One morning she arrived for class early. The carved doors of Webb Hall were so heavy that, before class, a slight Christ-figure of an Azorean janitor tied them open against the wrought-iron railing. This morning he hadn't been around yet. The doors were not locked and the large brass ring was slightly oily when she gripped it. Inside, the windowless foyer was a leathery brownish black, and for a moment Dinah had the dizzying feeling of pitching forward.

Sometimes it was hard to tell if you were really awake in such darkness.

She noticed a concentration of dark as tall as a grandfather clock in the farthest corner. But before she had time to be frightened, there was a voice, wryly sympathetic. "No need to worry."

"Hello?" said Dinah.

He leaned against the inner door and a dull shaft sanded with grains of dust split the foyer.

He held out his hand and Dinah was aware of a tangy, animal smell. Her own body? She tried to back away, embarrassed. But he caught her, suddenly playful, as if they'd known each other since childhood. His hands on her bare arms were a uniform, cool texture. He spoke calmly. "You're early."

Of course she was. She was never at the right moment. She was all the way from California. She would soon forget her parents.

Her father's heart eroded as an old canyon, her mother's German customs at Christmas and Easter.

Inside the hall, the windows were narrow and cloudy, pasted with a decoupage of the wings of insects. The air was dense and chilly. Dinah thought of the gravel pits she visited with her father. He was forced to do roads, as a landscaper. If she closed her eyes she could still feel the truck jounce over the lot like pioneer hardtack.

They sat together. It would have been even stranger if they didn't, thought Dinah. She opened her book. Silence. Sitting still was rushing forward. He clasped his hands behind his head and tipped his chair back.

Soon enough students began to filter in, first the oddballs and the studious, then toward the sound of the bell the coffee-drinkers and chatterboxes. The professor announced his arrival with the groan of an interior door so that before he reached the podium the hall had fallen silent. Dinah had not managed to read a single sentence. She knew James Webb was watching her. She turned and his chair struck the slate as if from the impact of her gaze upon him. She licked her lips. Something smelled acrid like fresh urine.

There they were, in his lap: a pair of hand-sewn, deerskin driving gloves.

4

From an early age Marguerite understood the basic premise. Grandmother Webb must have hinted, and the cousins were at once blunt and ferrety. The scholarship girl from the gaudy West and the aristocratic, old-money Easterner.

"We would have been friends," Marguerite ventured, once, shyly. She meant if they'd been girls together. And then she was embarrassed. As if the fact that Diana was her mother was a strictly benevolent coincidence.

Sort of on the sly, she's developed a mild antagonism toward her students. The extroverts from New York and New Jersey; the male and female paper dolls from Hong Kong with British boarding-school accents; the anachronistic loners from Vermont or Nova Scotia; this semester, the singular auditor with virile red beard, woodsman of Washington.

And Jonathan. She's had grad students before, she's had "adult learners" from the "broader community." He seems different. She tries to put her finger on it. He's absurdly confident for someone so unmanly. His sanctimonious enthusiasm: he'd be an ideal puppy, with a highly developed understanding of humankind's nobility and a gift for pairing his owner's scattered shoes. She can't seem to stop herself. She imagines how effortlessly he must have fooled his mother into thinking he was a sensitive child.

Her dingy apartment has an under-the-stairs pantry. She ducks in and grabs a bottle by the neck, snaps the perforated seal. She can take care of herself, it's basic. Besides, vodka is a lot cheaper than therapy. A gluggy pour, at the beginning of a bottle. She distributes her empties among the neighbors' recycling; her dear old landlord of the grape harvest needn't be incited to judge her. If she saved the bottles up for a week the number would be alarming, but she knows better. She's thinking about Jonathan. His silky hair— as if his hair hasn't gone through puberty.

In her mind's eye she stares at him, enthralled, dumbly. Those dumb, beast-like dinosaurs. She knows they felt deeply. She knows Mr. Goff did, and she knows her mother. She pours again. The ice cubes rattle and bleed.

Ginkgo leaves turned the yellow of wet paint and Dinah thought the New England fall was a beginning rather than an ending. Boys stepped aside to cup flames for their cigarettes after a late afternoon lecture and girls flashed their white, cramped legs. Dinah had already purchased a powder-blue wool dress coat that she carried over her forearm. She could pay the department store in monthly installments from her work-study. The early evening was staged with low indigo clouds that tamped down the sunset.

The hall had been terribly overheated. One of Dinah's new acquaintances had wondered aloud, indignantly, if they were supposed to be ashamed they were bored, beautiful, between eighteen and twenty, in ribbed tights and lambswool sweaters. In fact Dinah *was* ashamed, of her powder-blue coat, of her father watering jewel-green lawns in a powder-earth climate. She imagined him at the window of his truck: the skinned hills and the giant cloverleafs where there were once pocket neighborhoods. There was a white patch on Dinah's mother's cheek that suggested the skin was peeling painfully like a root vegetable.

Just then, as if he had known she was pushing those thoughts away at that very moment, James Webb signaled from under a lamppost.

He had a floppy haircut, dark hair that naturally tousled. He wore pressed khakis and a cricket player's green-bordered V-neck. Between his thumb and pointer smoldered what Dinah was sure was a Camel cigarette. She broke away from her clutch of girlfriends.

"When my father takes your arm," James whispered, taking Dinah's, "you are convinced that you, too, shall have crushed mint in your rum drink." He laughed in her ear. "My father is the kind of man who plans to die no matter what he does." He paused. "Do you like that?"

They walked briskly, in unison, as if they were in an old movie. "You should see the cronies. You really should, Dinah." He made a face. She hoped he hadn't heard her breathing. "Mooning around the club like it's the bedroom of a longstanding mistress."

Behind them, she thought, the entire sky packed up its colors.

"Stabbing their jellied eggs, towels like rabbit stoles around their shoulders——" And then, almost curious: "I like that you don't know all this."

He seemed to be examining her, but he smiled to himself, Dinah noticed.

It's all in Marguerite's head. Gone to her head; if she doesn't eat something soon she'll have a splitter before she even gets tipsy. Long before she gets sober. When was the last time she got "tipsy"? Not only that her interest in Jonathan isn't reciprocated, but that it may not be in her heart at all—wasn't she talking about her headache? And she's pretty sure she doesn't want to bed down with him. Still, she forces a handful of salted almonds and bolts out the door before she can overthink it. She's heading back to campus for an eight o'clock reading.

The car is so cold her blood feels glassy. Her metatarsals, in last-minute flats, are actually throbbing. It's possible she's obsessed with the fact that the vehicle doesn't even begin to warm up in two miles. The steering is stiff, the chill of the grave from the dashboard vents, the engine sounds like a cello under a frozen blanket.

Creative writing department readings are generally held in an inhospitable, drafty black box on the newer, uglier, southern end of campus. Marguerite parks and fords the dark street. She affects her Brahmin stalk, she need not recognize people. All-weather smokers choke the sidewalk entrance and right away she sees him. He doesn't smoke, but he's talking animatedly to a skinny girl with an enormous nest of dreadlocks. Frozen baby birds in there, Marguerite imagines. The girl has hunched shoulders like a raven.

"Marguerite!" he calls out instantly. Happily, if not heartily, and she's forced to wave, then join him and the sullen nest-head.

In the skirt of light from the propped-open door of the black box, Jonathan's own coat of hair is loose and shiny. His mouth hangs slightly open. What does he see? She imagines herself, a hereditarily lean twenty-nine-year-old, architected by patricians, finished in graduating tones of blond like veneer samples. When she's drinking she looks like a sunset. He has a plastic cup of wine—could he be nervous before his reading?

A stage manager in Army Navy pokes her head out and points to Jonathan. Marguerite finds herself suddenly deflated. It takes her by surprise, she hates to see him going, and she doesn't know if she can stand in the cold of the theater, or sit, as the case may be, through the whole reading, until the inflammatory wine at the end, and crackers.

But the girl with the dreads is holding the door for her, and to escape now would take an effort. She finds a seat at the top of the bleachers. The reading starts almost immediately.

"Hi," Jonathan greets the audience.

"Hiya," someone replies from the bosom front of the theater.

He smiles appreciatively. "I wanted to start—" He stalls a little with his papers. "I have this story I've been playing around with." Renews his smile. He may have practiced without exactly knowing he was practicing. Once again she has an image of him in his bathrobe, and she doesn't need any literary critics or psychologists to tell her she finds him vulnerable. Almost grudgingly she admits to herself that his delivery seems natural.

"A story," he says, "about my m-mother."

He laughs at himself, his stutter. Then he looks up more carefully from his pages. "She died when I was seven."

Marguerite's ears are sort of ringing. Her coat is stunningly hot and heavy. Suddenly she's aware of making an enormous amount of noise when she tries to free herself from it. All at once, as if in the heat of the moment, she realizes what a cheap coat it is, a faux ski jacket, she's even let it get stained, she's not a child. She didn't see it coming. His mother. And here she is hunkered in the back, half drunk, cheaply jacketed. No way she's looking around her. It would be unbearable to catch someone's eye and have to make a sympathetic expression regarding Jonathan.

He continues. "I have this photograph of her." He raises his eyes, shoeless, puppy, velvet, as if the audience can see in his eyes the photograph. "It's captioned by *her* mother."

He arranges his voice in a documentary voiceover. "*At eighteen Leslie Klaveness left home for New York City.*" He can't help smiling. "I always loved the kind of bittersweet third person. It made me think my mother must've had a close friendship with her mother. The same sense of humor. You could say I was a little jealous." He pauses. "In the photo, though, my mother is so serious. She's pulled to one side," and he shows the audience with his rather slight body how massively cumbersome the luggage. "There's this heavy shadow over her chest that never fails to remind me of an X-ray vest." Then he shrugs as if to say, how can he help himself? "It always strikes me that when you're eighteen, twenty more years of life seem like plenty."

Marguerite lets out a little puff of air, she can't help it. Are they to take it she died at thirty-eight? Marguerite would never offer up her mother. She can't seem to regulate her temperature. She's cold again, and she pulls the noisy jacket against her lap, finds the pockets.

"After college I went to New York," says Jonathan. "I had this little inheritance from her. I rented an apartment on West Eleventh Street. I thought it was a pretty quiet and tree-lined block for my money."

He pauses, he gets a few laughs; he must, of course, have a whole bevy of admirers in the audience.

"The defining feature," he says, "and let me tell you, I knew I was unconscionably lucky to have found an apartment with any f-*fea*ture—was a marble fireplace. It looked like tapioca." A hint of writerliness. Marguerite recoils.

"My father sent me a package of my mother's artifacts. *I had always meant you to have these.* It was so novelistic. There was a day book, and a pair of tortoise combs, which should have gone to my sister, and a bundle of early letters from *Barb McLaughlin—childhood friend? To Leslie,* my dad had scribbled. All the envelopes had been discarded."

He pauses significantly. Marguerite has to admit she's poised. "To save space?" says Jonathan. "The envelopes that would have had her address on them."

He takes a sip from the same plastic cup, which now appears to be half filled with water. "Anyway," he says, "this is how I wanted to start my reading. With this letter. I—I'm going to recite it," he offers humbly.

"Dear Leslie,

"I enjoyed your charming description of the rooms on West Eleventh Street overlooking the Jewish cemetery. A "pocket," as you call it! Of course I did not know that the Jewish people kept their own. Me, I'd prefer to lie in a quiet valley. I'm sure you are very fortunate to have a landlady like Bernice, whom you mentioned, looking out for you. Although it is hard from my point of view to imagine any "dog-eared Bohemian" in charge of an entire building! You know how I, the most practical girl in Pennsylvania, can hardly keep up with the housework.

"A marble fireplace! Well you should ask Bernice to be sure about the chimney before you go drying your hose or, as you say, burning your papers. Send me your papers, instead, Les! I'll keep them for you until you're famous!

"We did have a chimney fire here because of nesting swallows...

"You see?" says Jonathan, sliding his glasses up with a knuckle. Even from her nosebleed seat Marguerite can see he's gotten sweaty.

He leans forward. "Picture me setting the letter down beside me. I'm sitting on the bare wood floor, I have no idea at all how to obtain furniture. I barely know how to feed myself. I don't have to go to the single west window, across from the fireplace, to see my mother's view." One last pause. "I've already spent hours looking down on that pocket cemetery."

5

Dinah Holly stared at the green and white linoleum, every stain obvious in the harsh glare of the university-run coffee shop. James maneuvered his chair so he could stretch his legs out beneath the little white table. He squinted at her and her heart raced like a rabbit's. Her hands were warm from the thick white coffee mug—he had bought her a hot chocolate.

Yes, driving gloves; and at twenty-two he kept martini mak-
ings in the kitchen of his off-campus apartment. His walnut hair,
his cigars, his gentleman's manners juxtaposed with an adorable,
adolescent thuggishness...his father was the president of a bank
with branches that overarched the Eastern Seaboard, he told her.
His family's "summer cottage" was eleven bedrooms and a man-
sard roof, high hedges and a whole Stonehenge of chimneys.

Dinah imagined herself grazing on seaward lawns, twirling
batons of crabstick among those sloshy Daughters of the Revolu-
tion (James called them drakes and tomcats) with inverted lips and
dresses as thick as linen tablecloths. She loved the unctuous smell
of boxwood, mothballs, and the Atlantic.

James shared his apartment. Cousin Henry was possibly a graduate student, possibly not this semester. He had the same thick roll
of hair as James, the same wafer-white chest with rosebud nipples.
They had the same compulsion to clear their throats, which every
time made Dinah start, but Henry Webb had a shallow laugh like
a shale shelf, three inches of water.

His neck was skinnier and his hands, with nails the same rosebud pink, were smaller than James's, as if they could pick locks,
poke things into knot-holes. He had a weakling's bag of tricks,
James said, and the unpitiable nature of an asthmatic. At the beach
club, Henry had been known to spit into the beverages of cousins
who beat him at tennis, examining the foam of his own saliva before handing the concoction over.

The three of them drove around on weekends. They made fun
of the provincial surroundings, the mom-and-pops, small dirt
roads that squirreled through the forest. James and Henry re-
counted beach club antics from last summer or the summer before.
They declared that mental illness was *rampant*, genetic.

"Our grandparents!" cried Henry, the natural braggart, "were second cousins!"

They brought any kind of liquor. They drank it out of the bottle until Henry took Dinah aside and insinuated that she, being the girl, was expected to provide the ice and chalice. James drove steadily when he was drunk; when he was sober his driving was a mean streak. He'd go for miles in the wrong lane, until something happened to Dinah's equilibrium and she lightly fainted.

Sometimes, at Henry's suggestion, they swerved off the road and walked for a while into the forest. Henry jumped about laterally as if in tennis, and was always drawn to the sound of water. The woods had ample veins of it.

When they came to a pool in a stream or a Guinness-thick beaver pond they sat down to rest and James eyed her until she couldn't stand it. She rose self-consciously and went to him. Sometimes they had forgotten the liquor in the car, they were so drunk when they left the car in a ditch or a pull-off, and then the sound of the forest gradually became scratchy and close and James's desire for her drained like color from his face while her longing for him increased. He pushed her away and Henry watched carefully.

She could never quite figure where they grew up. They laughed: the beach club, New York, dark Satanic boarding school, and "Damnit, Henry, do you remember that time in Paris?"

It seemed to Dinah that there was no layering of time between generations. The grandparents were superimposed on the grandkids, the given names were the same, all the Jameses and Henrys, and everyone lobster pink, Lamarckian, from summers on the Atlantic.

James would always kiss her goodbye when they dropped her at her dormitory, but if he kissed too much, his lips became covered with something like flour. Dinah's were chapped, too, from the unfamiliar furnace heat. In fact her bottom lip had split in the night, and she'd woken up to the hissing and clanking radiator, the taste of blood, smell of iron.

He took her to the beach club in the wrong season. The place was nearly deserted, and Dinah imagined the ruins of a Roman settlement: actors in sandals, dusty nubs of stables, a snaggle-toothed tower against a rougy sunset. She told him—shyly, sparkling—and he was pleased as any tutor.

The foreign help had long been visa'd back—in James's father's day they were Irish, now they were all from Eastern Europe. Relishingly James described for her the Slavic girls with tight scalps and the springy boy gymnasts occasionally called upon to fill in a game of tennis; he caricatured for her the matriarch of the next-door cabana, breeder of Shetland ponies, with a forelock of thick strawberry-blond hair absolutely unaffected by rogue coastal weather; and her ponies, sulky dwarves with oversized teeth their owner called "bone structure."

The cabanas were closed and they looked like nothing more than a row of public restrooms. The sea was heavy after a storm, mud brown, churned up and hollow-smelling like a rotted-out tree trunk. The sand had been scoured and then pummeled with rocks and there were ugly, soupy rivers running widthwise.

James showed Dinah the hedges of honeysuckle that extended to marsh grass behind the cabanas. He led her along the rabbit paths; had she ever tasted honeysuckle? You pulled the stamen through the slender horn. Early summer, he smiled apologetically. Each flower gave up a bead of sweet, lymph-colored liquid.

Did she know horsetail? Did she know he had loved her since the dinosaurs?

The wind was like sandpaper against the cement boardwalk. As if he were brought to his knees by it, James said, "Don't go back for Christmas."

Once Diana was a parent chaperone on a school field trip. The maritime nature center was close by; nonetheless, the fourth graders were required to board the nauseating midmorning school bus. There were presentations on pollution, ospreys, oysters, whales. There was a booth for listening to the mating calls of certain seabirds, and there was a life-sized model of a right whale.

The right whale was so called because it was the right whale to harvest. Diana wasn't like the other mothers, who read in uninflected voices. Even the teachers edged closer to listen. Her voice was rushy and melodic, the same as when she told Marguerite stories in their loft over ginger ales and gin and tonics, that narrow ribbon of dark between them.

The right whale always swam against the shore, Marguerite's mother continued. Ideal for the whaler: no fortnight upon fortnight leaving wife, children, and difficult mistress. Its blubber, melted and boiled, was ninety barrels of oil. It had baleen like fine dry grass before a fire. Every part had a use except its heart, which was four hundred pounds, read Diana.

Afterward they ate their bagged lunches in the sand and crispy seaweed. Not only her friends, but classmates Marguerite had never spoken to clustered around her beautiful mother. Marguerite had to make space for them.

On the ride back, Marguerite shared a booth-like seat with her mother in the mid-body of the school bus. She longed to talk, but she was too prim—or too cold—to breach her mother's privacy.

And then all of a sudden her mother seemed to be crying. The right whale, larger than a school bus. How handy for the whale hunters; it floated along dead for hours on account of its prolific blubber. Marguerite drew back into her growly window corner. When she closed her eyes against her mother she saw the grainy photographs from the nature center: the giant mammal pulling the dinghy by the very harpoon it would be killed by within a couple of hours. The whale swam so fast it turned the dinghy into a modern-day speedboat.

Speeding toward the horizon, all the way to the vanishing point...

They had just turned into the school lot and the melee of dismissal when someone rose over the seatback wielding a Polaroid camera. Marguerite and her mother, looking up through a membrane, nebulous, their eyes at once indistinct and magnified.

Marguerite pushes the ugly photo away from her on the table. She has a slim envelope of photographs she keeps unceremoniously with her files. Telephone bills, old SAT scores, her mother. All to scale.

It's five o'clock somewhere. She cringes when anyone says that. Laugh-track material, and to Marguerite, drinking is no laughing matter. She has a headache that feels like a tumor, and weird referencing pain in her upper stomach. She swings through the kitchen—glass, ice, jug. She makes an echoing half circle for the lemon.

Speaking of scale.

Quetzalcoatlus of the Late Cretaceous had a thirty-nine-foot wingspan. What a stupid coincidence. The same length as a school bus.

The scale of loss...she can't stop thinking about Jonathan Hughes' mother. She can't stop thinking about her loss compared to Jonathan's.

The pressure on the earth, the skid, the bite in a fossil track reveals the speed of a powerfully hungry Allosaurus, in one illustration.

What is it about their extinction? It's not just death, but the God of death. The remainder. The hard and final thing that is irreducible. Quetzalcoatlus, imagined from a few spare wing bones, inverse creation.

In those few months between Mr. Goff's scavenger hunt and her mother's vanishing act she never read the children's dinosaur encyclopedia. Was she so terribly busy? She never asked her mother to read it to her, either. Now and again she must have paged through: dutifully, guiltily, impatiently. She might have vaguely wished to put Mr. Goff behind her.

How much would she have lost going to the landlord and asking a few simple questions about his hobby? What's five minutes out of childhood? But she never did, and it occurs to her now that after her mother left there was so little between her and the retired couple that she failed to say goodbye to them on the single occasion that her grandmother brought her back to collect, Grandmother Webb insisted, only her "good" clothing.

Mr. Goff was working in the backyard. Those very borders where the bones had been lightly buried were now filled in with phlox and rose and black-eyed Susan. Marguerite was surprised to see that he was beginning to walk with his neck turtled forward.

Two hundred and fifty million years ago the equator ran up and down instead of around like a girdle.

No, it didn't, but there was only Pangaea, the mother of all continents, the single mother supercontinent.

Horsetails full of spores, fern tufts, and scaly conifers.

Dinosaurs like kangaroo-lizards hopped around with strands of vegetation hanging from their orifices.

There were no great worries like polar ice caps.

A fossil exists of the underwater birth of an Ichthyosaurus. A bone-lattice baby coming out midstream, mid-extinction. No letters, no records of her existence.

Grandfather Webb once suggested he hire a private detective. Marguerite was so shocked and distracted by his kindness that she only wanted to reply in kind—in kindness. "Oh, no," she fumbled. "That would be too much trouble."

6

Her grandmother calls before she's out of bed, eleven thirty, still morning.

"Mah-gret." As if the name were one syllable, with a little foot on it. "Dinner with Hope Grosvenor last night, and her boring husband."

Her grandmother is not in a Masterpiece Theatre production. They both know she amuses herself putting on certain airs for her granddaughter's benefit. "Hopesic's nephew has had no word from you, Mah-gret." The nephew is a young lawyer just launched at the "only" firm in Providence, and Marguerite was to suggest lunch at the plate-glass lobster-and-rib-eye emporium on the ground floor of his building.

"He hasn't?"

Grandmother Webb blows like a horse. Marguerite empties a can of soup into a saucepan. Is the glop more than mildly disgusting? She never makes food for anyone. She pours out a little white wine she keeps for this kind of morning.

After what she absorbed last night, she has a many-headed headache. The wine is cheap, but silvery. She decides it's the color of a banana—very pale—and thus perfect for breakfast. Screw the soup. She washes it down the drain with Palmolive to cover the meaty odor. Disgusting, absolutely. She'll glow with health in a minute. But she has to admit that she doesn't have it in her to sleep with a lawyer.

She slept with a teacher, at boarding school.

Maybe Jonathan Hughes slept with a teacher too, his puppy eyes velvety as sleep—she can see it. Like flying above the path in a dream, suddenly she can see everything.

Her English teacher was a lipless bachelor of thirty-seven, age of resentment and dissymmetry. His PhD was wasted, and he believed, perhaps needless to say, that he should have been teaching college. Something was owed him, compensation for tenth-grade *Frankenstein*, twelfth-grade *Great Gatsby*. Being a man of literature, he was entitled to his liberalism, in an unexamined, belligerent fashion: how stratospherically far he was above bourgeoisie convention. Nothing he did could be anything less than unstintingly original.

His apartment was in a painted brick house in town, a short walk off the boarding school campus. There was a clutch of metal mail sleeves at the front porch, and it thrilled Marguerite to see his last name on one of them. As if the man she loved had staked a claim in the world. She put little notes inside it; she believed they were cryptic.

She had nothing to compare it to, so she would never, then, have said the liaison was unimaginative. It seemed natural each one retreated, during sex, to his or her own private world. She would say to herself: I am holding a man's penis in my hand. Or her lips were forming a seal around it, it tickled her tonsils. When he grabbed her hair she felt abruptly sad, always, but she knew very well she wasn't a knock-kneed little victim.

Au contraire (as she used to say, constantly, determined to mock everything), she had a feeling of triumph when he slid out of her. She was on the pill, juice spilled all over. "Look at the mess you've made!" she'd exclaim. She would pretend she was maternal, or whorish, or anything to entertain herself. He used his T-shirt to wipe her.

They never discussed school. They weren't intellectual intimates. Marguerite imagined they were pawns of the large-heartedness of love. She told herself love was Love, she told herself the smell of his cinnamon chewing gum was Love also.

They carried on for almost four months, and she became absurdly comfortable in his presence. She would let her clothing drop as soon as the door closed behind her; she would slouch around thin and nude whether or not they consummated. She had the idea that he liked to hear anything she had to say. That she, in fact, had the upper hand in conversation, because she could make him laugh so easily.

He could not make her laugh. She told him frankly that he was not in the least bit funny.

Another glass of wine, a nice big brimmer.

Good thing she chose Comp Lit over Women's Studies. Wasn't a victim? Now she has the stomach to finish washing the saucepan from the soup misadventure, and she tips the thin vomit down the drain with a tap water chaser.

As if her status were determined by whether or not she enjoyed it. One girl claimed he was hung like a goat, and thereafter they all called him Billy. Boarding-school girls sardined together, marinating in each other's fishiness, became experts on whatever is the opposite of awe. Awfulness. The girls on her hall pored over magazines with pink-toned photo shoots of uber organs. He liked a certain degree of slickness, and so he had Marguerite come before he entered her. "Come, little girl," he would say, and she would, immediately. She crushed her own breasts against her chest as if someone were hugging her.

She liked imagining herself adult enough to keep a secret. She thinks now, all of a sudden, that she didn't like him, and he must have known that.

The front door of his apartment opened straight into the living room, the kitchen alcove was on the left, with the rather crumbling bathroom behind it. His bedroom was behind the living room, with an illicit washer and dryer in the closet, stacked one on top of the other. Never once did he offer to do Marguerite's laundry. One evening there was a knock on the door as they were feeling each other up on the sofa. In fact they sat facing the door, the world, like the farmer and his wife in *American Gothic*. Outside the frame, perhaps, if indeed they were a painting, Marguerite was naked on the bottom and he was one-handedly, rhythmically, spreading her open. She made a clicking sound that was only slightly distracting.

It seemed as if the knock was right there in the room with them, and they both recoiled. Marguerite's first thought was that it was her mother. She stuffed her heart back down like a jack-in-the-box and grabbed his damp T-shirt to cover her fuzzy triangle. Maybe because of her ever-increasing and self-perceived ease with sex she had been lulled into forgetting the danger. Maybe it was the head of school. The police. Or just an unwitting neighbor. Did someone want to borrow a cup of sugar? she whispered. He motioned for her to stay quiet.

Finally the knocker ceased, discouraged, and Marguerite turned to her lover. "When are you going to make an honest woman of me?" she said, almost without thinking.

One weekend, James took Dinah to New York City.

She stood between the double doors that divided one room of their suite from the other and watched him unpacking. It seemed

QUETZAL 243

to her he'd brought everything. A suit for the opera, flannel pajamas, shirts for morning, afternoon, and evening, professionally folded. He looked up at her and flinched. She noticed his thick, wood-colored hair was clumped and almost matted where he had a cowlick in the middle of his forehead.

He said, "I've forgotten something important." He was rummaging through the suitcase. But he seemed more surprised than bereft, and it was forgotten.

He couldn't get enough of her. All weekend he kept bearing her back to the bed. They skipped the opera, the bed had its own brocade curtains. Every time she woke up, in the morning or in the middle of the night, James was propped up on one elbow wiggling his foot and gazing at her. "I love you so much I can't sleep," he whispered.

But by Sunday afternoon he had fallen silent. It was almost as if he would have forgotten to get in the car and drive back to Providence if Dinah hadn't said it. Then she had to drag their suitcases out to the hall and shove them in the elevator by herself, and how would she know how much to tip the concierge or the doorman?

The car seemed enormous, a cold, echoing chamber. Dinah realized she had no idea how to drive it. "What is it?" he mimicked. Only she hadn't actually said anything. He looked at her triumphantly and the car swerved and fishtailed, throwing off gravel.

"Scared you. Scared us both," James said, mildly. "You know, we could keep going. I could drive you all the way to——" Dinah saw that he was trying to locate something. Where she was from, that's what he couldn't remember. For a moment she believed that she couldn't remember either, and that was love, wasn't it. Being unable to remember where you came from.

Very quietly James started, "I've just lost it——"

He walked around the car and opened the door for her in front of her residence hall. He placed her luggage on the ground beside her. His picked up her hand as if it were a blank and squeezed it.

Another scene: he teased her, If she went back to California, he'd freeze the harvest! Oranges, avocados. Brightly flowering ice plants lined her childhood walk—he said, *ice* plants?

There was a Bird of Paradise with a spiked orange comb that stalked the house's shadow. She showed him a playful snapshot: back to back with the prehistoric-looking flower, her arms crossed tightly over her stomach.

Blue-flowering rosemary, whole hedges of it.

As a child Dinah had put her thumb over the round tinny mouth of the hose and sprayed water into the hibiscus In spite of her father she let the water dump down on the bleached, thirsty sidewalk. The sun was like white noise in Los Angeles, and the trees and the hibiscus were outlined in heat. Her wet footprints on the walk must have sizzled and evaporated.

Another Webb cousin was coming for the weekend. All was well again: "I'm going to show you off, darling," James hooted. Henry came out of the bathroom with a towel around his waist and another around his shoulders. How had James described those men of his father's generation? Festooned in scarves and bowties and ascots. Henry scuffed into his heel-bitten moccasins.

James had scribbled pages of notes for the final paper in Economies of Power. The notes were rolled into a tube and rubber-banded. James shot a rubber band at Henry.

"The boy has had those damn slippers since when, Henry?"

"Since my mummy gave them to me," said Henry. James snorted.

"Have the whites come back? I didn't leave you any towels," said Henry.

James looked through the tube of notes. He passed the tube to Dinah, perched on the desk beside him. "Have at it." He was failing out of college and going to work for his father. "I'm that kind of son," he had explained reasonably. "There's always one in every batch of us."

James said, "Let's make it a Christmas party for Ol' Charley." They were eating ham sandwiches they had made for themselves for dinner. There was only a week left in the semester. James wouldn't bother with finals. Threads of snow had begun to blow about in the afternoons when the sky, it seemed to Dinah, became simultaneously dark and pale.

That afternoon he'd blundered into the bathroom drunk when she was washing her armpits. She'd taken down the top of her dress in front of the mirror.

"Goddamn it, Dinah," he said loudly, but also peevish. "Don't they have showers in your dormitory?" He put his hands on the doorframe to steady himself.

There were often no towels even though they subscribed to a laundry service. She had never seen one hung to dry or air after a boy had used it. They paid for the heat themselves, and so had decided simply not to use it. Once Henry had taken her hand and pressed it on a cold radiator when James wasn't looking.

Dinah's dress was tight, binding in the armpits, which had made her sweat in the first place. She couldn't pull it up easily. She had thin arms and full breasts. Indeed her breasts seemed to push against her clothing lately. She was hot even though the weather was getting colder, even though she was from California. She had dark freckles on her torso, a neatly tucked-in belly button. Now James covered his eyes impulsively. From behind his mask he said, deadpan, "My strangely alabaster Californian." He grinned and took his hand away from his face. She was still naked.

"A sight to behold," he said, not looking at her. She could tell he was forcing himself to take a step forward, over the threshold. "I'd help you but I'm terrible with those," and he wiggled his fingers, "fasteners." She saw that he tried to smile.

Still she was quiet. He stepped inside the bathroom and closed the door behind him. He came up behind her and put his chin down on her shoulder. His face was ruddy in the mirror, even mottled. In fact he had one of those faces that appeared lopsided when reflected. They looked out to look at each other. His eyes were round holes, frightened. Dinah's eyes shone. Her breasts were goose-fleshed, the brown nipples hard and stem-like. Cool water dripped down the sides of her ribs from her armpits. Finally James reached around and held her breasts hard against her.

Henry took James's car in the snow and bought pine roping at a florist. The boys sang Christmas carols and hammered nails into the rented walls and lintels. They draped the scented pine over doorways and windows. They bought a Christmas cake with holly rosettes in green icing, and they decided to throw everything together in the punch bowl. Henry hunched forward stirring and sniffing like a witch over a cauldron.

Cousin Charles swished out of a taxi that honked for the sake of honking. He rapped on their unlocked door and called out, "Father Christmas!" He was taller than James and his mouth was fuller, more feminine. He wore wire-rimmed glasses and stooped like a misanthropic schoolteacher. Dinah imagined for a moment that the three male specimens were fanned out entirely for her choice in marriage. She was necessary to their survival: *new blood*, Henry had teased her just yesterday, practically a vaccine against madness. But the suspense only lasted a frivolous instant. James twirled her to him, and Henry dropped the needle on a twirling record.

It was midnight when Henry popped downstairs to invite the landlord to the party. He brought a glass of punch with him, or maybe a mug, white with an ivy-green stripe around it, something they'd lifted from the university coffee shop. The landlord, a bachelor, didn't need convincing.

At two o'clock in the morning Henry eeled his way through the crowd to tell Dinah that James had taken Old Charley to the hospital and might not be back till morning. Henry put his hand on her shoulder and pushed her deeper into the throng, toward the drinks table. "Appendicitis runs in the family!" he had to shout. "Runs the family! Come on, another drink and be merry!"

Figures moved backward and forward along predetermined planes of conversation. The punch had numbed Dinah's tongue completely. Whenever she turned around Henry was watching her. She had to sit down somewhere, but Henry grabbed her hand and pulled her playfully off the loveseat.

And then, it seemed sleep had only borrowed a moment, and waking, Dinah felt her bare legs against the blanket. In fact she was naked below the waist, and the blanket was a crust of mothballs and there was the university crest beneath her fingers. Henry was propped up on pillows beside her. He was looking straight ahead, and his mouth was moving.

She was still drunk. Her stomach was funny and her ears were, too. That was why she couldn't hear Henry. Had she simply stumbled into the wrong bedroom? She closed her eyes and reeled. When she opened them again she was surprised to see that Henry wasn't talking to her, actually. He was talking to James, in the doorway. James, in his driving gloves and overcoat. Where was he going?

It seemed as though Henry were trying to say something in her defense. How peculiar. Henry was saying, not to her, but to James, that he, Henry, loved Dinah.

James disappeared from the doorway. He must be in one of his moods. He'd been up all night, thought Dinah, orienting herself carefully, with Cousin Charles. Henry was sort of cradling her. It would be rude if she pushed him away, although she felt that she wanted to vomit. He was explaining something.

She couldn't pretend she hadn't noticed, Henry was saying.

Yes, she thought he had looked a bit sick spilling out of the taxi.

No, Henry was saying, not Charles. "You can't honestly say you haven't," said Henry. "Come on, Dinah." His body was next to hers, the same and different from James's. What did she mean, the same? What was she doing? It was too dark in Henry's bedroom to see where her clothes were, panties and slacks; it was as if her bottom half were under water.

"You know what I'm talking about," Henry was saying. Henry tensed his face into an eerie, plaster smile in imitation of James's at the end of that New York City weekend. "And then the unjustified, insupportable sadness!" Henry's indignation sounded almost practiced. "You can't explain James's moods, Dinah," Henry insisted. He paused and searched her face. "Unless you're a doctor."

7

Jonathan Hughes turns in another piece that really is transparently about his mother. He sees literature through the lens of her absence, he argues. He's working on what he calls a song-cycle. Marguerite says, "An elegy?" Her dignity—she maintains—requires that she raise an eyebrow. He raises one back at her. Her pulse quickens. But still, he's the wettest straight man she's ever encountered. The most sentimental mammal, like a whale, although he's not large,

and he doesn't sing, unless you count the song-cycle. He most defi-
nitely will not be hunted into extinction for his oil. She entertains
herself imagining how passionately he burns to be a writer, with a
capital W, and so on. His parents were probably so good to him it
was like having four parents. She catches herself. He stops by during
her office hours and lodges in her half-closed doorway. His chest
spreads out like an ocean, or like a little boy's chest.

"Hey." He smiles. Marguerite tells herself that he can't help it
that his voice is a lovely woodwind mid-register.

Her ears pop when she's nervous. "Come on in," she says. She
can't meet his creature eye, though. She's pricklingly aware that
she's been overthinking again—everything. Her bottom half *is*
the chair, and she watches helplessly as he surveys her bookshelf.
What a cliché, but her soul feels bare, unattractively puffy.

"I'm teaching my own course next semester," says Jonathan.

Still without really looking: "Good for you."

She chides herself, there's no need for retaliation. But he
doesn't look hurt—bemused, maybe. Maybe he thinks she's petu-
lant. She hopes he doesn't think she's jealous.

Why does she feel like picking a fight? A monkey could do
creative writing. He waves toward her books. "I have to come up
with a reading list."

Out of all the books in the world. As if the world were his oyster. Is that what a whale thinks? He fails to close his mouth when
he's done talking, his lower lip hangs open, all the nerves are in his
brain, but he's too young not to be self-conscious.

She says, "What do you write about?"

He blinks. She gets a tiny spasm—she can't quite tell remorse
from embarrassment. Suddenly it occurs to her he may use them
all—her, her class—as raw material. She sees him as a carnivore,
she sees him working on a screenplay.

He's saying something about the dynamic between form and content, the dialectic—it's nothing she hasn't heard before, and she finds herself sort of hovering, once more, over his long, girlishly lustrous brown hair, delicate glasses. She's seen him playing Frisbee with a loose pentagon of undergraduates. Once, in the fall, a stocky girl in a bikini top and cutoffs sailed the disc straight into the glare of an elm at sunset. Despite herself, Marguerite stood riveted at the edge of the quad as Jonathan borrowed a football from a couple of Madras-wearing future brokers and aimed it at the treed saucer.

And just like that, after their next class, he asks if she'd like to get a drink together. Her surprise shows, she guesses, and he covers his tracks: "It's nothing."

He turns to pack up. "No, sure," says Marguerite.

He straightens, he's as bright as a mirror. "Caffeine or alcohol?"

"Are you kidding?"

There's a bar on campus. Marguerite has only been a few times, she likes to think of herself as more of a dinner party drinker, although when was the last time she went to a dinner party? The truth is that she drinks alone in her apartment. The Grad Towers are seventies bloc style, dinosaurs of raw concrete with narrow, recessed windows and orange aluminum accents. There are dank interior courtyards, exposed concrete staircases, and empty bridges that connect the four thick-ankled buildings.

They don't have much to say, walking a couple of quiet blocks, but Marguerite feels almost high-spirited in the Friday December darkness. Stamping a little bit in the cold, she tries to stamp out her compulsion to dissect the unaccustomed cheeriness.

A security guard is more or less a belly on a thin folding chair in the open doorway. Marguerite can hear the tink of cues against lacquered balls and a bartender singing along with low music. She wonders what the security guard thinks about this particular assignment. Versus busting frat kids with six-packs in deep bushes?

The place, it occurs to her, is oddly preemptive. She can't imagine it existed in her mother's day, not to mention her grandparents'. It strikes her that the university can't appear to profit from student drinking; on the other hand, if it charges too little for the drinks, how are students expected to avoid becoming alcoholics? She doesn't share her train of thought with Jonathan. They offer their IDs to the guard—is Jonathan as nonplussed as she to be nearly thirty? He wears a black pea coat. So does Marguerite, it's practically a uniform.

She takes in the foosball and darts, microwave nachos and cold cereal sold in mini boxes. She feels good-humored and not disingenuously curious: did the trustees and the architects sit down together and decide to hide a great big watering hole in a windowless crater?

Jonathan pulls out a chair for her, and she wouldn't have guessed it would be so pleasant to feel taken care of. Or else she's quick to forgive. He folds his coat over his own chairback. "Marguerite," he says warmly. "What can I get you?"

And suddenly, in his absence—it's like she's had the wind knocked out of her. She has nothing to live for. She's exhausted. How will she hoist a glass of elixir? How will she lift her eyes off the scarified table, as sticky as a freshly licked stamp? It really is the dregs of the semester. One drink and she'll excuse herself. If she doesn't already have a good case of mono she'd welcome one; she doesn't need a drink, she needs a grave.

She can see Jonathan ordering at the bar, his low ponytail, did he dream of having long hair when he was a child? She really doesn't think he was denied anything. Not spoiled, but empowered. She sees him enchanting his mother. One drink, then she'll make her escape.

Getting out in front of it with a plan enlivens her. She conjures up her fish-spined advisor in Paris. He's plotting a side trip to Majorca or Morocco, it's getting dark at four o'clock in Paris, too, remember. She sees her advisor hoping the attractive undergrad he installed in Providence will remember to leave at least one sink dripping so the pipes don't freeze when she decides, at the last minute (relationship repaired with high school linebacker boyfriend), to go home for Christmas. She can hear her advisor remark to his prize-grabbing Swedishka: "You think Marguerite Webb is sleeping with Jonathan Hughes yet?"

Where's Jonathan? Would it be unforgivable if she got up and checked on the status of their drink orders?

Her advisor once told his wife, "Marguerite is too cold a person to ever really get literature."

"Not to put you on the spot," says Jonathan, when he returns. "But I'm a little bit in love with you."

"Wow," she says. For some reason they both start laughing. Then they clink glasses, "Chin chin," she says, and they start laughing all over again. She has a headache—so what. A headache like billions of tiny green flowerheads: dinosaur moss was the same as our moss. Horned turtles were having their day beneath the armored sun. *Testudo atlas*, eight thousand pounds. Not as heavy as a car. Not close to as heavy as 18½ Maple, their little cottage.

Marguerite read the encyclopedia in bed under the covers; Grandmother Webb staked out some distant corner of the floor plan. Each dinosaur was scaled to the shape and size of a human being: in some cases the human form barely reached the knees of the beast. She read until it put her to sleep, which she soon discovered was better than falling asleep crying.

She dreamed of the little boneheads below, their crowns of bone-thorns, sipping uncertainly from the yellow lake. All kinds of debris kicked up into the dusky atmosphere.

An Edmontosaurus on its side, red spaghetti uncoiling across parched rock outcropping. A beak like a duck and the long, thin neck of a sea serpent. God had not yet been created in order to create more adorable-looking creatures. Herbivores would have died first, when plant life could no longer support them.

Because the circumstances of their deaths were apocalyptic, their whole lives seemed tainted by apocalypse. Time, too. One second was the gulp of a year. A million years was a single day with a red sun and a river of lava...

Quetzalcoatlus flies across the gray sun. There is so much dirt in the sky that the earth may be, in effect, buried.

The quetzal, Mrs. Goff had once told her, was the national bird of Guatemala, where they lost their only child.

Jonathan pushes out from the table island and points to her drink again. "Yes?"

Yes. Baggy clothes, white shirttails out the back of his sweater. Would his hair have lost that gorgeous sheen if he'd played more football? She's entertaining to herself when she's drinking, she suddenly remembers. She shouldn't have another. She should, absolutely. She's no longer tired. She used to smoke. She wants a cigarette now, desperately, she'll bum one off the waifish art history girl shooting pool with her three boyfriends in the corner.

Another cliché, but it really is hard to know how much time has passed in this deep interior chamber. She's reached the bottom of the glass—three times? Who is she kidding. Seven?—where the cocktail straw scrapes and the fibers of lime are already drying.

She decides she's too drunk to dwell on it. Drunk enough to divine her mother's secrets.

Mr. Goff, the cathedral ceiling of his forehead, his figurine of a wife tucked in beside him. Mr. Goff, hungry for knowledge, in love with Diana. How did he explain the fact that she would take no money from the outrageously moneyed family of her child's father? He must have known it was her decision.

Now the campus bar is full, and friendly. People are beginning to order the nachos and, Marguerite notes woozily, instant noodle soup in Styrofoam. The bartender pours the boiling water. No doubt somebody is drinking away his or her college education, albeit in three-dollar increments; somebody else is writing a paper on the bar itself, sourced and footnoted, contextualized, cross-disciplined, cross-referenced.

The messier she feels, the more everything seems to connect, and it's all for the best, she's quite certain. Jonathan returns with drinks like crystals. "I'm still a little bit in love—" he smiles. She's in a state of spongy acceptance. He smells good, whiskey-laundry.

He doesn't say a word about her choice of drink when he sets it before her on the little table. His drink is amber. She appreciates the simple manners.

"So the seminar's gone well for you?" she manages.

She's always liked him, she's her very own retroactive fortune teller. Love at first sight is always in the past tense. Riding the swells of her vodka and cranberry, feeling a little bit bloodless, she believes everything she tells herself.

She pushes her hand toward him across the table. Her hand comes to a stop when her arm is fully extended. He draws one finger down each of her fingers.

Footsie on the table. Handsy. With their claws. Did the dinosaurs? He does have a wet mouth. He makes clucking sounds between phrases. Unselfconscious. She's happy for anyone, she tells herself, who's so close to his original, infant nature.

He smacks the table gently. "Think about that," he says. About what? She has no idea.

"I'm going to relieve myself," he says, "then I'll be back and I'll bring you another another." He grins. He probably has to go badly. It's as if she blinks and he's gone. She's unsettled, open in all the wrong places. She can't really remember anything they've talked about.

Time expands to fill the empty space at the table. A minute is an hour. Feels like an hour. Marguerite's thoughts pull away from each other, harden, and become separate thought-rocks.

She feels herself sober. She realizes she's at the point in the night where, no matter how much more she drinks, she'll only sober.

She closes her eyes. Allows herself to imagine her mother standing outside on a tiny Juliet balcony, it's barely a foot deep, a cheap stucco façade, the apartment they rent in—say—Carmel, California. She's always liked the way it sounds like candy. Half the cars are coming and half are going, from her mother's balcony.

The velocity of the world should cancel itself out, thinks her mother. When she thinks of her daughter.

Marguerite hears the blender from the bar chewing up ice and freezer-burned strawberries. There's no fat-padding around her eardrums. Everything is exposed to her bony hearing.

She closes her eyes again. She hears sand—remembers playing in the sand beneath an enormous white cloth sunhat.

She's four, maybe. Crabbed over, excavating, her expression intent, proud, even engorged with the adulation of the entire human race in the form of her mother. Her mother isn't in the snapshot, but Marguerite is certain she took it. Marguerite's expression reflects her.

Why did her mother do it, allow it, whatever you want to call it: just lie there? Diana wasn't sore yet but she would be.

Marguerite should have known that a woman who would just lie there, disconnected, would be equally capable of just leaving.

8

Henry was family.

And in the weeks that followed, he was fawningly, meticulously attentive. He took Dinah home to meet his wild, daddy-long-legs sister Margaret. Margaret affected a swoon, irreverent, bawdy, slavish: "Oh let me corrupt you!" she would cry as she presented Dinah with a pair of diamonds one day, the next day opera tickets. She, too, took Dinah to New York City. She had a cultivating spirit. She would have made a benevolent, even playful colonialist. Dinah could picture her as a schoolteacher in some outback, falling in love with a fourteen-year-old native.

It was Margaret Webb who assembled everyone: maids Dinah couldn't keep track of, an old-fashioned butler, a neighbor who'd given Dinah a turn around the paddock on horseback, Henry and Margaret's parents. There was a roaring fire in the study, silver trays of cocktails that caught the glint of it, and it seemed to Dinah that they were all clapping heartily and toasting her pregnancy even before Margaret brayed the announcement.

("The Christmas party?" Henry had suggested. He had pulled her in and whispered hotly, "Our first try, Dinah." She didn't have to say anything. "God, well then this is meant to be, isn't it!" blurted Henry.)

She changed her name to Diana. She would write the spring semester from the guesthouse, so as to finish out her first year of college. Everyone said she was darling, and of course she would want to finish, because it was true she had taken a scholarship.

Through the spring she became even closer to Margaret, who was a cunning and sophisticated eight years older, and had been living in New York City and spending too much money, since college, on a series of confidantes. Margaret had been home redeeming herself at the time of Diana's arrival; she had meant to stay shut up and dry out in her girlhood room through August. But now she recalibrated. "What would you do without me, darling?"

"Oh come on," said Diana, delighted.

"I can't just let my little brother's wife languish," Margaret admonished her own higher nature.

Long afternoons they ate smoked almonds and Margaret drank gin while Diana splashed white wine in her seltzer. If Diana wanted the sea air Margaret would balk, then spoonily capitulate and drive her down to the beach club. Margaret declared the water putrid borscht. "It'll make you contagious," she warned, grinning. She would stand on the boardwalk with her arms crossed, watching Diana.

It wasn't long until Margaret confessed her infatuation. Diana was so surprised, and flustered, that she felt obliged to match Margaret with her own secret. She looked down at her lap, the tightening belly, and said shyly, "All right. And I'm still in love with your cousin."

"My cousin," repeated Margaret uncertainly. "James?" Then, "I knew it!" Margaret put on a great show of satisfaction, even relief. "You unfaithful wench!" She blared her smile.

"Anyway, if it's a girl," said Diana, taking Margaret's hands (Diana had never blushed so much as those months she spent with Margaret), "I'm going to name her after you, Margaret."

"James if it's a boy?" Margaret said quickly.

Suddenly Diana grew very quiet. She closed her eyes on her companion, the darkly draped library where they sat on mahogany benches, the low drum of the full-length grandfather clock inside its mirrored case.

"Di?" There was Margaret. "God, Di. I didn't offend you——"

"No," Diana whispered. She knew her loose hair looked especially sumptuous in the cherry light of the Webb library.

The beach club is a cove of fine white sand bookended by cliffs topped with twin white mansions from the Roaring Twenties. One is a museum with extremely elusive hours, and the other belongs to the Cousin Charles Webbs, who've broken it up into apartments for the various family factions.

The crescent cove is walled by a continuous row of bunkers called cabanas. "Ca*bon*yas," say the clubbies, although as a group, they're utterly unmusical. The doors are painted Chardonnay yellow with wood trim like meringue, browning with sea mold.

The children play up and down the cement boardwalk or in the pool that's invisible to the ocean (as if the ocean would be offended), and at lunch the mothers bend their elbows or shake out aspirins and duck behind sunglasses. There's a formal dining room that requires sweaters the color of lemonade, geranium, mint julep, but the children take grilled cheese or chopped salad boarding school style at outdoor rattan tables.

The spring Marguerite was eleven—lofting quickly into summer, linden trees all papery seed wings and brushy greenish flowers—her aunt Margaret came up from New York City. It was the first time Marguerite had met her. Six feet tall, knock-kneed like a colt, slanted like a sketch drawing of a fashion plate. Gin had melted the fat from her frame and distended her stomach like a rosehip. She wrote for a magazine and she smelled like the chrome pages of ads for perfume and lipstick. She had a bedroom voice—sultry, throaty—with which she dispensed decadent, intimate presents a mother would be too shy to give and so would haughtily deem inappropriate. Marguerite and her cousins hid them away like love notes.

All the little girls flirted with her shamelessly, dropping their white towels on the beach when she approached, flouncing by her table at lunch with their naked salads balanced on one hand, soft-knuckled, dripping with a charm bracelet, but it was clear Diana was her real project. Marguerite watched her draw a single eyebrow across her own forehead. "Is it Diana Kahlo now, darling?"

What did it mean? Marguerite wondered. "Are you going native?" teased Aunt Margaret.

Another time Marguerite heard her say archly: "Charming, the way you wear Marguerite on your sleeve like an extra heart, Diana." But she pronounced Diana's name like a bauble.

"Hey Marguerite!" she would summon. "Did you know Mummy used to pick avocados and oranges off the vine in Los Angeles?" She turned her huge square smile upon Diana, but there was something grating in her laughter. And if a Gentleman of the Last Generation— that is, the last generation that would not be required to work—came tacking toward them, varicose veins like nests of worms in his bare legs, his hairless forearms a cannibal pink, Aunt Margaret would grin slyly and whisper, "That one wouldn't even ask for a dry smooch at bedtime, Diana." It didn't take Marguerite long to figure out that her aunt was trying to marry her widowed mother back into society.

One evening before supper Marguerite and her mother went down to the water. Diana was the only female member of the beach club who would swim in the ocean, and there was always a little dent of shyness in Marguerite's pleasure: were people watching? Red tide made a slurry of the shallows, a thick fur of blood-colored seaweed that would coat them after swimming.

Diana wasn't a skeleton like Aunt Margaret, and she didn't have Margaret's height, but she was only thirty-one that summer and she looked fit and lovely in her dark blue swimsuit. She had a generally serious temperament, but on the beach she turned playful and silly. She skipped and splashed and patted the wet sand as if it were the sleek hip of a dolphin.

The Cousin Charles Webb mansion was pearled in the early evening light and the sunset divided the sky into upside-down cliffs over the water. Out a ways, Seagull Rock was plastered white with frost-like bird droppings. Birds circled and plunged and exploded in separate dark droplets. Marguerite danced around her mother, even tugging the ribbon that hung from her hat as if she were a much younger child, chatting aimlessly, happily about the evening's clambake.

But all of a sudden, like a wind change, Marguerite noticed that someone was coming swiftly, deliberately across the beach, straight toward them. Not down from the cabanas, or from the fire pit where caterers swarmed to prepare the clambake, but Neptunish from the water. He was waving urgently, and his unbuttoned white dress shirt knocked about his bare chest like the broken wing of a seagull. He was tall and held himself unnaturally straight from the waist up. His hands began jerking wildly as he approached them.

Diana pulled up short, and Marguerite, of course, halted with her. She looked up at her mother. Well, were they meeting him? Diana had stopped but Marguerite had the strange sense that her mother's whole being was in motion.

"You're—you're a beautiful pair!" shouted the man with the flapping shirt. He was jogging to meet them, then faster, as if he would lose them if he didn't.

Up close, his face was waxy and his hair was gray, but he seemed almost childish, unguarded. His loose pants were rolled up to the knees and his eyes were pink as if he'd been swimming with them open underwater. Diana took her hat off. Her long hair uncoiled slowly, plum-colored in the sunset.

"I saw you swim out to the rock," he said. Diana shook her head but it was true. Marguerite had also watched her.

He patted his shirt pocket and drew out cigarettes. He held the pack suspended, staring openly at Diana. Then, with a half smile, and half embarrassed, "Won't you take me to California?" There was the tiniest bit of singsong to it.

Diana looked out to sea. The wrong sea, the Atlantic. "This is Marguerite." She put a hand lightly on Marguerite's shoulder.

When he bent down stiffly, the blood in his eyes startled Marguerite just a little. "Do you like my beach?"

Her mother gave a short laugh. He jerked his hand through his hair, flinching. He looked out over Diana's head. "Are you by any chance named after our cousin Margaret?" It took Marguerite a moment to realize he was addressing her.

She said, "I'm named after my aunt." The only thing she ever said to him.

She found Aunt Margaret and a gin and tonic at one of the alcove bars between the pool and the dining room. "The spinster aunt!" cried Margaret. "Of course, I'm required to babysit. Who needs a fucking clambake?"

"Who?" Great Aunt Taffy was with her, at once muddled and adamant.

"*I* don't need any more mollusks or blue cheese dressing," said Aunt Margaret.

The bartender set down a Shirley Temple. Marguerite felt her aunt eyeing the drink lewdly. "Just the two of us without Mummy—won't we manage?"

For a cover-up Aunt Margaret wore an oversized Oxford shirt, not unlike the white dress shirt the man on the beach had been wearing.

"Why aren't these clambakes ever rained out?" said Taffy.

They heard a car peel out of the parking lot behind the cabanas. Margaret cocked her narrow head. Marguerite stood up quickly.

"Well that sounds fun," said Margaret.

Aunt Margaret had promised her a subscription. "At least my namesake should appreciate beauty's contrivances," she said. "What does Diana know, with her *natural beauty?*" Now she took Marguerite's face in her hands and squinted. "We'll leave hair and makeup for another day, sweetheart."

A handful of clubbies were idling around the fire pit. Outside their circle stood a short, dumpy man in swim trunks and a yellowing T-shirt. His beard clung to his rounded chin like lichen. His round nose was inflamed with sunburn as if prior to this day he'd been living underground as a potato. He had a bright red line of sunburn, too, just above his eyebrows. Margaret stretched her lips as they approached him.

He tried to angle away from them, but Margaret bore down, and she was a full head taller. The interloper had to stumble backward to look up at her.

"Believe me," he said. "I'm aware I'm not invited."

But Margaret held out her long hand to arrest the little paw in a handshake. At least she meant to smile. "From here on out, you're a guest of ours," she said. She looked at her niece. "The Two Margarets." She kept his hand as she waited for him to say something. He would rather have been shunned and silent.

"It's a real embarrassment," he gave up finally.

"Oh?" said Margaret, releasing the handshake.

"One of your members took my car, I'm afraid. I'm stranded." He paused, hoping his confession was finished.

"One of our *members*."

"And on a Saturday night," he continued, changing tacks, feeling sorry for himself. He looked out at the ocean.

"Well." Now she was all business. "I'm sure we can find you a cocktail." She broke into a real smile and waved to attract the attention of a waiter. "They don't really see you till they know you," winked Margaret.

When the man had his drink he was ready to laugh with her. "Jeez it's awkward," he confided. "You know, I'm not a doctor or anything. Just the chaperone."

"Ah," said Margaret knowingly. Marguerite understood she would have to wait for an explanation.

"They like to get out once in a while. Just like the rest of us." He said it in a kind of generous spirit, to his credit.

Margaret merely nodded.

"To top it off." He drank. "Sunstroke."

Aunt Margaret lifted her glass. "Well here's to sunstroke." She drank. "And a night off for Diana."

Jonathan leans forward. "You asked me what I write."

She nods, she's soberly drunk, drunkenly sober, omniscient as God, vague as God also. She feels as if she's been crying for hours. At this moment all she sort of needs is for him to like her. Squishy, egoless little life forms become mouths and sharp elbows. Self-sabotaging, hard-drinking Marguerite: no wonder her mother left her.

She places her fingertips on her shoulders, an inane and invented gesture that will never be repeated. She can tell he likes it.

He leans back a little. Now Marguerite crosses her legs under the table and tries crossing her fingers on command: she can still do it, but any inkling of where she left her car is eclipsed by vodka.

A small flock of girls in saggy jeans, down vests, and lumpy backpacks circles the table next to theirs, which all this time has been empty. The backpacks seem to tumble off the girls' shoulders of their own accord, as if this is the very thing that backpacks are made for. A girl with an emaciated white ponytail and white lashes locks her mittened hands on their extra chair. "May I?"

Her mittens are the red of Christmas. Her white eyebrows take over the world, Jonathan and Marguerite are completely wiped out. Then she settles into her group and her voice is common, indistinguishable.

Jonathan digs his elbows into the table and Marguerite leans in to close out the intruders. She concentrates on keeping her face open. He moves in too, and his intent makes him startlingly handsome.

"So," she says. "You didn't really end up in the same apartment as your mother."

"The O. Henry?" says Jonathan. Before she knows it they're both laughing. He takes his glasses off and wipes his eyes. The unexpected irreverence of it! She gulps and almost chokes with laughter, which sets him laughing all over again. Finally he pushes his drink away and the glass skates a little on some liquid. Have they been spilling their drinks all evening?

They float from the room. The security guard is reading a cheap paperback, a cover like black nail polish. Marguerite could easily forget how to exit this tower.

She follows Jonathan down a dim hallway that becomes another dim hallway. They come to a fire door with a low red light and Jonathan pushes it open. Time is so screwy she's half expecting daylight. She imagines herself craning around, looking for that star of sunshine.

They're outside, and it's dark. They're outside, but they're not out of the Grad Towers. They're on a high bridge somewhere in the middle of all that Godforsaken architecture and it's cold and the giant concrete pillars are radiating an even more intense coldness. There are three-foot-high planters with dried-up box-woods a corpse shade of yellow and flurries of frozen cigarette butts. It's like being inside a concrete basket. The light comes from a buzzing streetlight and Marguerite realizes she has no idea which street they're facing. Benevolent, Thayer, Charlesfield?

"I can't believe I found you," she hears Jonathan saying.

For a moment it makes sense, and then it doesn't. He paws one foot up on the edge of a planter.

One dinosaur, thinks Marguerite, represented many. One set of bones came from many skeletons. As if a thousand Quetzal-coatluses contributed. Their taut-skinned wings reconstituted in the imaginations of a thousand scientists: maybe they looked like enormous egrets.

Suddenly Jonathan loses his balance and his foot skids off the edge of the planter. He wobbles, puts his arm around her waist for stabilization. His coat is open and she slides her hand around his waist underneath it.

ACKNOWLEDGMENTS

With great thanks to the folks at Dzanc.

I've been lucky to have crossed paths with fine editors at intrepid literary magazines that continue to publish unusual work—thanks especially to Ronald Spatz, Carolyn Kuebler, Lynne Nugent, Laura Furman, Rebekah Hall, Minna Proctor, and the poet Sarah Gambito, who's been there since the beginning of writing time.

And in memory of Hedy Dowd Suraski, 1975-2012.

Stephanie Alvarez Ewens

KIRSTIN ALLIO's novel, *Garner,* was a finalist for the *Los Angeles Times* Book Prize for First Fiction. She is a recipient of the National Book Foundation's 5 Under 35 award, a PEN/O. Henry prize, and other honors for her short stories and essays. She's currently a Howard Foundation Fellow at Brown University, and she lives in Providence, RI with her husband and sons.